D0295763

BULLSEYE

As the most powerful men on earth gather in New York for a meeting of the UN, Detective Michael Bennett receives intelligence warning that there will be an assassination attempt on the US president. Even more shocking, the intelligence suggests that the Russian government could be behind the plot. Tensions between America and Russia are the highest they've been since the Cold War, but this would be an escalation no one could have expected. The details are shadowy, and Bennett finds false leads and unreliable sources at every turn. But he can't afford to get this wrong. If the plotters succeed, the shockwaves will be felt across the globe.

BULLSEYE

by

James Patterson & Michael Ledwidge

Magna Large Print Books
Long Preston, North Yorkshire,
BD23 4ND, England.

British Library Cataloguing in Publication Data.

A catalogue record of this book is
available from the British Library

ISBN   978-0-7505-4499-3

First published in Great Britain by Century in 2016,
part of the Penguin Random House group

Copyright © James Patterson 2016

Cover illustration © Collaboration JS by arrangement with
Arcangel Images

James Patterson has asserted his right to be identified as the author
of this work in accordance with the Copyright, Designs and Patents
Act, 1988

Published in Large Print 2017 by arrangement with
Random House Group Ltd.

Magna Large Print is an imprint of Library Magna Books Ltd.

Printed and bound in Great Britain by
T.J. (International) Ltd., Cornwall, PL28 8RW

For Emmett and Debbie O'Lunney

PROLOGUE

SNOWED IN

ONE

There were snowdrifts at the curbs and snow-buried benches in the parks and snowcaps on the street signs and fire hydrants and on the newel posts for the subway entrances. There were four inches so far, and they were thinking maybe ten when all was said and done.

Four inches was laughable somewhere like Maine, but in Manhattan on a dark early November evening, it cancels plans and sends people indoors.

The two black-clad figures on the BMW R 1200 RT sport motorcycle that rolled slowly north up Amsterdam Avenue near 135th Street not only knew that; they had planned on it. They'd been waiting on the cold snowy conditions for the last month.

The Beemer's engine thrummed steadily as the City College of New York campus appeared on their right. First the big, ugly, modern, box store-like classroom buildings. Then the older, original, Harry Potter-like Gothic ones.

The driver did controlled swerves from time to time, careful not to get a pile of road salt under the motorcycle's studded snow tires. An experienced winter biker, he knew that even with the studs, salt was slicker than ice.

He and the rider behind him were dressed identically in the latest in cold weather riding

11

gear. Gore-Tex Tourmaster electric jackets and riding pants over EDZ thermals, Windstopper gloves and neck warmers. Black glossy Scorpion snow helmets with the tinted no-fog visors firmly down.

Every ounce of gear was specific to the mission. They had even specifically selected the heavy BMW for its low center of gravity, which aided in stability and traction.

Then finally there it was, two blocks ahead.

The corner of West 141st Street.

The driver had been over what was going to happen next so many times that he could have drawn the scene west down 141st Street with his eyes closed. The old, once-stately five- and six-story prewar apartment houses on either side of the narrow, descending, one-way side street. The ancient shoe repair place on the left, the Caribbean hair salon on the right. Both business entrances sunk down a flight of steps below the sloping sidewalk, as on a lot of Hamilton Heights' quirky up and down streets.

They'd played it through time and time again, until it was boring. Over and over, slowly. Listing everything that could possibly go wrong. Because it wasn't just surprise. It was surprise plus doing. Doing lots and lots of stuff you'd already pre-planned while the other guy sat there going 'Wait, what is this?' for that split second you needed to get the hammer down on him.

Suddenly the rider said in their two-way Bluetooth helmet radio, 'Hold up! The car isn't there. Shit! There must be something wrong. Maybe we should abort.'

12

They'd planted a remote camera in a car across from the 141st Street target; the rider was monitoring it via smartphone.

'Calm down. It's okay. They're just late because of the snow,' the driver said as he drifted the bike over and stopped at the left-hand curb half a block from 141st's corner. 'We're not aborting. We just have to wait a second. This is going to happen. Right now. I can feel it. Keep watching and tell me the second you see it.'

As he waited, the BMW's driver closed his eyes and ran through the scenario yet again. Amsterdam was the highest point in the neighborhood, and the path down 141st to the target was like going down steps: the first long slope off Amsterdam to the flat of Hamilton, and then another down slope to the flat of Broadway. The target building was on the final down slope of 141st between Broadway and Riverside Drive, midblock south side, on the left.

The abandoned apartment building had two wings, with the entrance between them way back off the street, through a canyonlike corridor. That was why it was so formidable. The target could see anything and anyone coming well before the front door could be reached. Two police raids had been tried over the past two years, and the place was always clean by the time they got inside.

The softest point, they'd discovered from their extensive recon, was right around now, when one of the grandmas usually brought the crew home cooking. The three guys on lobby duty would come out and give *abuela* lots of showy love on the sidewalk in exchange for aluminum pans of stewed pork and eggplant, as the fourth guy hung back by the propped-open front door.

One thing the driver liked was that they were above the target. That they would swoop down on it. There was an instinctual power to being above that truly thrilled him. He also liked the surprisingly smooth, graceful sucker punch speed of the Beemer, throttle open downhill. They would be in theater right quick. Speed and surprise from above were two excellent angles of advantage.

They certainly needed every advantage they could get, since there were seven in the well-armed drug crew. They had two AK-47s in the cook apartment in case of emergency, and they all carried straight blowback Glock 18 machine pistols in 9mm caliber.

The damn Glock 18s bothered him. They were excellent for close combat. No bulky stocks or long barrels to bang against corners or stair banisters. And they were looking at the closest of combat in the crumbling prewar building's coffin-wide hallways and slot-canyon-of-death stairwells.

Worse, the Glock 18s indicated tactical intelligence. And that kind of intelligence made him think that no matter how much they'd planned it, there might be something they'd missed.

But that was part of it, too. It was actually better to assume you missed something so as to keep your eyes open.

He glanced forward, up Amsterdam, at the snow drifting in the cones of the streetlights. Bits blowing this way and that, shifting and reshifting in the gusts.

No need for cocky in this line of work. You had

to know that even great plans had a funky habit of changing on you.

'I see it! It's there,' said the rider, suddenly pounding on the driver's back. 'The car – the Chevy. It's pulling up out in front. Go! Go! Go!'

The spinning tires of the BMW threw up a fat rope of slush as the driver ripped back on the throttle. Then he let off on the brake, and they were hitting the corner and going straight down.

TWO

The cooking lab was in the east wing of the building, on the third floor. It was in a type of apartment known as a junior four, a one-bedroom with a formal dining room off the living room. The dining room was usually separated with French doors, but since the cooking lab was set up there, they'd taken off the doors and Sheetrocked the doorway.

In the lab, just to the right of the kitchen door, was a barrel of sodium hydroxide, a big white fifty-gallon industrial drum of the stuff, plastered with bloodred DANGER: HAZARDOUS MATERIALS diamonds. In front of the drums were two lab tables where two HCL generators were going full tilt.

The generators were chemistry industry standard, a bubbling, dripping, steaming mousetrap setup of hot plates and beakers and rubber tubing and inverted funnels. The HCL rig was for turning solids into liquids and liquids into evaporated gases that were separated and condensed back down into newer, much more lucrative solids.

Hustling busily between the barrel and the lab tables and the kitchen was a tall and wiry, handsome, black-haired Hispanic man. He was the drug crew's head, Rafael Arruda. No dummy, Rafael, he wore a super-duty gray-hooded hazmat suit with full respirator, two pairs of seagreen rubber medical gloves over his hands, and plastic nurse booties over his vintage Nikes. All the seams taped nice and tight to avoid the highly caustic fumes and chemicals.

He was whipping up some MDMA, the main ingredient in the drug ecstasy. He'd already cultivated about three ounces of the drug's blazingly white crystals in the plastic-lined collecting tin beside one of the generators. About thirty grand worth once it was cut and packed down into pills.

He'd shoot for a half pound tonight, before he pulled the plug around one or two and went home to his wife, Josefina, and his daughter, Abril, who had come home for the weekend from Georgetown, the school that he himself had attended, majoring in chemistry on some rich oil guy's Inner City Golden Promise scholarship fund.

His promise in the field of chemistry had paid out all right. At least for him. When he wasn't cooking drugs, he was a tenured professor and cohead of Columbia University's under-grad chemistry department and lived in a four-million-dollar town house in Bronxville, beside white-bread bankers and plastic surgeons.

It was about seven thirty when he noticed the

16

clogged dropping funnel in generator one. That happened from time to time with the new, iffy stuff he'd gotten from a chemical supply house in Canada. The stuff was cheaper, especially the hydro, but it was becoming more and more obvious that it was subpar with impurities, probably Chinese-made.

If it wasn't one thing, it was another, Rafael thought as he immediately lowered the heat and replaced the inverted funnel with a fresh one. You had to pay attention.

As he arrived at the kitchen sink with the dirty funnel, Dvorak's Symphony no. 9 in E Minor, known as the *New World Symphony,* began playing in his headphones. He loved this one, the slow oboes and clarinets and bassoons, sad and yet somehow strangely uplifting. Salsa was his favorite, but way back since high school, it was nothing but calming classical while he worked.

He was lifting the bottle brush from the depths of the original prewar porcelain kitchen sink when the bassoons cut out, replaced by an incoming text beep.

His family and guys knew never to bother him when he worked, so he immediately looked down at his phone on his belt.

He prided himself on his stoic calm, but he suddenly felt a chill as he read the three words down there on the screen.

BOSS COME QUICK!!!! it said.

Rafael pulled the plug on everything and tore off the hood and respirator and earbuds as he came out into the hall of the apartment and went into the count room next door. In it were two bull-

17

necked towering Dominicans. One had a slicked ponytail and one was bald, with a thin beard, and both wore camo fatigue pants and black Under Armour under puffy silver North Face vests.

They were his crew captains, fraternal twin brothers, Emilio and Pete Lopez, with whom he had grown up. They stood staring dumbfounded at the laptop that monitored their closed-circuit security video downstairs.

'What the hell is going on?' Rafael said.

'We don't know. Nate just radioed up from the lobby,' Emilio said, thumbing nervously at his beard. 'A bike – a motorcycle or something – just wiped out into Louis on the sidewalk, and he said two dudes in helmets jumped off it and were fighting with Jaime and Jesus.'

'And now no one's responding,' said Pete, shaking his head. 'Nate won't answer his radio or his phone.'

Nate again! Rafael thought. He was Josefina's cousin and a pot-head total screwup, the weakest point in his armor by far. That's it. He was going to fire him. Right after he personally kicked the living shit out of him.

'Where are they?' Rafael said, scanning the screen's security grid. 'Jaime and the rest of them. I don't see them. They're not in the street.'

'We don't know,' said Pete.

'Did you scope out the front door?' Rafael said.

'Of course, bro. That's just it. No one came in, or we would have seen them,' said Emilio.

'That doesn't make sense.'

'We know,' said Emilio, wide-eyed.

'Jackass – come in,' Rafael called down on the

Motorola. 'Nate, you there? Hey, jackass!'

He unkeyed the radio and listened. The rasp of static. No Nate. No nothing.

What the hell is this? he thought.

'What are you guys doing just standing there?' Rafael cried up at the towering Lopez brothers. 'I sent you to that training course why? For exercise? Shit is going down now! Get out the vests and choppers *now*.'

'You think it's the Romolos, maybe?' said Emilio. 'Over that thing with that girl who got killed? Or is it the cops?'

That's when it happened.

In a silent instant around them came darkness.

The lights, the monitor, all the juice – all of it was suddenly gone.

THREE

Rafael felt panic arrive, a cold petrifying pulse of it that began in his stomach and radiated out. To his balls and knees, to his chest and brain.

'Holy shit! What is this?' cried Pete in the dark.

Rafael bashed down the welling panic and finally, with a shaking thumb, got the flashlight going on his phone. He went out of the count room to the apartment door and cracked it.

No. F me. Not good.

The hall was dark. The entire building was out. Someone had shut their whole shit down!

He almost wet himself as the gunfire suddenly

started up. Thundering up the dirty worn marble staircase came the sudden deafening blasts of a Glock 18 going off in a long magazine-emptying, full-auto burst. A faint flicker of muzzle flash accompanied the sudden jackhammering, the pulsing glow of it against the cracked stairwell plaster like firelight on the upper reaches of a cave wall.

Think, Rafael thought as he quickly closed and bolted the door.

Do not panic. You are intelligent. You have a plan. Do the plan.

'Who is it? Cops?' said Emilio as Rafael came back into the count room.

'You hear any bullhorns? It ain't the cops!' said Rafael, opening the gun closet and reaching for the second shelf. His hands passed over the tube of a flashlight until he found what he was looking for.

The night-vision goggles.

He had all kinds of shit in there. Dried food, a portable propane generator, enough ammo to outlast Judgment Day.

Now, apparently, it was here, he thought as he pulled the strap of the goggles over his head.

'You want to play blindman's bluff in my house?' he said as he clicked on the goggles and everything was suddenly illuminated with a pale-green light. He unclipped the Kalashnikov from the wall rack.

'Then you got it, bro. Let's do it. Come out, come out, wherever you are, you son of a bitch.'

FOUR

Rafael sent Pete and Emilio up and over the roof to come down the west wing while he went down the east wing stairs.

The wrapped-tight canvas AK strap cut hard into his forearm as he came silently down the quarter turns of the stairwell. He tried to remember the shooting techniques. Was he supposed to blur the target beyond the front sights? Or was that just for a pistol? Fricking impossible to remember all the training they'd had from the course two years ago. He checked the safety. It was on. He shook his head, clicking at the button.

As he came across the final stair head of the first-floor landing, he caught the scent of gun smoke. A lot of it. The tangy, almost sweet smell, rank as a gun range. He tightened his grip on the gun as he came across the landing to the final turn, his back against the abandoned apartment doors, barrel trained down through the balustrades. There was no one through the posts. No one on the final stair flight, and then he was coming down, his AK sight center-massed on the open lobby doorway.

The first thing he noticed when he peeked through it was that the heavy wrought-iron-and-glass front door of the building was ajar. A triangle of the outside sodium security light spread over the floor's dirty mosaic tiles. Bits of snow swirling in the yellow beam, a faint layer of snow already gathering in the grout.

'Rafael!' Pete suddenly called out across the lobby from the other stairwell.

Rafael almost tripped over the bodies as he came through the west wing doorway.

There were two of them. One of them lying flat in a pool of blood on the dirty tile, the other to the right, sitting up against the wall. The chests of their motorcycle shells were wet with blood, and the tinted face masks of their motorcycle helmets were smashed to shit, just riddled with bullet holes.

'Ha-ha! That's what you get, you fucking amateurs. That's exactly what you get,' said Rafael as he hawked and spat on both of them. Whoever the hell they were.

He glanced at Nate, also covered in blood, by the bottom of the stairs, the Glock 18 on the tile beside him.

At least the jackass had done something right for once in his miserable life, Rafael thought.

'Rafael! Do CPR! Nate's dying! Come on, do something!' said Pete, who was kneeling at the bottom of the stairs beside Nate.

'He's still breathing, I think,' said Emilio, pressing his ear to Nate's mouth as Rafael arrived.

'And so are we!' said the prone motorcycle guy behind them as he sat straight up like a monster in a horror flick.

Rafael, standing in profile to the suddenly risen figure, had just registered that the man had a suppressed automatic pistol in his hand when Pete's bald head blew apart as if it had been dynamited. Pete's instant death was followed quickly by ponytailed Emilio's as the other reanimated dead body by the wall shot him with a suppressed pistol.

Rafael screamed as he swung the rifle up and then abruptly stopped screaming as a third and final suppressed .45 ACP lead slug instantly carved a brand-new orifice through his temples.

'Is it him? Is it him?' said the rider excitedly as the driver leaped up from the pool of fake blood behind his trusty suppressed Heckler & Koch Mark 23.

Instead of answering, the driver knelt and removed Rafael's wallet, trying not to look at the hot mess that an ounce of lead makes when it's sent traveling through a human head at the cruising speed of a 747.

'It's him,' said the driver, calmly pocketing the target's driver's license and checking his watch. 'Our work is done here. Time to go.'

FIVE

They scooped up their brass, left the BMW bike out on 141st, and went out at a quick, steady pace through the back of the building, taking a garbage alley that led out onto Riverside Drive.

Three blocks south, parked alongside Riverside Park, was the preplaced getaway vehicle: a beat-up dingy white work van with the baffling and meaningless words THE BOWLES GROUP LLC poorly hand-painted on the door.

Once inside the rear of the van, the driver finally

pulled off his helmet. He was a fit-looking white guy in his late thirties with close-cropped blond hair and light-blue eyes that were striking in his otherwise easy-to-forget plain and pale face.

He scrubbed the sweat from his hair with a towel and then put his pale-denim-colored eyes to his stainless steel Rolex. It seemed like it was last week that they were up on Amsterdam, but the assassination had taken eleven minutes from start to finish. Eleven!

He looked over at the rider getting changed beside him. Then he reached around and cupped her perfect left breast. Her right one wasn't so bad, either, he felt. She turned and smiled at him, an improbably gorgeous woman in her early thirties, petite yet athletic, with white-blond hair and large greenish-brown doe eyes. His pet name for her ever since they met was Coppertone Girl.

Coppertone Girl made a quick twisting move and then he was somehow down on his back with something hard digging into his crotch. He looked down. It was her .45!

'I'll do it. You know I will, you pig,' she said, her green eyes cold behind the white-blond shards of her bangs.

Then she kissed him hard.

And they both started to die laughing.

It never got old, this fired-up feeling afterward. They'd walked the rope with no net, and now they were back on sweet, exhilaratingly solid ground.

They kissed again, and then he pressed in her pouty pink lower lip with his callused thumb. She bit his thumb playfully, and then he was jumping over the front seat and turning the engine over.

An hour later, they'd put all the gear and the van back at the South Bronx safe house and were showered and changed and rolling back into Manhattan in their new Volvo crossover. They actually found a parking spot right in front of their Federal-style brick town house, in SoHo on Wooster Street between Broome and Spring.

They stood holding hands on the sidewalk for a moment. Nothing but the famous chic neighborhood's incredible beaux arts nineteenth-century cast-iron buildings in every direction. The cobblestones, Corinthian columns, and delicate wrought-iron railings dusted in the still-falling snow were like what might appear on the cover of *'Twas the Night Before Christmas.*

Not bad for an Indiana shit kicker, the man thought, drinking in the billion-dollar view down his block.

Not bad at all, he thought, looking at his exquisite wife, now in a candy-blue Benetton down coat, cream mini-sweaterdress, and black leather leggings.

He knocked the snow off his shoes on their doormat and keyed open their front door.

'Mommy! Daddy! You're home!' their four-year-old daughter, Victoria, squealed, a blur of pink footie pajamas and strawberry-blond curls as she ran in from the family room, sliding on the gleaming hardwood in her Nana-made wool slippers.

'Yes! We! Are!' said the husband with equal excitement as he pretended to let his giggling daughter tackle him.

'That was a quick movie,' said Jenna, the baby-sitter, bringing up the rear, holding a sheet of still-raw cookies.

'We arrived late, with all the snow, so we just decided to get some dessert instead,' said the wife.

'Dessert? Wow. You guys just live on the razor's edge, don't you?' said their ever-sarcastic NYU film student sitter with an eye roll.

'Oh, that's us. We're real wild,' the husband said, laughing as he hung his car coat in the front hall closet and snitched a glob of raw oatmeal cookie dough.

'Yep, we're complete psychos, all right,' agreed his wife as she lifted Victoria and blew a raspberry on her cheek.

PART ONE

HAIL TO THE CHIEF

CHAPTER 1

Early Saturday morning, a lone figure stood center stage in the storied culinary arena of the Bennett family kitchen.

That figure was, of course, *moi,* your friendly neighborhood cop, Mike Bennett, but unlike an iron chef, I found myself where I often do when I make the mistake of going near pots and pans – namely, very, very deep in the weeds.

I was doing pancakes, Mike Bennett-style. Well, I guess technically you could call it Ina Garten-style, as I had her latest cookbook open on the kitchen island in front of me. Unfortunately, things weren't going very well. Poor Ina was covered in flour, and she had a lot of company. There was flour all over the island, on the stools, on the floor next to the egg I'd dropped. There was even flour on Socky, the cat, who was licking at the broken egg.

As I stood there sweating and whisking and wondering if cats could get salmonella poisoning, I detected a distinctive aroma. I turned to the stove, where the sausages were burning in the too-hot cast-iron pan.

Dagnabbit! I thought as the next batch of toast popped. How was I supposed to put everything hot together at once? I wondered. And how come you never saw this crap happening on *Diners, Drive-Ins and Dives?*

'Are you okay in there?' my kids' nanny, Mary Catherine, called from the foyer, back from a walk with Jasper, our border collie. 'Correction. Are you still alive in there? What's going on?'

'The making of culinary history, Mary Catherine,' I said as I hopped over the cat and turned down the stove. 'Sit tight. All is well.'

'It doesn't sound all that well,' she said. 'I'm coming in.'

'Don't you dare. It's your day off, remember?' I said. 'Put your feet up, relax, and soak in the tranquility.'

That last remark was made with pointed irony, of course, this being the slow-motion not-so-quiet riot known as the Bennett household. As I burned down the kitchen, there was quite a din coming from the living room: the sound of buzz saws and laser beams, and the *gloop-gloop-gloop* of something dripping followed by a cacophony of what sounded like evil Tweety Birds laughing, all at 747-at-takeoff decibels.

The older of my ten kids were luckily still sleeping or plugged into headphones, but the younger ones, Eddie and Trent and Shawna and Fiona and Bridget and Chrissy, were sprawled out in front of the boob tube, watching some Saturday morning 'toons – mind-meltingly stupid, probably magic mushroom-inspired ones, by the sound of them, brought to my kids by the fools at the forbidden Cartoon Network.

Isn't it hard enough trying to raise kids without edgy television execs trying to fit them for straitjackets? I thought as I made a mental note to change the parental block code again. That Eddie was worse

30

than a safecracker when it came to unraveling the TV combo.

In between burning breakfast items, I was watching a little insanity-inspiring footage myself. I had the local CBS news site on the flour-covered iPad propped beside Queen Ina. On it, a report was scrolling that showed politicians. Actually, it wasn't so bad. It was a story about the newly inaugurated president, Jeremy Buckland.

Surprisingly, I found myself liking Buckland. Maybe it was just a superb acting job, but he really did seem like a straight shooter. He'd been an Eagle Scout, a decorated war hero in Iraq one, a test pilot. The former governor of Pennsylvania also seemed smart and funny and deadly serious about making the country and world a safer, freer, happier place for everyone involved.

His wife was a nice, pretty, black-haired woman named Alicia, and they had four kids: three middle school-age daughters along with the true star of the show, their cute little five-year-old boy, Terrence. The kindergartner had captured the world's loving attention by carefully imitating one of the full-dress marines at the inauguration.

I guess it was a good thing Terrence was so cute, because the news report was saying that the prez was due in town today for a series of upcoming UN meetings that were going to clog up city traffic as tight as concrete in a drainpipe.

'You're up early,' I said as my oldest son, Brian, came in.

'Yeah, I know. I heard some old guy yelling,' he said, elbowing me as he grabbed the OJ out of the fridge.

I glanced down at my flour-covered phone as I heard my text ringtone.

'Fu – I mean, rats,' I said, looking at it, then at the tablet's screen.

'Furry rats?' said Brian groggily, draining his glass.

I took off my apron and hung it around his neck.

'There are times in life when a man has to pass the baton to his son, Brian. I'm all out of batons, so I'm passing this spatula. Your beloved nanny is in there, and she and the other multiple members of this family are very hungry and counting on you. Feed them well, my son. Watch the toast. Don't let it win.'

'What? Cook breakfast? Me? I, eh, I have practice.'

'Practice? You have a game at one. It's eight.'

'Um, sleeping practice.'

'Don't worry, kiddo,' I said as I headed into the dining room. 'You have that skill down pat. Again, beware of the toast, and may the force be with you.'

'Mary Catherine,' I said as I came into the dining room waving my phone. 'How can I break this gently?'

'Work? On a Saturday morning?' the blond Irish beauty said, wide-eyed as she gave me a look.

I hated that look. In addition to being my kids' nanny, Mary Catherine was also my ... girlfriend? Significant other? Like everything else in my life, I guess you could say it was complicated.

But does it have to be? I wondered, not for the first time.

'On a Saturday morning?' she repeated.

'It seems so,' I said as I closed my eyes and bowed my head solemnly.

'But we were going to go skating in the park. The kids were looking forward to it. Have all the other flatfoots in the entire city perished?'

'It's Chief Fabretti or I'd ignore it.' I shrugged. 'It's important. Something is up, I guess.'

'When is something down in this town, I wonder?' Mary Catherine said as I slunk out of there.

CHAPTER 2

A little over an hour later, I was in Queens, sitting in a large open room on the second floor of an ugly brown concrete-and-glass building off a service road in the south part of the small city that is JFK International Airport.

The building was the Port Authority Police Department JFK Command Center, and outside the window next to me, bursts of white exploded up into the crystal clear air from the massive airport plows working the snow from one of the airport's four runways.

Between the runway and the PAPD building, there was what looked very much like a parking lot, but on it, instead of cars, were several small white bullet-nosed corporate jets, and from the planes came groups of mostly male passengers.

Some of them were tall and slim and wore dark business suits, and some of them were tall and bulky and wore olive-drab military fatigues.

Every once in a while, one of the curious incoming passengers would enter the room I was sitting in and pass on through to one of the conference rooms at the far end, where various closed-door meetings were taking place.

The tall gentlemen were Secret Service, I knew. The guys in the suits and polished wing tips? Presidential protection agents. The guys in the drabs with the long gun bags? Secret Service CAT – counterassault team – tactical agents. From the news report I'd seen this morning, I surmised that the Secret Service people were the forward contingent prepping for the president's imminent arrival in NYC for the General Assembly at the UN.

What I didn't know was what I was doing here. I was working in the Major Case Squad, not Dignitary Protection. My boss, Chief of Detectives Fabretti, hadn't said much in his text except for me to get here forthwith.

As I sat pondering the continuing mystery, I realized that I'd actually been in this building and squad room before. It was in 2001, when I'd been in the NYPD's ESU SWAT A team. We'd been assigned to assist the NYPD's Dignitary Protection squad to protect George W. Bush when he came to New York three days after the Twin Towers fell on 9/11.

I was actually right there among the firefighters and phone guys and welders in the crowd at the pile down at Ground Zero when he gave the famous bullhorn speech.

It was a pretty unforgettable moment, the president standing on the pile of devastation, his rousing words lost after a moment in the overhead roar of the two F-16 fighter jets flying air cover around the perimeter of Manhattan.

But the fact that I was now here, back in this room, going over that dark rubble-strewn memory, wasn't exactly boding well. What was adding to my growing worry was what I couldn't help but notice about the Secret Service personnel. Usually, the Secret Service guys are somewhat laid-back when POTUS isn't around, but every one of them walking past looked stressed and tense and quite concerned.

After a few more minutes, a conference room door opened, and Neil Fabretti stuck his head out and waved at me.

I thought the room would be packed, but besides Fabretti, there was only one person inside, a stocky redheaded guy sitting at an Office Depot discount conference table talking on his cell. Though he was wearing a suit, he didn't look like one. His rusty-colored hair was military short, with sidewalls the color of a Carhartt coat.

'Mike,' Chief Fabretti said as the guy got off his mobile. 'This is Paul Ernenwein, the new anti-terror ASAC at the FBI's New York office.'

'Pleased to meet you, Paul,' I said as he almost broke my hand with his meaty one.

'Here's the story, Mike,' Ernenwein said with a Boston accent. 'Right when Air Force One went wheels up, we got a credible threat that a hit is going to be attempted here in New York City.'

I almost jumped out of my shoes, then just stood there, stunned and blinking. I knew something was up, but wow. Talk about a sledgehammer to the face.

'A hit? An assassination attempt?' I said.

Ernenwein slowly nodded his large red head.

'It's a long story, but an extremely reliable Russian mafia informant has provided credible information that a hit is going down now. And I mean right now, perhaps on POTUS's entry into New York. It's a long saga, but we actually think the Russian president Alexander Grekov himself might be involved in this assassination attempt.'

I tried to absorb that. It wasn't easy with all the alarms still clanging inside my head.

'But why not abort if the president might be in danger?'

'POTUS refuses,' said Ernenwein, biting his lower lip. 'Look, all we know is that Grekov is trying to start up the Cold War again. The president ran on putting a stop to it, but he needs help, and he has a meeting this morning with some of our shakier NATO allies. Any suggestion of weakness, that he has to hide on our own soil, would be disastrous. He told us to do our jobs and to protect him.'

'If it's true that there's a hit team already in New York, we have to find them yesterday,' Fabretti said, staring at me. 'I want you as our front man in the task force with the FBI to help track them down.'

'Of course,' I said as another whining corporate jet roared in beyond the window.

I took a breath as I stared at it, trying to ramp up to speed.

A second ago, I was making pancakes, and now we were ... what, back on the brink of WWIII?

This was crazier than Cartoon Network.

CHAPTER 3

Usually, the NYPD takes exclusive care of all air cover on presidential visits, but since such a dire threat was so imminent, it was all-hands-on-deck time, and every police aircraft and tactical team in the tristate area had been called in to assist.

When I learned about the manpower shortage, I mentioned to Fabretti that I had actually been a spotter on a sniper team when I was in the ESU. He made a call, and I found myself teamed up with a sniper from the Nassau County SWAT team whose partner was out of town. Then, twenty minutes later, I was out on the airport's cold, windy tarmac with my overcoat collar up as a whining Nassau County PD Bell 412 helicopter touched down in front of me.

Sitting in the backseat behind the pilot was the sniper I was there to assist. His name was Greg something Polish that I didn't quite catch. Definitely not Brady. He was a slim, cocky, thirtyish guy with a shaved head and lots of tats. He had even more lip than ink, if that was possible. I don't know what it was, the five-alarm stress or adrenaline or if he was just a natural-born jackass, but he started being a jerk from the very second I strapped in beside the pilot.

'You're my spotter?' Greg said in the chopper's headphones. 'Where'd you pick it up, Korea or 'Nam? And nice tie. I didn't know this was dress

37

formal tactical response, or I wouldn't have left my cummerbund in my other kit bag.'

'Hi, Greg. My name's Mike Bennett,' I said, smiling back at him where he sat in the chopper's backseat. 'I know this is last-second, for everybody to get chucked together like this. Believe it or not, I worked on a sniper team in the NYPD's ESU for a few years and know my way around a spotting scope. I'm also pretty familiar with the area around the UN. Let's say we get the president to where he has to go, okay?'

'Whatever,' my new charming friend, Greg, mumbled in reply.

With that, the chopper's rotor whine rapidly increased in pitch, and we were ascending up and out over Jamaica Bay to the airport's south. As we stilled to a hover, beyond the fishbowl canopy I could see a half dozen other hovering police helicopters in a loose string along the airport's perimeter.

Down alongside the runway beside the Port Authority building, the presidential motorcade was assembling. Even from a couple thousand feet, I could make out the military armor-plated limo they called the Beast, which the president would ride in. There were actually two of them. In front and back of the huge Cadillac limos were over a dozen other black Suburbans that would carry other White House officials and the Secret Service CAT tactical guys. Ahead of the feds was the NYPD-provided sweep team, a highway unit car in front of an NYPD Intelligence Division command car in front of a bomb squad vehicle and a tow truck.

As we waited and hovered, huge, seemingly too-close passenger aircraft flew in and out of JFK what seemed like every five seconds. Listening to the pilot's hectic radio sizzle, I started to get nervous. There were a lot of chefs here in this rapidly developing situation, a lot of stress and amped-up emotion. It was precisely at times like this that mistakes happened, I knew. When, say, a new air traffic controller gets ahead of himself and decides to shift a hovering PD chopper right in front of an incoming DC-10.

'There she is,' the pilot said suddenly over the headset as he pointed to the left.

And there she was.

I sat gaping at Air Force One, coming in from the east for a landing.

The sight of the iconic aircraft struck a strangely powerful emotional chord with me. Was it patriotism? A sense of hope? Of vulnerability? My memories of 9/11?

Whatever it was, I suddenly felt like I was a Boy Scout again. Like I should salute the plane or maybe recite the Pledge of Allegiance.

God bless America, I prayed silently to myself as the huge aircraft gently touched down on the runway below.

Please.

CHAPTER 4

The blind was the size of a jail cell.

It had the feel of a jail cell as well, with its concrete ceiling, the rear concrete wall, the cold concrete floor. The blind's side-walls and the front were made of plywood that was spray-painted black on the outside to fit in with the industrial roof space's black painted concrete. In the forward plywood wall was a hole the size of a computer monitor with a black piece of cloth duct-taped over it.

The assassin checked his watch, then pulled the curtain off and looked down into the angled eyepiece of his Swarovski ATX hunting telescope.

The first thing he noticed as he looked out on the world was the morning's air quality. It couldn't have been better. It was a cold twenty-nine degrees Fahrenheit and bright and clear as freshly Windexed Waterford crystal. *Good bombing weather*, he thought. Both the wind direction and speed were perfect, a light, gentle, eight-miles-an-hour west-southwest at his back.

From his perch fifty stories up looking east, the view field in the scope offered the clearest, most incredible view of Manhattan north of the Empire State Building. One could actually make out the curvature of the earth there in the distant horizon of Queens.

He panned the scope north to south across the

gray carpet of building tops, the 59th Street Bridge, the black obelisk of the Trump World Tower. He stopped when he got to the Chrysler Building; that was on his right. It was so close and vivid in the advanced optics of the four-thousand-dollar scope that it seemed like, if he wanted to, he could reach out and prick his thumb on the glistening silver needle of its spire.

He panned the scope back a skosh to the left, and then angled it slightly down and thumbed the zoom.

Then, a few moments later, there it was in glistening focus. The target. The reason he'd been pissing into Gatorade bottles for the last two days.

The United Nations building.

Technically, the iconic glass skyscraper was called the United Nations Secretariat Building. In his scope, the sparkling rectangle of blue glass was so sharp-edged it looked two-dimensional, like a shiny forty-story glass playing card stuck into First Avenue.

He zoomed and tilted lower again and framed in his kill zone.

The bookends were the edge of the Secretariat building's concrete sidewalk guard shack on the left and an apartment building on 43rd Street on the right. The in-between target zone was a segment of the UN building's iron-gated circular driveway and reflecting pool. He centered the scope over the fence just to the right of the building's front door entrance, where the VIP cars stopped.

The target zone had already been ranged in

41

with a PEQ laser sight at a little under thirteen hundred yards away. The bullet path would be a descending one on a slight diagonal, right to left, approximately one cross street block in width. Because of the diagonal, the kill gap was tiny, a thin slot between a residential building on the corner of Second Avenue and 43rd and the north edge of an old prewar building called the Tudor Tower that was on the cross street directly across First Avenue in front of the UN.

Threading that needle would have been bad enough, but adding to things was a jutting roof structure on the UN's Permanent Mission of India building between Third and Second on the north side of 43rd Street. By his calculations, his descending bullet would have to clear it by less than half a foot on its way downrange to the target.

Another X factor was some small American flags on a lamppost at the dead end of 43rd and First Avenue that the bullet had a chance to deflect off. But the worst of all was the sculpture in the pool in front of the UN building itself. The damn sculpture drove him nuts. It was called *Single Form,* an abstract, ugly twenty-one-foot piece of bronze that looked like a giant dog tag that could potentially be between him and the presidential limo.

If all went well, he would have maybe three seconds to get the shot off as the president went from the armored car to the front entrance of the building. Three seconds to gauge and sight and squeeze. Three seconds to hit a hole in one from atop a five-hundred-foot cliff thirteen football fields away.

He took his eye off the scope and checked on the

42

electric blanket wrapped around the barrel of the long dark rifle resting on its bipod beside him.

Some guns are quite beautiful, but his world-famous thirty-pound Barrett M107 mounted with Zeiss 6 – 24 x 72 scope was about as elegant as a bulldozer. It was almost five feet long with the suppressor. Even its ammo was huge and clunky. The ten .50-caliber BMG API (armor-piercing incendiary) rounds loaded into its detachable box magazine were each over five inches in length and weighed over a quarter of a pound.

But what it lacked in form, it made up for in function, and then some. The Barrett was technically known as an anti-matériel rifle. With confirmed kills at over twenty-five hundred yards, it could shoot through one inch of armor plate or a foot of concrete.

Some might think that a Barrett loaded with APIs was a bit overkill, and that, say, a .300 Winchester Magnum or .338 Lapua round fired from a lighter rifle would have been adequate. And it might have been, but for the cold weather conditions. Because even with the warming blanket, he would be firing from essentially a cold bore, which sometimes reduced the range considerably.

Besides, this wasn't some match event. He was only going to get one shot if he was lucky, and he had to maximize every possibility that he would kill what he hit.

There were two, maybe three other people in the world who would even think of attempting the incredible shot. But he wasn't attempting it. He was going to do it.

He would kill the president not because he was

the best shot in all the world, he knew.

He would kill the president because he was the best shot who had ever been.

The assassin removed the electric blanket and clacked back on the Barrett's bolt slide, jacking the first huge .50 BMG into the chamber.

The bullet would be put in a museum when all was said and done, he realized as he glanced at the long gun. Maybe even the Smithsonian.

He pictured visiting it one day with a grandchild, seeing it there like a relic or a moon rock in some crowded gallery.

He was a very visual thinker and he smiled as the image of a huge mushroomed .50 mounted in a shadow box lingered in his mind.

It warmed him to think that the work of his precious hands would be preserved forever and ever under thick panes of alarmed glass.

CHAPTER 5

We arrived in Manhattan five minutes in front of the motorcade.

It was incredible how fast the limos and SUVs moved through Queens, somewhere between seventy and eighty miles an hour. Well, I guess not that incredible, since they had every highway and byway blocked off and the entire road to themselves.

They were supposed to have taken the Van Wyck to the Long Island Expressway to the Midtown

Tunnel, but at the last second, they had changed their mind about the tunnel for some reason, and now they were due to come into Manhattan over the 59th Street Bridge in a minute or two.

We were pointing west in a low thousand-foot hover somewhere over Yorkville just to the west of the bridge, waiting on them. In the helicopter, I sat to the pilot's right, and on my right was the east side of Manhattan's endless wilderness of buildings and windows. Park Avenue, Fifth Avenue, the green mat of Central Park ahead.

Due to the helicopter's vibration, a high-powered spotting scope was pretty much useless, so I was using just a pair of 10-power binoculars to scan the windows and rooftops. It was a beautifully clear day, hardly any clouds in the cold blue sky.

I had my gloves off, and I blew on my hands from time to time to warm them. The pilot's heater blew on the upper half of me, but beneath the metal footrests, it must have been open in places because my feet and lower half were freezing.

'What's the range on the inner perimeter around the UN again?' I said as I stared down at the congested Monopoly board of buildings.

'A thousand yards,' said Greg, the sniper, over the chopper's interphone.

Three thousand feet, I thought, looking down. The UN was to our left, between 42nd and 43rd Streets on First Avenue. Cross street blocks were each two hundred fifty feet, I knew. So that meant what? The interior scan perimeter was twelve blocks north and south from around 30th

45

to 54th Street, and then west to Lexington.

How many windows in that area had a vantage on the sidewalk in front of the UN? I thought, looking at grid after building grid of them. Too many to count, let alone watch. Plus a sniper would be far back in a room, probably up on some platform, and would need only a slit of an opening.

'Wait. I see something,' I suddenly said, scanning over by Park Avenue. 'Go over to Park by the MetLife Building.'

'Where?' said the pilot.

'The MetLife Building,' I said, pointing to the left. 'That big fifty-story headstone-looking thing on Park Avenue.'

'Are you crazy? That's too far out,' said Greg.

'I don't care. I saw something, some movement,' I said as we flew closer.

'Where?'

'Underneath the rim of the roof, that black area beside the sign where the satellite dishes and equipment are.'

After another minute, I heard Greg, the sniper, laugh.

'What's the power on your glasses?'

'Ten,' I said.

'Here. Use mine, supercop. They're a sixteen,' he said, shoving his binocs at me. 'We can call off the air strike. I think we're good.'

Just as I looked, something dropped out from underneath the rim of the massive office building and unfurled.

Greg continued cracking up as I saw the red tail feathers and realized I was looking at a hawk.

CHAPTER 6

In the blind, the assassin put on his noise-canceling headphones and knelt down on the wood pallet platform beside the Barrett.

He lay prone and scooted in around the humongous rifle, embracing it like a lover at a picnic. He nestled the gunstock into his right shoulder joint ever so gently, like a newborn that needed a burp. His cheek went to the cold plate, his palm to the grip, and his finger to the metal comma of the trigger.

As he always did, he first closed his eyes and tried to actually physically feel the tension draining from his body as he breathed. With every release of breath, he envisioned it as a warm, glowing liquid spilling out of his pores through his clothes and flowing over the platform's sides.

He went through his checklist. Perfectly relaxed, naturally aligned, and oriented to the target. Check, check, and check.

He opened his right blue eye an eyelash length from the polished curve of the Zeiss's scope, his focus and concentration tightening like a slipknot. In the scope, the universe condensed itself into a circle picture of a sidewalk guard shack, an iron fence, a circular driveway, a reflecting pool, and a bronze sculpture.

His body was perfect stillness. His mind was perfect visual awareness. He was entering the

47

zone. He could feel it. He was dialing it in.

Flashing lights crossed the meridian of his scope as the motorcade pulled up in front of the building. The lead vehicles slowed, and the huge presidential limo slipped in through the UN's opened gate. He tracked it around the circular drive, all the way around the pool, and watched as it stopped well before the entrance to the right of the sculpture.

The doors popped a split second later, and there he was. Voilà! Like a rabbit out of a hat.

It was the new president, Jeremy Buckland, his famous face coming out of the car, dead center into the cross of the scope's reticle.

The assassin held himself. He was in the midst of inhaling a breath, and he needed to wait for his exhale, for that still zone between the oxygen coming in and the carbon dioxide going out, where everything leveled so he could squeeze.

He never got there.

It just happened. Something happened.

There was a bluish-gray blur in the scope, and the president was gone.

What?!

He looked up over the rim of the scope.

It was a helicopter. A helicopter had come from nowhere and was now level with his position. He hadn't heard it approach because of the head-phones.

The Bell 412 had police markings and was twenty feet out off the building's edge, pointed directly at him. There was a cop in it next to the pilot, pointing binoculars, again, right at him through the hole in the blind. The cop was look-

48

ing right into his face.

The assassin stared in horror for a moment, then did the only remaining thing he could do.

He shifted to his left and center-sighted the huge Barrett rifle onto the helicopter and squeezed the trigger.

CHAPTER 7

It was one of those surreal moments when you say, *Wait – this is impossible. I'm dreaming.*

I'd just told the chopper pilot to head in closer on the east side of the MetLife Building for a second look, when under the rim of the roof, I spotted something with the binoculars.

It wasn't movement this time, but a box, a weird black box tucked in behind a bunch of wires and a satellite dish. The pilot moved a little more to the left, and through a slit in the box's front I suddenly saw what was inside.

It was a man.

Behind a rifle.

He was wearing earphones over a black balaclava ski mask and black coveralls, and he was lying prone beside an enormous black rifle.

I had just enough time to drop my jaw when he swung the rifle right at us.

'Sniper!' I yelled at the moment the muzzle flashed.

A second later, the entire helicopter's glass canopy shattered and cold air was rushing in my face, and we were spinning crazily. You could tell right away that there was something very wrong with the chopper. It felt incredibly top-heavy, hanging down and over to the right side as we wheeled and wobbled. An alarm was sounding in the console over the suddenly much louder *whumps* of the overhead rotor. All I could do was sit there and panic as, outside the shattered windshield, the sky and the buildings whipped past in a chaotic blur.

I looked up and saw the hole in the cabin ceiling spilling oil. Then I turned to my left toward the pilot to see him fighting with the joystick.

'My eyes! I have glass and blood in my eyes! I can't see!' he said, and then there was a horrendous metal groaning, and I rocked hard in my seat and blasted the side of my head against the cabin's bulkhead as we suddenly smashed into something and rolled over to the left.

'What happened? What happened?' yelled Greg in my ear as a horrible metal snapping sound came.

I learned later that it was the rotor and tail blades snapping off as they hit the concrete deck of the MetLife Building's roof, where we'd just crash-landed. Somehow, I quickly unstrapped and got my door open and dropped over and out between the toppled helicopter's skids. Greg, the sniper, was right on my heels, and a moment later, we pulled the bleeding pilot out and ran away from the still-whining, smoking chopper as fast as we could.

Not yet truly believing we were still alive, we found a stairwell door and opened it and set the injured pilot on the landing as we watched the chopper, spinning and smoking at the edge of the MetLife Building's roof. I looked out at the incredible skyline of Manhattan behind it as I shook my head. If I hadn't already believed in miracles, I would have been converted right then and there.

'There is no way in hell we should still be alive,' Greg said as we heard a click. It was a door, a door opening in the stairwell one floor below us.

Greg and I turned from the chopper and looked in over the stairwell's railing.

And saw the guy.

The guy in the balaclava – the assassin – standing there one floor below us, staring up.

CHAPTER 8

When I saw that the shooter had something down behind his leg, three things happened at the same time.

I grabbed Greg by the back of his vest, I started to backpedal, and there was a shot.

We tripped over the still-sitting pilot's legs and landed back out on the roof. I pulled myself up and drew my Glock. I was about to help Greg up when I saw the hole between his nose and cheek and the blood spray on the concrete beneath his head.

He was dead.

My heart jackhammering in my chest as I wondered what in the name of God Almighty was going to happen next, I pointed my Glock straight at the stairwell doorway. I walked around the pilot as he crawled back out onto the roof, and I quietly stepped into the stairwell and took a deep breath and peeked back over the railing, Glock first.

I let out the breath. No one. Just a bare concrete floor. The shooter was gone.

I listened. There was no sound of running farther down the concrete stairwell. The shooter must have entered the floor just beneath, I thought with a nod.

I took out my phone with my free hand and thumbed Return Call.

'Mike, what happened?' Fabretti said.

'Shooter in the MetLife Building on the second to top floor,' I said as I began to take the stairs down two at a time. 'He's six feet tall. Black coveralls. Wearing a ski mask. He's armed and highly dangerous. He just killed a cop. I repeat: just killed a cop. I'm on the roof coming down after him. Seal off the MetLife Building lobby and send EMTs up to the roof for the pilot.'

'The pilot? What? Aren't you in a helicopter?' Fabretti said.

'MetLife Building!' I hollered, and dropped the phone back into my jacket pocket as I pulled open the door at the bottom of the stairwell, carefully staying well to the left side of it. I waited and waited, then glanced in through the doorway behind my gun.

Over the Glock's sights, I scanned a long, empty, fluorescent-lit industrial corridor with some unmarked doors on each side. Behind the doors on the right, there was the sound of machinery clacking and humming. There was a strong smell in the warm air. It smelled like a garage, like motor oil.

It's where the elevators are, I thought. The motors for the massive building's elevators.

I stood there, staring down the bright, empty industrial hall as my heart continued doing roadwork in my chest. I thought about Greg, dead on the roof, and about the Dallas cop Oswald killed after shooting Kennedy.

I was still thinking about all that and just about to take my first step into the hall anyway when a gun and arm appeared like a magic trick around the right corner of the corridor's far end.

The gun started going off, and the concrete of the stairwell wall beside my head started exploding. There were three shots, then four, then five, and concrete grit dusting my face and concrete dust stinging my eyes as I ducked and dropped back and kicked the door shut again.

A small piece of cement must have cut my face because when I touched my cheek, I saw blood on my finger. I coughed and crawled back some more as two more shots ripped jagged holes through the fire door.

'Shots fired!' I screamed into my phone. 'I'm up on the floor where the elevators are. Second from the top. Get SWAT up here now!'

CHAPTER 9

Mona Garcia, a twenty-eight-year-old recently naturalized immigrant from Belize, was in maintenance elevator number two and had just opened the door to the thirty-third floor when she heard the overhead thump.

She looked up as the ceiling hatch of the elevator car shrieked open. A man was standing there on top of the car. A man in black with a black ski mask and nice blue eyes.

Those blue eyes were the last thing she ever saw as two Federal Hi-Shok hollow-point .45-caliber bullets entered the top of her forehead.

The assassin dropped down into the car through the hatch and glanced into the hall behind his Springfield Range Officer M1911. Seeing that it was empty, he placed the RO down on the pebbled steel floor of the elevator and quickly unclipped the climbing harness from the ropes he had rigged in the elevator shaft two days before.

The ropes were his emergency escape route, which he'd just used after slipping into the shaft through a gap beside the elevator machinery up on forty-nine.

He glanced at his watch.

He had at most three minutes to get out of the building before it was completely sealed.

He dragged the cleaning woman's body by the ankles out into the empty maintenance hall and stepped back into the elevator. Then he hit the button for the basement as he reached for the zipper of the coveralls.

'Help you, Officer?' said a maintenance man, a skinny, pale, blond young white guy standing out in the hall with two other Spanish-speaking cleaning ladies, as the elevator opened in the basement. He was gaping wide-eyed at the Springfield the assassin held openly by his leg.

'Listen up,' the assassin said with a cop command voice from beneath the brim of the NYPD ESU ball cap he was now wearing. It went with the rest of the convincing NYPD tactical uniform that he'd hidden beneath the coveralls. 'We got shots fired up on the street. A cop just got shot, and the perp ran into one of the train tunnels. You got access to the Grand Central Terminal train tunnel from the basement here? I need to get to the tunnels.'

'Yeah, I think so,' the kid said, blinking and nodding rapidly. 'Through the boiler room there's an old access door.'

The assassin already knew that. It was how he had entered the building two days before.

The young maintenance guy unclipped the radio at his belt.

'You want me to call the building manager?'

'No. No time. Show me now. There's no time to waste,' the assassin said, grabbing the guy's elbow and urging him along.

CHAPTER 10

East 50th next to the Waldorf Astoria, where the president was staying, was completely blocked off when I arrived there on foot with antiterror FBI head honcho Paul Ernenwein at around five thirty that evening.

It had begun to snow again a little, and through the swirling bits and gloom, I saw more cops per square inch in the street and on the sidewalk around the famous block-size art deco hotel than on Saint Patrick's Day. Unfortunately, a lot of news vans were parked three deep on Park Avenue as well, I noticed. We'd kept details to a minimum so far, but the helicopter crash and the shootings of Greg and the cleaning lady were already being broadcast fast and frantically out there in connection with the president's arrival.

Paul and I had just come from working the three different crime scenes at the MetLife Building: the sniper's nest; the crash scene on the roof, where Greg had been shot; and the freight elevator, where the shooter had killed the cleaning lady. We were still putting interviews and details together and combing for evidence, but the basic depressing bottom line so far was that we didn't know who the shooter was or, more important, where the hell he was.

Paul had gotten a call from one of his bosses saying that we should head over to the Waldorf to give the head presidential protective agent a personal briefing, so we'd decided to walk the five Park Avenue blocks. You could actually see the silhouette of the crashed helicopter still on the roof from the street, I noticed when I looked up. Figuring out how they were going to get it down from there was thankfully someone else's job.

After we credentialed our way past two checkpoints, we walked through the 50th Street entrance of the hotel's top-shelf premier section, called the Towers of the Waldorf. Its lobby was amazing, an Old New York, gleaming, opulent jewel box of creamy marble and paneling and gilt moldings. I'd never been there before in my life, but I knew that, like the Empire State Building, the Waldorf had been built in the art deco skyscraper heyday of the early thirties. I thought that at any moment, Mr. Monopoly would come around the corner in his top hat and spats.

Instead, Tom Kask, the Secret Service team head, arrived. He was a big guy – six five, maybe – well dressed and lanky, with slicked silver hair and a cold, remote look on his face. If I had to judge a book by its cover, I'd say he looked like a big dumb jock bully.

'So you're the cop who lost him?' Kask said, looking down at me as he arrived.

'No,' Paul said calmly as he showed him some of the crime scene photos from his phone. 'He's the cop who found the guy with the Barrett fifty cal that you jackwads missed. Mike here is the guy who probably saved the president's life, and even your career, Tom, if you think about it.'

There were a bunch of factors to explain why his

guys hadn't seen the shooter, the incredible distance being the most glaring, but it didn't matter. They, the glorious Secret Service, had screwed up royally, and a lowly NYPD cop had done their job for them.

'Sorry. That came out wrong,' the big bastard Kask said, not looking very sorry at all. 'It's that kind of day, you know.'

'Yeah, you're right. It did come out wrong,' Paul said, continuing to give him hell with his Southie Boston accent.

I was beginning to like Paul. He'd been totally hands-on in helping the PD and FBI response teams at the crime scenes – not exactly a common occurrence for an FBI boss. Not bad for a Red Sox fan, either, I thought.

'Anyway, Tom, we're still smack-dab in the middle of this,' Paul said, putting his phone back into his pocket. 'Anything else?'

'Actually, yeah,' Kask said. 'Follow me. He wants to see you. Well, *him,* actually.'

'Who, me?' I said. 'Who wants to see me?'

'The president. Who else?' said Kask.

CHAPTER 11

With that, Kask led me around a corner of the incredible lobby.

We walked past two more Secret Service presidential detail agents and an impeccably dressed desk clerk into a waiting elevator. The doors closed, and the button for 29 lit up by itself somehow, and we started to ascend.

Kask ignored me and began checking his phone while I did my best not to gape at the impressive surroundings. I'd been in elevators for work before, just never a lacquered, bird's-eye mahogany-paneled one that was inlaid with art deco sunbursts and chevrons.

The elevator doors opened onto a small Oriental-carpeted foyer where four tall spit-shined Secret Service agents stood at attention. Between them was a set of bright-white double doors with the words WALDORF PRESIDENTIAL SUITE written in gold script.

Before I could ask someone to pinch me, I watched as Kask opened the door without knocking, and I saw President Buckland for the first time.

Beyond another small foyer, the president was sitting in a little living room on a love seat with his hands behind his head. His eyes were closed, and he was nodding as an aide read him something. Then he opened his eyes and saw me and stood up and smiled.

'Thanks, Tom,' the president said to Kask, who immediately left. 'Detective Bennett, I believe I owe you a thank-you,' he said, offering his hand.

I stood there for a second, staring at his hand, stunned by it all.

'Yep,' I got out as I finally shook his hand. 'I mean, no, of course not. No, sir. Are you kidding me? I'm just glad that you're okay. I'm just glad to help.'

'Oh, thank you so much, Officer,' the First

Lady said as she came out of another room. 'The whole thing must have been terrifying.'

She was Snow White classically pretty, with her dark hair and pale skin. She had on a cream-colored pantsuit but was wearing slippers, I noticed, and I found myself amazed again that all this was actually happening. That I was standing in the Waldorf's presidential suite enjoying a chat with the commander in chief and his wife.

I'll never forget this, I thought.

I couldn't wait to tell the kids and Mary Catherine.

'*Officer,* Alicia? Really? It's *Detective*. Detective Michael Bennett,' President Buckland said, rolling his eyes. 'You think you'd remember the name of the man who just saved your beloved husband's bacon. I mean, did you even vote for me?'

'You'll never know, Jeremy, will you?' the First Lady said, winking at me before she headed back toward the other room. 'Thanks again, Detective Bennett.'

'So, Detective,' said the president.

'Please call me Mike, Mr. President.'

'If you call me Jerry'

'Okay, Jerry,' I said, finally at ease. I definitely liked this president's style.

'So, Mike, I wanted to talk to you to get your firsthand opinion. I hear advisers say things that they themselves were told, and on and on like a game of telephone, so I wanted to talk to you. You saw this guy, right? In your opinion, this guy was the real deal? He was going to kill me?'

I nodded. 'I was in the blind. Looked through the scope myself, sir – I mean, Jerry. It was dialed in right on you. He'd been there a couple of days, it seems. Not to mention the way he killed my partner. It was a hell of a pistol shot. My partner never had a chance. Then he got away with rappelling equipment in the elevator shaft. That's about as professional a killer as I've ever encountered.'

'Mr. President,' said his aide from across the room. 'This just in off the AP wire.'

The president turned.

'The Russians have made it clear that they had nothing to do with any threat against the president. They find the suggestion insulting, the bastards.'

The president's demeanor changed for a second. He looked down at the table we were standing beside. The emotion was there for a moment – raw hurt, slightly afraid. When he looked back at me, it was gone, and he was smiling.

'I'll let you go, Mike,' the president said. 'Miles to go and all that, but I'll never forget what you did for me and for your country.'

'Mr. President,' I said.

'What happened to Jerry?' he said as Kask appeared again.

'Mr. President, I'm going to catch this guy,' I said.

CHAPTER 12

The assassin licked away the last of his chocolate *crémeux* and dropped the spoon and closed his eyes as he leaned back in the tufted banquette.

The restaurant was called Elise. It was on a cobblestoned street on the outskirts of the meat-packing district, and it served Michelin two-star French molecular deconstructive cuisine that was as absurdly good as it was expensive.

The decor was seductively dark in the dining room and bar below, with dramatic lights thrown upward onto gorgeously textured high white limestone walls. With his back to the wall in the darkness, even a man like him could relax, the assassin thought. At least for a moment.

He had just consumed a four-hundred-dollar nine-course chef's tasting menu that pulled out all the stops: a parade of caviar and white truffle risotto and fried sweetbread piccata and herb-roasted tenderloin of wagyu. All of it arranged like museum-quality art and matched with pre-posterous precision with the best wines of Burgundy and the Rhône.

He had gone hungry more than once as a young child, and since then, he had never failed to treat food with its proper reverence. To eat meant more than just filling his belly. It was a communion with ... something. Life? Death, perhaps? He didn't know. He was no philosopher, but food was something just ... more. It was more than simply a combination of pleasant sensual experiences.

Ecstatically stuffed and drunk, he listened to the surrounding murmur of the expensive restaurant. The plate clacks and conversation and discreet laughter. The festive rattle of the bartender somewhere off to the left, shaking ice cubes. Music to his ears.

'Can I get you anything?' his wife said. 'A hot towel, perhaps? Maybe a pillow and a blanket?'

'Absolutely nothing,' the assassin said, opening his eyes with a smile. 'That was...'

'Expensive,' his wife said with a frown.

'Oh, yes, it was. And well worth it,' he said, swirling his twenty-one-year-old Elijah Craig single-barrel bourbon.

He'd picked up an addiction to the American spirit three years ago on a job in Osaka, Japan, of all places. The Japanese were nuts, but he was all over their fetish for mastery. Maybe he'd been Japanese in a previous life.

'I don't understand. The mission failed,' she said.

He looked at her.

'Sweetheart, the helicopter landed on the roof. I mean, I'm one for planning for eventualities, but I didn't see that one coming. I come out and look up, and there's the cavalry. You know how close I came to getting pinched?'

'All too well.'

'But I didn't,' he said, winking as he sipped at the smooth fire of the bourbon. 'If that's not something to celebrate, I don't know what is.'

'How about finishing the job? You know, getting

paid? That helps, with the way you blow it.'

'Darling, I had him,' he said, kissing her hand. 'His face was right there. We were in. He can be had. We'll get another chance. You'll see. In the meantime, I just got an offer I can't refuse. A quick little job here in town. You in?'

She rolled her eyes playfully at him.

'Ever the sweet-talker, I see,' she said, smiling. 'Count me in, as usual.'

CHAPTER 13

Around midnight, I was doing what I always like to do after helicopter crashes and meeting US presidents.

I was kneeling on the floor of my apartment bathroom, pinning the family cat, Socky, to the tile floor.

The Sockster had been sick the last couple of days – some upper respiratory thing – and he wasn't eating or hardly even drinking, so Mary Catherine and I had to, per the vet's order, syringe-feed him. Mary Catherine was on syringe duty while I wrapped him up tight in a bath towel. I was wearing kitchen gloves as I held him down to avoid getting clawed.

With good reason, too, because Socky didn't seem to be enjoying his force-fed meal in the slightest. In fact, he sounded a lot like a Harley at full throttle as he squirmed.

'So anyway,' I said to Mary Catherine over the

ungodly howls as she slipped a paper towel bib over Socky's head, 'I'm standing there, and the door opens and there he is! Buckland's sitting five feet away, talking with one of his advisers.'

'No!' she said, staring at me.

'Yes!' I said, nodding, still hopped-up from the day's excitement. 'If I wasn't currently using it for lion taming, I'd show you the hand that shook the hand that shakes the world.'

Mary Catherine smiled as she tried to squirt cat vitamin water between Socky's fangs.

'You're not so bad yourself, Detective Bennett. You saved his life, you did.'

'Well, keep that to yourself, please. They're actually trying to keep that under wraps for now, a full media blackout, and it's working for once. Plus I don't want the kids to know that I was in the helicopter crash. Not yet. They have enough to worry about.'

'It's so hard to believe somebody would want to kill Buckland after his landslide election,' Mary Catherine said, shaking her head. 'How many states did he win? Forty-four? Forty-five?'

'Forty-six,' I said. 'Maybe that's just it. He said he was going to shake up the status quo, and he's got the mandate to do it You have to think that there are a lot of folks with entrenched power at home and abroad who are feeling pretty rattled right now.'

'Rattled enough to put a hit on a sitting US president?' Mary Catherine said.

I looked at her.

I didn't even want to mention the Russian tip from the FBI. That an attempt on Buckland's life might have actually come from the Russians and that some new vicious revamping of the Cold War could right now be under way. It was too terrible to contemplate. I almost wished that I didn't know.

Socky hissed, got a claw out, and raked my gloved wrist before I was able to subdue him with the towel.

'I don't know, Mary Catherine,' I said with a shrug. 'Who knows today? Anything seems possible.'

'Well, all that matters now is that you're home in one piece,' she said, smiling.

'Couldn't agree more,' I said. 'Now let's just hope Socky here will let me stay that way.'

CHAPTER 14

Next day around four thirty, I was uptown in Hamilton Heights, standing on the third-floor fire escape of a building on West 141st between Broadway and Riverside Drive.

Taking in the lay of the land, I decided that it had to be one of the most architecturally interesting crime-ridden neighborhoods I'd ever been to. There were stone row houses with Greek-columned entrances and apartment buildings with Juliet balconies. I noticed there was an equal number of reno Dumpsters and beat-up, tinted-windowed cheap Nissans and Mazdas in the street in front of the buildings.

Like everyplace else in the perpetually sky-rocketing rent zone that is NYC, even the Heights seemed to be in the midst of gentrifying. Too bad I wasn't looking to flip an apartment, I thought. A shooting had occurred here the week before, when an entire seven-member drug crew running an ecstasy lab in the apartment behind me had been slaughtered.

Such things happened from time to time in New York, of course, but the weird thing about it was *how* it had happened. Apparently, suppressors had been used. The power line to the building had been cut. In sum, it had the earmarks of a professional hit.

Just like the attempt on the president.

We were still stone cold in the leads department on the MetLife Building assassin's whereabouts, so we were looking at anything and everything that might be related.

'Don't jump, Mike. It's not that bad,' Detective Jimmy Doyle said as he and Detective Arturo Lopez came out of the drug apartment and stood beside me by the snow-topped railing. My buddies and protégés from my special assignment in Harlem a while back were among the many Thirtieth Precinct detectives who'd caught the seven-body case.

'Yeah? Tell that to Chief Fabretti,' I said, flipping up the lapels of my overcoat as a cold wind sliced in off the Hudson to my left. 'Now, one more time from the top.'

'Shots fired call comes in at eight fifteen,' Doyle said, Magliting the clipboard he was holding. 'Responding officers were here in five. Straight off the bat, they see the first bodies slumped in the exterior sidewalk stairwell down there on the left, then head into the lobby. The other four they spot just off the lobby at the foot of the east stairwell.'

'All dead? Not dying? Dead?' I said.

'All seven well dead, with one-shot-kill head shots by' – Doyle flipped through some pages until he got to the coroner's report – '.45-caliber ACPs.'

'Whoa. And nothing was missing up here in the cookhouse?' I said. 'How much did you find again?'

'Nine hundred thousand in tens and twenties. Twice that in product.'

'Just sitting there?'

Doyle nodded.

'DEA had a theory about the crew but not much else,' said Arturo as he made a snowball. 'They called them the no-name crew. By the setup here, the experts think they were easily one of – if not *the* – biggest ecstasy suppliers in the city.'

'Under the radar. The drug boss, Rafael Arruda, was a smart man.'

'That's *Dr.* Rafael Arruda to you, Mike,' Arturo said as he chucked the snowball into the parking lot across 141st. 'He was a Columbia University professor, after all.'

'Unbelievable,' I said. 'What's the family dynamic again? Could it have been the wife?'

'No. The wife of the Ivy League's answer to Pablo Escobar checks out,' Doyle said. 'She was his high school sweetheart. Goes to church every morning. You should see his house. He lived up in tony Bronxville. His daughter was home visiting from Georgetown.'

'Canvass?'

Arturo gestured out at the surrounding buildings with both hands as he nodded. 'We busted our ass, but nothing.'

'All the windows facing the front, right?'

'Yep. Every vantage on the front sidewalk, where it went down. No surveillance cams pointing this way, unfortunately, and we got only a few people to open doors. They hadn't seen or heard a thing. Which makes sense. It was the night of the big storm.'

'What time did you start the canvass?'

Doyle looked at his notes again. 'Nine thirty,' he said.

'What time you got now?'

'Four thirty. Why?'

'Time to bust your ass again,' I said. 'Call patrol and do the canvass all over again right now.'

'How's that? It's been a week,' said Arturo.

'That's why you need to do it again. It's been exactly one week since the crime. Someone who saw it could have left before you guys arrived on scene to question them. For whatever reason. Work. A date. People are creatures of habit, right? One week later, they'll be home right now.'

'Hey, that's smart,' said Doyle, looking at me. 'Have you done this detective thing before?'

CHAPTER 15

The gallery was in West Chelsea on West 30th between Eleventh Avenue and the West Side Highway, directly across from the fenced-in Hudson Yards Penn Station Amtrak train yard.

The opening night installation was called *Solar System:* ten massive modern neo-expressionist canvases integrated with various materials. Burlap and stainless steel. Flesh-colored porcelain and black rubber. Brass and cardboard. The largest painting, titled *Needing to Know #11,* was embedded with a mosaic tile of cowhide and fractured plexiglass.

It had taken the artist, Soyi, a twenty-seven-year-old Korean prodigy from Queens, six years to complete them. They were meticulous yet somehow chaotically, primitively powerful, restrained while being simultaneously aggressively expressive. At least that's what all the critics who had come to sponge the vodka and caviar were talking about.

Matthew, the dealer and gallery owner staring out at the paintings, hoped they were expressing, 'Hey, billionaire! I'm what you want on the wall of your new penthouse!'

Matthew turned as a pudgy blond woman waved by the door after grabbing her coat. He smiled and winked and waved back at Hilda Breen, the critic from *Art in America* who had called Soyi a 'definite new force in the art world.'

But would all the critical hype mean a sale? Matthew thought, sipping a vodka and tonic as he watched a pathetic and scarily dwindling number of people orbit the paintings. His client, Soyi, certainly needed a sale badly. Her unemployment was running out, and she was threatening to throw in the towel and go back to waitressing at her uncle's restaurant in Flushing. Soyi had been so nervous about her show's opening night that she'd actually fainted about an hour before and had gone home with her mom, the poor thing.

Matthew bit his lip as he thought about Soyi. Great reviews in the blogs and trade rags like *Artforum* and *October* were definitely scintillating, but keeping a brilliant young artist from a mind-deadening day job would be even more brilliant, Matthew thought with another swig of vodka.

It was his downtown-born-and-bred wife, Sophie, who had passed on the dealing bug. She'd gotten it from her father, a former artist who had owned a gallery in the famous 420 West Broadway in SoHo in the seventies. He'd been friends with Warhol and had briefly represented works from Warhol's famous Factory. He was actually now living in Palm Beach and mind-bogglingly rich from all the Warhols he had been given.

They were definitely not yet following in Daddy's footsteps in the big-bucks department, unfortunately. The bills were piling up. Art was a big-money business, but so were the NYC rents. They were a constant strain, galleries: searching for cheap areas that then increased in value, forcing the galleries to find somewhere else to gentrify. It was hard to figure where the next area would be since even rents in Brooklyn were getting patently ridiculous.

'Stop sulking!' said his wife, suddenly linking arms with him. 'Think positive, now, Matthew. Smile. Light this place up like Times Square. That's it. Turn on the charm. Sell, darling. Sell!'

'Yes, dear,' Matthew said through his wide grin. 'Has our final chance left?'

'Not yet. See? He's over by *Crimson Falling.*'

Their final chance was a tall, blond, bearded German gentleman who favored vintage jeans and plaid work shirts and who was known in the dealer world as the Berlin lumberjack. Not much was known about him except that he was a whale collector with edgy tastes and seemingly endlessly deep pockets.

'He seems interested,' Matthew said, still grinning to beat the band. 'Not just interested. Look at his eyes. He's mesmerized.'

'Mesmerized?' Sophie said. 'He looks bored.'

'I've seen that look before. He's just straining to appear so, the crafty German. If he's bored, why is he standing there?'

Retrieving his next vodka tonic five minutes later, Matthew was barely able to contain his surprise as he turned to see the Berlin lumberjack at his elbow.

'Okay, fine. I need them,' he said in a deep voice.

'I'm sorry?' Matthew said, coughing Ketel One.

'No. You're not,' he said, rolling his eyes. 'I need them. All of them. How much?'

Before Matthew could open his mouth, the

72

man continued.

'Now be careful, my friend. Do not be stupid. Do not gouge. There may be other people in the world intelligent enough to see the value of this work, but unfortunately for you and fortunately for me, they are not in this gallery space here that is bleeding you thirty thousand a month in rent. Choose wisely. Remember the goose with the golden eggs.'

Matthew did. But he knew he had him. He immediately came up with a ridiculous number.

And multiplied it by three.

CHAPTER 16

An hour later, they'd shoveled everyone out the door and called an ecstatic Soyi with the news.

'We did it!' Sophie said, kissing Matthew after they hung up. 'We actually did it again. A three-pointer at the buzzer. As usual, we dodged another, um ... bullet.'

'Never doubted it for a second, babe,' Matthew lied.

Finally with a chance to sit down, they were opening a bottle of champagne in the office when Sophie's phone made a strange beep.

'What is it? A text?' asked Matthew as he struggled with the foil atop the bottle of Cristal they'd been saving just for this very occasion.

'No, an e-mail,' Sophie said, looking. 'News alert.'

Matthew nodded. He knew what news she was monitoring.

The hit they'd done on Rafael Arruda up in Hamilton Heights the week before.

'Well?' he said with studied casualness.

'It's nothing. A piece in *New York* mag about the life and times of the dearly departed, brilliant drug-trafficking professor. The cops are, as usual, clueless.'

'Have I told you that you were amazing that night?' Matthew said, leaning over and kissing her neck.

'Maybe,' Sophie said, smiling. 'But tell me again anyway.'

Before he could say a word, Sophie's phone buzzed again.

'Hold that thought,' she said. 'I'm getting a call. It's a FaceTime. It's Victoria.'

Matthew, drunk on vodka and victory, felt a skyrocket explode in his heart when he looked over his wife's shoulder and saw his daughter's baby-bunny-rabbit-cute face suddenly appear on the screen.

It was for her. All of it. She would have the best of everything, always. The best for the best.

He knew that he and Sophie had in many ways failed. What kind of parents would do what they did? They'd participated in such ... utter darkness. But in his heart, he knew that Victoria made it worth it. She was the sunlight that made it all worth it. Her angel's face burned away their sins with every smile.

'Mommy, Daddy! Did you sell them? Did you sell Aunt Soyi's pretty pictures?'

74

'Yes, we did, Victoria. Every one,' Sophie said.

'Hooray!' Victoria said. 'So are we going to Grandpapa's? Will we swim, Mother? All of us? Will we swim in the ocean like last time, with the glasses? Will we look for Nemo and Dory?'

'Soon, baby, soon,' said Sophie.

'Can I have a pretty new swimsnoot? *Pleease?*'

'Of course,' said Matthew, smiling at his daughter's face. 'Heck, make it two!'

'Hooray!' said Victoria again.

Hooray indeed, thought Matthew as he finally got the champagne foil off and popped the cork.

PART TWO

ALL IN THE FAMILY

CHAPTER 17

'Dad, don't do it. It's not worth it,' Ricky said. 'Please, Dad.'

'He's right, Dad. We need you,' said Eddie, pretending to cry. 'What will we do without you?'

'If this is good-bye, Dad,' said Trent, giving me a quick hug, 'I just want you to know it's been nice knowing you.'

'Exactly, and make sure you have your insurance card in your wallet,' said Jane.

'Ha-ha. Tee-hee. Very funny, you wisenheimers,' I said as we all did a Bennett family fire drill around the van out in front of Holy Name school the next morning.

All the younger kids were disembarking from the van for school, but Brian was switching to the driver's seat. His road test was coming up, so for practice, I'd been letting him drive to his high school, Fordham Prep, in the Bronx.

The other kids, of course, were really helping out as usual by sharing their confidence in his driving skills.

'Don't listen to them, Brian,' I said when we were finally alone in the van. 'You can do this. Now, check your mirrors, okay? Don't forget to look over your shoulder. Good. Nice and easy now, son.'

The van roared as Brian gunned it out onto 96th Street.

'Brian, no! That's too much!' I screamed.

There was a violent screech as he slammed on the brakes. A box truck's horn blew in my ear as it whipped around us close enough to almost shave off the side view mirror. More horns sounded over the pounding of my heart. Brian's face was as white as a sheet. Mine was, too, as I swiped away the beads of sweat that were already gathering on my forehead.

Driver's ed NYC-style was definitely not for the faint of heart.

'Don't worry. Happens to everyone. You can do this, son,' I said.

'Nice job, son. I knew you could do this,' I said when we were safely stopped in Fordham Prep's parking lot thirty white-knuckling minutes later. 'See you at dinner, kiddo.'

'Wait, Dad. Actually, Coach Downey wanted to talk to you about something. He was going to send you an e-mail.'

Coach Keith Downey, Fordham Prep's athletic director, was also an old friend. I checked my phone and saw that he wanted to know if I could pop into his office one morning this week.

'He mention what it was about?' I asked Brian.

Brian shrugged as he shouldered his bag.

No time like the present, I thought, getting out and following Brian into the school building. It sounded pretty suspicious.

It turned out it *was* pretty suspicious. I found Coach Downey in the library, making copies.

'Mike, hey, thanks for stopping by,' the short and amazingly stocky Irish American said, smiling widely.

Coach Downey and I had gone to St. Barnabas grammar school in Woodlawn, where we grew up. He was a couple of years younger than I was, but I'd worked with his older brother busing tables at Villagio's, the only Italian restaurant in the predominantly Irish neighborhood.

'Hey, Keith. What's up?'

He put down the stack of papers in his big hands and looked me in the eye.

'No bullshit, Mike. I got a favor to ask you. If you can do it, great. If you can't, that's fine, too. It's about Marvin Peters. You know how he carried the football team last year?'

I nodded. 'Talented kid.'

'Three-letter athlete,' Coach Downey continued. 'One of the best this school has ever seen. What you might not know is that he lives in a shit project in Morrisania.'

My job had made me familiar with that section of the Bronx for all the wrong reasons. It was a crime-ridden area dominated by drugs and prostitution.

'His aunt Althea was keeping him on the straight and narrow, but as Brian probably told you, Marvin's aunt died two weeks ago. So another relative is scheduled to come up from the Carolinas to live with him, but it's going to take a couple of weeks. He's looking at foster care until then unless we get him set up somewhere.'

'Let me guess,' I said. 'You want to know if there's any room at the old detective who lives in a shoe's place?'

'Hey, sorry for asking, Mike. I know things are pretty tight at the Bennett villa. I'm actually asking everybody I can think of. I don't want to let this kid fall through the cracks, you know?'

'Two weeks?' I said as I took out my phone.

'Three, tops,' Coach Downey said, putting his hands together in prayer.

'Hey, Mary Catherine,' I said, and explained the situation to her. 'Thanks,' I said a minute later, and hung up.

'Well?' said Coach Downey.

'Tell him to come home with Brian today. Hope this kid likes togetherness, not to mention left-overs. Turns out there's one last free bunk in the old shoe after all.'

CHAPTER 18

Two hours later, I was at my morning's second academic meeting.

Unfortunately, this one wasn't so benign.

'Are you sure you don't want to come back later, Detective?' an annoyed thirtysomething personal assistant asked me from the other side of the stately high-ceilinged wood-paneled office I was sitting in.

'I'm absolutely positive,' I said, crossing my feet as I flipped through a Columbia University directory for the third time. 'It's okay. Don't worry about me. I have all the time in the world.'

I was at Columbia, trying to track down every-thing I could about the decedent, professor-drug dealer Rafael Arruda. I couldn't stop thinking about the professional way he had been hit. And that it might have something directly to do with the president's shooter on the MetLife Building.

'But again, I must stress how highly irregular this is,' the PA said. 'Vice president of academic affairs Hynes doesn't handle things like this. You're in the wrong department.'

There was a lot of that going around, I thought. I'd just been to the chemistry department in Havemeyer Hall, across the quad, where I'd spoken to two other administrative people, Dean this and Department Head that, about trying to find some information about Dr. Ecstasy, and they kept saying I had to speak to somebody else.

My head was truly starting to spin from the academic bullshit runaround, so here I was, digging in my heels at one of the big kahunas' offices.

'Then again, maybe I'm in the right place,' I replied with a shrug. 'Who's to say?'

'Like I said before...' Ms. Short began, but then the door opened behind her and a slim, attractive middle-aged woman with wavy brown hair and a crisp camel hair coat walked in.

'Hi, Vice President. I'm Detective Bennett. Could I have a few words with you?' I said, showing her my shield before the PA or anybody else could bullshit me some more.

The vice president surprised me with a wide, friendly smile. 'Of course,' she said. 'Please call me Reba. Come in.'

I thought her inner office would be as stuffy with dark wood paneling and bookshelves as the outer one, but the decor and walls had a clean, modern, soothing California aesthetic. There was a cream-colored distressed desk against a denim-blue wall and a comfortable slipcovered couch. Light flooded in from an oversize window onto a miniature driftwood sailboat propped on a coffee table.

On her desk was a photograph of a blond girl of about eight, a glassy canopy of teal-blue water over her head as she surfed.

'Wow. Great picture. Hawaii?' I said as I sat down.

'The Maldives, actually,' the surprisingly pleasant Reba Hynes said, smiling at the photo. 'My daughter, Emilia, really loves the water. We joke that she has gills instead of lungs.'

She tilted her head as she leaned back in her chair, still smiling at me. She had sharp, intelligent gray-green eyes, I noticed.

'Detective, I normally don't do this,' she said, 'but I take it you're here about Rafael? Dr. Arruda, right?'

Normally don't do what? I wondered, squinting. Cooperate with the police?

'Yes,' I said. 'I'm trying to find out all I can about him.'

'What is your particular interest, if you don't mind my asking? Are you in the narcotics division? I believe we already spoke to some precinct detectives.'

'No, I'm in Major Case, currently working on a joint task force with the FBI,' I said. 'We're investigating a national security matter that may tie in with the murder.'

Reba Hynes suddenly sat forward in the upright position with a semiconfused expression on her face. 'Oh, that's getting a little ridiculous, now,

84

isn't it, Detective? First, Rafael is some sort of drug dealer, and now you think he was a spy or something? I knew Rafael personally. He was one of the most popular professors on campus. Plus his narrative, his background, where he came from to achieve all that he's accomplished...' She waved her hand dismissively at me.

She folded her hands on her desk and looked me directly in the eye.

'Rafael was with some friends in the wrong place at the wrong time. It doesn't make any sense for him to have done the things he's accused of.'

'Well, we're very interested in finding out who killed him,' I said. 'I'd like to speak to his students and colleagues. They might be the link to finding his murderer.'

'I'm terribly sorry, Detective Bennett,' VP Hynes said, frowning. 'We can't release any information about students. We take our students' privacy very seriously.'

'Not even to help solve the murder of one of your professors?'

'No, not without a subpoena. I'm sorry,' the attractive academic said, giving me her pretty smile again. 'Now, if that will be all, Detective, I have a million meetings today.'

CHAPTER 19

But it wasn't all. Not even close.

Instead of hightailing it off campus, I grabbed a quick lunch at the nearest Columbia cafeteria. I was jazzed to see that it had a Starbucks counter, so I picked up a turkey wrap with my Venti black.

As I tucked in at a corner booth, I watched as my new buddy, President Buckland, appeared on the TV over the counter.

On the news this morning, I'd seen that there had been a dustup in Russia near the Ukrainian border. A school and hospital had been blown up, and Grekov was claiming it was from a Ukrainian mortar attack and was rattling his saber.

Grekov was shameless in his desire to put the old USSR back together, with the Ukraine as his first target. His invasion strategy was straight out of Hitler's playbook: claim that because there were ethnic Russians in the Ukraine, Russia needed to support them by invading. Hitler had said the same thing about Czechoslovakia. And before he'd invaded, he, too, had staged false flag border attacks inside the German border, which was exactly what Grekov's newest maneuver was looking like.

But President Buckland was all over it, I saw. As I watched, he started a slide show with satellite surveillance photos that showed Russian military trucks and soldiers coming in from the north to the supposedly Ukrainian-attacked hospital and school.

Take that, Grekov, I thought. Wow. That was a bold move. Buckland was calling out Grekov's bullshit for all the world to see.

Was that why that hit man had been there to shoot the president? I wondered. Grekov knew he now had a formidable foe in our new president; did he figure the best way to beat him was to clear the playing field?

Doyle called me a minute later. 'Hey, Mike. Major score last night on the recanvass. A super up the block showed us a security cam we missed. I just e-mailed it to you. It captures what happened. It's incredible. Watch.'

I did. It was murky black-and-white. First, it showed three drug crew guys standing on the sidewalk. Then, a second later, they were flying like bowling pins as a motorcycle streaked into them. Two people leaped off the bike, already shooting. They were all in black, wearing helmets. One was smaller than the other, with wide hips. A woman? I watched as she put a bullet in one of the downed drug guys' temples, then casually walked toward the building's front entrance.

Were we looking at a male-female hit team? That was a new one. And two on seven? That took some major guts. Not to mention training.

I watched the video again. The hit team was so smooth, so calm, just taking their time. These were no rival gangbangers. These people were military or ex-military, major pros.

I looked up again at the president on TV.

Two pros take down a drug crew a week before

another pro tries to pull a Lee Harvey Oswald on Buckland?

I ran through the video of the hit team again and again on my phone. I sipped my coffee as I stared at them. I especially concentrated on the male.

I tried to match him up with the brief glimpse of the shooter I'd gotten at the MetLife Building. Both were about six feet with a slim build.

But was it the same guy? I wondered.

I just wasn't sure.

CHAPTER 20

Lisa Hunter was a pretty, full-bodied, olive-skinned girl with shoulder-length raven-dark hair and a lot of dark eye makeup. I met with the Columbia premed student at a little after two in the afternoon.

Lisa was one of Rafael Arruda's chem students. After lunch, I'd gone over to the bursar's office, and after talking to a surprisingly unfussy, co-operative clerk, I'd actually been able to track down a few names.

One of the students I'd interviewed told me that Lisa was rumored to have been Rafael Arruda's lover. If that was true, my long shot hope was that she might have some insight into why he'd been taken out by a team of professional assassins.

I sat with Lisa on the edge of a sunny windowsill in the back of an empty Havemeyer Hall chem-istry lab. Outside the window, across the quad, workers were brushing snow off the top of the massive dome of the campus's famous library.

'Is it too warm?' I said as I laboriously opened the big window beside us a crack.

Lisa shrugged as she kept her eyes down on her brown leather boots. She took a Zippo lighter out of her laptop bag and started playing with it. She wore a gray hoodie that was too big for her, and I thought she seemed very depressed and vulnerable. Was that why the creep Arruda had seduced her? I wondered. Her vulnerability? Probably. I felt sorry for her.

'So it's true about Rafael?' she said, her face going a little gray. 'I mean, Dr. Arruda. He's dead? He was murdered by drug dealers?'

As I nodded, an old-fashioned bell clanged loudly out in the empty corridor for a moment and stopped.

'I can't believe it,' she said, blinking. 'He was so smart. It doesn't make any sense.'

'Some of the other students I talked to said he gave them drugs. Namely, ecstasy. Did he ever give you any drugs, Lisa?' I asked.

'No,' she said, not looking at me. The rapid snap of her lighter was loud in the empty room.

'That's a lie,' she said after another second. 'Yes, he gave me drugs. Ecstasy, ketamine, even crystal meth once. I never even really did drugs before. He was really interested in their effects on me. Like, obsessive about it. He sometimes even gave me a survey sheet to fill out. Like it was an experiment.'

I'd heard the same thing from some of his other students. He must have been using them as guinea pigs for his drug batches, testing their strengths so he could price them accordingly. His own students. He easily could have poisoned or killed them. Arruda was a real piece of work, all right.

'We were sleeping together,' Lisa suddenly said as she looked out the window. 'You probably heard that, I'm sure. I thought I loved him. I guess I did.'

She snapped the lighter again and again.

'I'm so stupid,' she whispered.

'Lisa,' I said, patting her on the shoulder. 'Don't blame yourself. This guy was bad news. I'm not here to pry into your personal life – really. I'm just trying to find the guys who killed him. Were you two together a lot? Did he ever take you to his house, or maybe to an apartment in Hamilton Heights?'

'No, he would pick me up over on Broadway, and we would go to this motel in the Bronx. I'm from a small town in Rhode Island, and at first I thought it was kind of gritty and exciting. You know, like that old Police song "Don't Stand So Close to Me."'

She made a disgusted face.

'Then he started being a jerk to me after a month or so. But I couldn't stop seeing him.'

'Lisa, did he mention if anyone was after him? Maybe you heard him talk on his phone about someone or something he was worried about?'

'He was always cryptically talking on his phone,' Lisa said, shrugging again as she darted a pained look at me. 'Only in Spanish, though. He could be rude like that, speaking in Spanish in front of me to people, like I didn't exist. I was sad when I first heard the news, but I think I'm happy now,

90

Detective. In fact, I'm glad the bastard's dead.'

'Lisa, if this is too much for you to deal with, they probably have counseling services on campus. Maybe you should talk to someone.'

'Maybe,' she said with another shrug. 'I don't have a lot of friends here. New York, I mean. It's so cold at times. I'm thinking about maybe going home at the end of the semester. Get my head straight.'

'That might be a good idea, Lisa,' I said as another bell sharply rang out in the hall. 'Here's my card. Don't hesitate to call if I can be of help to you. You've been through a lot.'

'Thanks, Detective. Maybe I will.'

CHAPTER 21

After a day spent digging dry holes, I finally lucked out by walking smack-dab into the middle of Bennett pasta night when I got home.

Mary Catherine must have been part Sicilian somewhere way back in her family tree, because the Irish lass made the kind of meatballs and marinara gravy Martin Scorsese's mother would have been proud of.

I gleefully pulled up a plate and sat down beside our new houseguest, Marvin Peters, who'd come home with Brian. Marvin was a big African American kid, about six four, with double-wide shoulders and a boyish, round, soft face that made him look approachable despite his formidable size.

He looked like a friendly bear. He also looked a little shell-shocked as he sat staring at our frenetic dinner table.

'Quite a sight, isn't it, Marvin?' said Seamus, who was sitting on the other side of him. 'But I'd be doing more shoveling than staring, if I were you.'

'He's right, Marvin,' I said. 'You'll need to tap into some of your athletic skills at mealtimes around here if you want to feed yourself before it's all gone.'

'I can't tell you how much I appreciate you letting me stay with you, sir,' Marvin said, staring at me earnestly. 'All you guys are such kind people. I don't know how to thank you.'

'I do,' said Seamus as he swirled spaghetti on his fork. 'A Catholic school win in the all-city basketball finals this year should do quite nicely. Also, Manhattan College would be a grand school for you to play for in a few years. A grand school with a fine Catholic tradition, right here in the city of your birth.'

'Seamus, would you please stop recruiting Marvin at the dinner table,' I said. 'I can't believe I had to actually just say that.'

'What? A priest isn't allowed to support Catholic schools now?' Seamus said. 'We've been locked out of the all-city three years in a row. And Manhattan needs to make it back to the dance, and quick. Marvin here is fierce powerful, so he is. Just look at him. He's our meal ticket.'

'Seamus, do I actually have to send you to your room?' I said as everyone started to giggle. 'He's a real priest, Marvin, I swear. I know it's difficult to believe.'

'Oh, don't worry about it, Mr. Bennett.' He turned toward Seamus. 'I don't know about Manhattan College, sir – I mean, Father. I'll have to look into that. But I'll do my best for you to win this year in the all-city, if we get there. I promise.'

'Don't let Seamus bother you, Marvin. He just likes to tease,' said Mary Catherine, not missing a beat with our newest family member.

Marvin smiled his friendly-bear smile.

'Hallelujah,' Seamus said sheepishly.

CHAPTER 22

'Puller, ready,' President Buckland said as he gently shouldered his Mossberg over-and-under 12-gauge shotgun.

'Ready,' said his son, Terrence, a safe twenty feet to his rear.

'Okay, let's see one,' Buckland said.

There was the familiar *click* and *whang* of the remote-controlled trap machine, and then two clays were aloft in front of him. The little terracotta Frisbees bobbed a little in the cold air as they sailed for the tree line of leafless poplars and maples and white oaks, as if trying to get away.

As if.

Buckland tracked textbook smooth from the waist, and then, two quick shotgun blasts later, another two clay pigeons were subtracted from the world.

'You're on fire, Dad!' Terrence said as he gave his father a high five.

'It was some pretty sweet shooting, wasn't it, son?' Buckland said, glancing over at the First Lady, who sat smiling by the fire pit. 'One might even say it was done with perfect execution. Which only makes sense, my being the head of the *executive* branch and all.' He winked at his son.

Terrence groaned along with his mother. The three of them were at Camp David, the famous presidential retreat in rural Maryland, standing beside the snow-filled tennis court where they'd set up a trapshooting rig.

Some presidents jogged or golfed to blow off steam; Buckland liked to shoot things. The family actually had a regulation skeet course built at their personal vacation place in Pennsylvania.

'*Très* classy,' his wife said after Buckland picked up the tall boy can of Heineken at his feet and took a pull and burped. 'If only the press could see you now. Where's the paparazzi when you need them?'

'Now, now. No more stalling, scaredy-cat. I do believe it's your turn,' Buckland said.

The blasts of the First Lady dusting her two clays were still ringing in the air when the black Chevy Suburban pulled up behind their security detail back on the road.

'Were you expecting them?' she said.

'I'm sure it's nothing, honey. I got this,' President Buckland said as he started walking over to Secret Service head John Levitin, standing by the SUV's back door.

'Don't waste your breath,' President Buckland

94

said as he sat in the backseat. 'You drove all the way up here for nothing.'

'Mr. President, please be reasonable. We can't go back to New York. Not now. It's just not safe. We haven't tracked down the shooter, who, by all evidence, is a world-class sniper. These guys are wizards, sir. The amount of exposure they need is almost nothing. You need to back down.'

'No, it's Russia that has to back down,' President Buckland said. 'This situation we're facing, John, it's bigger than all of us. We have to show unity right now, not fear. Besides, even if it all goes to shit – and it won't, since you guys are the best – there are worse things than me being dead. Far worse. Like Russia taking over Western Europe.'

'I strongly, strongly advise you not to go back to New York right now.'

'I hear what you're saying. I'm listening. I really am,' the president said as he watched his wife kill a couple more clays and share a high five with their son.

'But I'm going to New York,' the president said as he opened the door.

CHAPTER 23

The beat-up white work van pulled into the empty parking lot of the Kohl's in the Caesar's Bay shopping center in the South Brooklyn neighborhood of Bath Beach at 3:47 in the morning.

Immediately, it rolled to the lot's waterside

guardrail beside the closed shopping center and stopped and stood idling. Beyond the guardrail, far off on the dark-gray water, were the yellow running lights of a ship. A large ship that had just sailed in off the New York–New Jersey bight into Lower Bay.

In the van's passenger seat, Matthew Leroux lifted the three-thousand-dollar FLIR Scout II thermal camera from his lap and thumbed the zoom. After some more pans and zooms in the black-and-white display of the infrared camera, he finally read *MV Vestervig* off the ship's starboard side.

'Is it her?' asked Leroux's wife, Sophie.

'It's her,' Matthew said.

The container ship *MV Vestervig* flew under the Panamanian flag and was owned by a Japanese shipping concern. It was a hefty Panamax-class vessel that had a capacity of forty-five hundred containers and was now heading inbound for the Port Newark–Elizabeth marine terminal, he knew. Having done nothing but go over the job for the last three weeks, he knew *all* about it.

'Isn't it ahead of schedule?'

Matthew checked his Rolex.

'A little,' he said.

'How long do you figure?' she asked.

Leroux put down the camera and looked out at the tiny lights on the water. He scanned up the bay to the right and bit his lip. Containers averaged about twenty-five knots, he knew. Plus you had to time this right. Couldn't be too early. Not a lot of wiggle room in this one.

'Give it twelve minutes on the button,' he said.

'From here?'

'From here,' he said, putting down the camera and climbing into the back of the van.

He'd just slipped into all the gear and re-checked the kit bag when his wife's iPhone alarm started ding-a-linging.

'Ready?' she said.

'Hit it.'

She zipped the van out of the lot and got them up on the ramp for the Belt Parkway west. Leroux held on to the back of her seat, looking out the windshield as they drove. The dark water on their left. The lights of Staten Island on the other side. There wasn't a car on the road.

Another mile up, they took exit 3 on almost two wheels to West 278 and then got in the lane for the lower level of the Verrazano-Narrows Bridge. Half a minute later, they were under the upper deck, girders steadily going by on the right beyond the low concrete divider wall.

They passed the first of the suspension bridge's two seventy-story towers, and then Sophie slowed and stopped the van midspan, and he jumped out with the bag and the ropes. A car went by on his left a minute after Sophie drove off. He didn't even glance at it. In his coveralls and reflective vest and bridge worker's hard hat, he knew he was wallpaper.

Twenty paces up from where he'd been dropped off, he found the premarked girder, set up his six-millimeter accessory cord anchor around it, and then clicked onto the two hundred feet of climbing rope and chucked the rope over the side. Under the sodium light beside the bridge's guardrail, he knelt on the concrete and looped and clipped the rope into his rappelling harness's maillon and tightened the lock. Then he climbed out over the rusted guardrail and leaned back out into the wind and space.

CHAPTER 24

On the outside of the bridge, Matthew descended a few feet out of sight of the roadway and waited, dangling there twenty stories over the dark water. When he tilted his head back, he could see the lights of Manhattan sparkling against the cold night.

It arrived less than a minute later. He looked down, and rolling beneath him was the mighty arc of the *MV Vestervig's* bow, followed by the orderly rows of colored containers stacked up from its hold like hundreds and hundreds of giant Legos.

The *swush* of the massive ship pushing through the water drowned out the whistle of rope through the maillon as he lowered himself in a slow, controlled rappel.

He stopped himself when he was ten feet above the top row of containers and stared at the wheelhouse coming at him. The container tops sliding by beneath his boots looked like the cars of several slow-moving trains. He lowered himself some more, and when he was five feet above the plain of rolling container steel, he let go with his brake hand and landed on his side on one of the container tops with a hollow thud.

He lay there for a full minute, listening for some outcry. The ship had a twenty-three-member crew, but only two navigation officers and an engineer worked the night shift. But there was nothing. Just the wind and the rhythmic slap of the water off the ship's moving hull. *Good,* he thought as he took his map out of the bag and clicked on his flashlight

Even with the exact bay row and tier on his ship map, it took him five minutes to find it, a battered blue Maersk box on the top row. He snipped through its high-security bolt seal with the cutters he'd brought, creaked open the container's swinging door, and stepped inside and swung it closed behind him.

'My, my, my,' he said as he passed his flashlight over what was inside.

It was a car. But not just any car. A sleek, museum-grade '67 Lamborghini Miura, cherry red with a mustard leather interior. It was worth well over a million dollars.

'Stop your drooling and get to work,' he mumbled to himself as he opened the supercar's door and pulled the latch for the hood. Under it, instead of the engine, there was a spare tire and the battery. Leroux reached into the bag and brought out the device.

It was a sheet of plastic explosive along with a small radio-controlled detonator and a microphone. After activating its transmitter, he reached in under the hood on the driver's side and sealed the device up against the chassis, just to the right of the left front wheel well. Then he wiped engine grease all over it until it was hidden.

After he was finished, he tested the device's signal, then closed the hood and the car's door and smiled. Now, unbeknownst to the owner, the occupants in the car could be heard – or, better yet, killed – at any moment.

He checked his watch.

'Okay, time to go.'

He came back out of the container and resealed it with an identical high-security bolt seal from his bag.

When he climbed back on top of the container's roof, he could see that the ship was already in the tight Kill Van Kull waterway that separated Bayonne, New Jersey, from Staten Island's north shore.

Some industrial tanks went by along the right shore of the shipping channel. Then he passed a smaller container ship, called a feeder, sitting at a dock before he saw the Bayonne Bridge.

With only one hundred and fifty feet of clearance from the bridge to the waterline, the huge *MV Vestervig's* radio and radar antennas would clear it by only twenty feet. He spotted the rope ladder hanging down off the bridge a minute later, and he walked over the tops of the containers and caught it and quickly scurried up to the bridge deck.

He had to wait a few minutes, hanging from the bridge's guardrail, after the ship was gone before Sophie arrived.

'How'd it go?' she said after he collapsed in a ball of sweat onto the floor of the van's rear.

'Swimmingly, darling. Just swimmingly.'

CHAPTER 25

The next morning at twenty minutes before nine, I was sitting and staring at a Norman Rockwell print.

It was one of my favorites. The one of the big state trooper seated beside the cute little runaway kid at the diner. I loved all the incredible colors and details. The deep blue of the trooper's uniform, the focal point red of the bandanna tied to a stick under the kid's shiny chrome diner stool. I thought it was a heck of a painting, but then again, I suppose you could accuse me of being a little biased in the cops and kids department.

The print hung on the office wall of Chief of Detectives Fabretti, who had texted me for a meeting on my way in to One Police Plaza. Beside the print on a whiteboard were crime scene photos. One was of the MetLife Building's roof, another of the assassin's blind that we'd found under its rim. Beneath them was a shot of the huge Barrett .50-caliber sniper rifle we'd been unable to trace or find even one print on.

I hoped the chief wasn't looking for an update on things, because there was none. It was pretty frustrating. We were no closer to finding the president's shooter than on day one.

'Yeah, yeah. Okay, I know. I'll call you back,' Fabretti said into his cell as he came in and loudly dumped the bunch of binders he was carrying onto the smooth glass top of his desk.

'The fricking president is making another visit to the UN. Can you believe this?' he said as he dropped himself into his tufted leather office chair. 'That was Paul Ernenwein. He just got off the phone with the Secret Service. Does Buckland have a death wish? I mean, some in the press like to say he's like the new JFK. You think he wants to end up like him?'

'When is he coming back?' I said.

'Two weeks. They said he has a big meeting with ambassadors from a bunch of the former Eastern Bloc countries and some NATO ones. They said he's trying to put the full-court press on Russia. Really up the pressure.'

'He's upping the pressure, all right,' I said, shaking my head.

'You said it,' Fabretti said. 'My blood pressure alone. Just having to work with those Secret Service prima donnas again after all they did to try and throw us under the bus is an outrage.'

'I'm with you there,' I said. 'Anything else, Chief?'

'Well, now that you ask,' said Fabretti as he took a sheet of paper out of one of his binders.

CHAPTER 26

In the last daylight of my long day, I stepped out of my unmarked into the parking lot of a big, ugly, yellow concrete building in Brooklyn. It was the last, most southern building in the South Brooklyn marine terminal, a massive industrial wilderness of rusting chain-link and corrugated sheet metal just south of the Gowanus Canal.

Icy wind off the bay roared in my stinging ears as I crossed the parking lot. I looked up at the looming silhouettes of a couple of massive dock cranes at the adjacent facility, where imported cars were processed and put onto freight trains.

This must be the old Brooklyn, I thought, turning up the collar of my coat. There wasn't a hipster in sight.

The inside of the building was even more depressing than the outside, if that was possible. It was a meat distribution center – basically, a giant refrigerator stacked with row after endless row of cardboard cases of frozen meat. Beyond a smudged window by the front door, workers in hooded winter coats piloted forklifts and pallet lifts between the rows, like lost souls doing penance in a frozen hell.

I found Pavel Levkov upstairs in a cozy, warm glass office overlooking the interior tundra of the warehouse. He was a medium-size bald man in his fifties, with gray eyes and a weight lifter's build. He didn't offer me a seat.

I'd actually been looking for him all day. He was a hard man to find. He had a list of cash businesses as long as my arm: a bunch of gas stations in Newark, a slummy motel in Coney Island, a garbage-hauling outfit out in Staten Island.

Though Levkov didn't have a record, he was linked to the Russian mob in New York. He was also linked to the informant who'd told the FBI about the MetLife shooter.

Apparently, the FBI's informant had split town yesterday, out of the blue, but not before telling his wife that if something happened to him, we should talk to Pavel Levkov.

So here I was.

'NYPD? What the fuck is this about?' Levkov said after I showed him my shield.

'How do you do, Mr. Levkov? My name's Detective Bennett, and I'd like to ask you a few questions. Actually, just one. Who put the hit out on the president? Was it you?'

The Russian immediately started laughing. I'd really hit his funny bone. He crossed his arms as he creaked his bulk back in his old wooden office chair, giggling.

'Yeah, it was me. You've found me out, Detective. Welcome to Dr. Evil's lair,' Levkov said with a theatrical wave of his meaty hand.

He sat forward then, leaning on his desk with his elbows. 'I'm just a businessman, Detective. Look at this place. Do I look like I'm getting rich to you? Look at my car in the lot, some piece of shit Jeep Cherokee with a bad transmission. How many times do I have to tell you people? I pay my taxes and pursue the American dream. That's it.'

'We have reason to believe that's not just it. Maybe you didn't set it up, but I know you know something. I need the shooter. He killed a cop. We're not gonna stop looking for him. You choose to stand between us and him, you're going to find your little grimy empire coming down around your ears. You need to give me something. If not the shooter, then a name that gets me off your ass and on theirs. Think hard. I'm actually trying to help you.'

'You're crazy, Detective. I voted for Buckland. I don't know who put my name in this, but you need to arrest them because they're pulling your chain.'

'Okay, Levkov. Let's do it the stupid way. Get up and put your hands behind your back.'

'What? Why?'

I took out the subpoena that I had been handed by Chief Fabretti for the over three thousand dollars in unpaid parking tickets the Russian had racked up.

'Well, Pavel, sometimes the American dream includes paying your parking tickets.'

CHAPTER 27

'So how do you like the madhouse so far?' Brian Bennett said as he huffed and puffed next to Marvin Peters; they were jogging in Riverside Park after school. 'You don't have to answer that.

It's only for a few weeks, right?'

'Madhouse?' Marvin said as they ran. 'You don't know how lucky you are, man. Your dad, and Father Seamus, and Miss Mary Catherine, and all your brothers and sisters. Not to mention this neighborhood. Heck, you livin' the good life, believe me.'

'Yeah? Tell me that again after one of the pee-wees gets into your stuff or the first time you slip on a Barbie roller skate in the middle of the night.'

Marvin just smiled.

They were coming out of the icy trail by the Riverside Drive sidewalk at 86th when Marvin spotted him. Hardly believing his eyes, Marvin slowed to a stop. It really was him, Big Flicka himself, just standing there by his big double-parked silver Mercedes, smiling.

'Hey, what gives, Marv? Getting soft on me?' said Brian.

Marvin didn't answer. All he could do was stare out at the street beyond the snow-filled park at the big, lanky, fifty-year-old black man in the black thousand-dollar Canada Goose down jacket.

As Flicka gave him a wave, Marvin remembered a snatch from some old stupid eighties song, 'Get Outta My Dreams, Get into My Car.' Only here in real life, it was like Flicka had just come out of Marvin's nightmare, and Marvin only wanted him to go back.

'Marvin, Marvin, you were a friend of mine,' Flicka sang soulfully. He had a nice voice. Ghetto legend had it that he actually did some backups on a couple of tracks in the nineties before he got caught for a body. 'Marvin, it is you, isn't it?'

Flicka said. 'I thought it was, and I was right. Look at you, son. It's been too long.'

How had the bastard found him here in Manhattan? Marvin thought. He must have spotted him at school and followed him here.

'Come here, boy,' Flicka said, tilting his head to one side playfully. 'What, you're not even going to say hi?'

Marvin didn't want to go but did as he was told. Because Flicka was effing crazy. Full-bore, hockey mask, chain saw crazy. You didn't know what Flicka would do until he was doing it.

'Tell your white boy to keep going his merry ol' way or I'll clip you right here,' said Flicka, still smiling like he was posing for a selfie. 'I'll do you just like I did yo' cousin, and the white boy, too. You know I will.'

'Hey, Brian. You keep on going,' Marvin said. 'I'll catch up with you later.'

'Maybe we should just head home, Marvin,' Brian said.

'I won't be long,' Marvin said.

'Okay,' Brian said. 'You're sure?'

Marvin nodded.

'Yeah, keep going, white boy,' his cousin's killer said as he opened the passenger door of the Merc. 'You don't want any piece of this punk ass's sorry problems. Not any piece at all.'

CHAPTER 28

Saturday morning, Matthew went into the famous Strand Bookstore on Broadway, down from Union Square Park, while Sophie got her hair done nearby.

He was deep in the stacks, flipping through a coffee-table book about depictions of pain in Renaissance art, when a big guy in a hooded wool toggle coat and Clark Kent glasses jostled him in the narrow aisle.

'You and your girlie art books,' Mark Evrard said under his tobacco breath.

'Yeah, well,' Matthew said, cocking an eyebrow at Evrard's Brooks Brothers fall weekend ensemble, 'at least I don't dress like one.'

'You're losin' it, a corn-fed Indiana boy like you, letting me sneak up on you like this,' Evrard whispered as he elbowed him. 'You have a minute?'

Matthew closed the book on the photograph of *Laocoön* that he'd been studying.

'You have a car?' he said.

'Yeah, but let's take a walk instead,' Evrard said, gesturing beyond the precarious sea of stacked books, toward the door.

They didn't talk as they went north up Broadway. Or even when Evrard led him across Union into an old pub a block past the park.

'Ah, if these tin ceilings could talk,' Evrard said when he arrived back at the darkened rear booth with their whiskeys. 'Does anything on earth beat one of these when-New-York-was-Irish joints?' They were the only ones there so early, besides the bartender.

Matthew nodded. 'What's up?' he said.

'Good job on the uptown shuffle, Mattie, not to mention your antics under the bridge,' Evrard said as he gently clinked Matthew's glass. 'You said you'd come through, and as ever, you're a man who does what he says.'

'Yep. That it?'

'Of course not,' Evrard said, slipping him a thick envelope under the sticky table.

It was the same kind of paper as the one for Rafael Arruda. Thick stationery. Scratchy. You could feel the threads in it.

Matthew tried to hide his shock and numbness as he tucked it inside his jacket.

He had thought they were done.

He'd thought wrong.

'So he's here?' Matthew said.

Evrard took off his glasses and rubbed at his dark doll's eyes and then put the glasses back on.

'He's here,' he said.

'The last of the Mohicans,' Matthew mumbled.

'The last,' Evrard said as he turned the thick glass tumbler in his big hand. 'And most dangerous.'

Matthew's eyes went wide as he figured it out.

'Wait, the president thing?' he gasped. 'With the MetLife and the chopper and the cop?'

'Yep,' said Evrard, nodding. 'He might have had him, too. Rumor is, in the blind there was a big ol' Barrett zeroed in. Who knows what would have happened if that cop hadn't got lucky.'

Matthew did the quick calculations in his head. Lex to First Avenue, little over a mile.

'Just mighta had him at that,' Matthew said with a whistle. 'How did he get in, though? I thought he was in Dubai.'

Evrard shrugged his grizzly bear shoulders in his prissy coat. Though he looked like an academic, the Chicago native had played defensive tackle at the University of Michigan before he tore his ACL.

'Who knows? Mexico? That barn door is wide,' Evrard said. 'It ain't like before. Everything's screwed up now, Mattie. Truly, madly, and deeply. Why do you think I'm sitting here with you?'

'And he's still here?'

'Far as we can tell. But check the paperwork. You have to talk to a guy first. But you know this bastard. He's just like you, Mattie. He likes to finish a job. You sure you're down for this? Should Sophie be sitting here with us?'

'No, we got this,' Matthew said, patting the envelope. 'Believe me. This one we've been waiting for.'

'Not just you,' Evrard said into his Jameson's.

'Then we're done,' Matthew said as if he were talking to himself. 'One last one, and it's all over.'

'To the ending,' said Evrard, staring into Matthew's too-blue sniper's eyes as he raised his glass.

'Of a nightmare,' Matthew agreed as he clinked and tilted and drank.

CHAPTER 29

The assassin's wife made a right off Pell onto Doyers Street in lower Manhattan's Chinatown and stopped and checked the address on her phone again.

Tucking her phone away into her large knapsack, she looked up into the fearsome face of a paper dragon draped in the tourist shop window in front of her.

'Oh, aren't you cute,' she said, walking past it alongside the graffiti-covered steel shutters beneath the dirty store awnings.

Around the bend of Doyers, across the street from the Chinatown post office, she opened the door of a small, ugly green brick building and promptly scrub-picked the cheap lock on its inside door. Quickly and quietly, she went up the small building's four narrow, sour flights and then opened the door to the roof. Directly outside the doorway was a black wooden water tower, and she quietly walked to it, ducked beneath its metal base, and knelt and unzipped her bag.

The rifle she removed from it was a suppressed short-barreled McMillan CS5 loaded with specially made 200-grain subsonic .308 ammo. She flicked out its collapsible tripod and stock and laid it on the gritty tar paper and put her eye to the scope.

Down below her was the crazy four-way

intersection of Chinatown, where Bowery met Doyers and Catherine and Division Streets. She glassed up Division Street and rolled her neck and got comfortable. Then she dialed her phone.

'In position,' she said.

CHAPTER 30

'Okay, love. Look lively,' her husband said from the van parked two blocks east, over on East Broadway.

Hanging up, he glanced at himself in the mirror attached to the rear van wall. He was dressed once again like a cop now, an NYPD beat cop, with the iconic yellow-and-light-blue patches on the shoulders of his midnight-blue jacket and a metal badge on his peaked hat.

Knowing there would be witnesses and maybe even phone video of what was about to go down, he had a fake mustache now and was wearing brown-tinted eyeglasses. But the key to his disguise was hiding his race, courtesy of his wife's expert makeover, which gave his skin a warm brown Hispanic tone.

'Okay, you got this. You got this. You got this,' he said, pumping himself up as he stared in the mirror. Then he rolled open the door and jumped out onto the street.

He threw out a hand to stop traffic as he hurriedly crossed East Broadway, and then crossed the sidewalk in two steps and pulled the handle of the Baijiu Liquor Shop door.

The old guy behind the counter reading a Chinese-language paper gave him a look of sheer bewilderment as he drew his Glock. Without a word, the assassin rushed toward the back and kicked open a cheap wooden door at the right-hand rear of the crowded store.

'NYPD! Nobody move! This is a raid!' he yelled as he rushed in behind the Glock.

Forty or fifty Asians, looking as shocked as the counterman, stared at him through thick smoke. They were sitting in groups of four at small green-felt card tables covered in purple-backed tiles. It was a mahjong parlor, a 24/7 illegal gambling house, one of the biggest in New York City.

He scanned faces, looking for the one he had already memorized, his target, Richard Yu.

He spotted him a second later at one of the farthest tables, a young guy with a New York Knicks varsity jacket and a mop top of spiky hair, like a crazy anime character come to life. He seemed younger than in the picture Pavel Levkov had given him.

What this girlish Asian kid had done to have a two-hundred-thousand-dollar contract on him was difficult to comprehend. But as was true for most old soldiers, his was not to wonder why.

'You, Spike! Stay right there! Hands! I want to see your hands!'

Yu peered back at him through his blade-sharp hair, then suddenly jumped up and hit a door to his right, fleeing into the back alley.

The assassin hit the edge of a table, sending Chinese character tiles flying as he ran across the

113

parlor and through the door after him. Surprisingly, Yu was already hopping the alley fence to the parking lot when he came outside.

Good, the assassin thought as he followed at a jog. *Run along, now.*

The parking lot on the other side of the fence had only one way out, he knew. Right into the middle of Division Street.

'Coming to you,' he called into his phone to his wife.

He heard the low report of the suppressed rifle off to the left just as he was coming out of the parking lot. He looked ahead to his right, down Division, and saw Yu running flat out in the street beside the parked cars and traffic. He was cradling his left shoulder with his right hand as he ran. He was dripping blood. Some was splattered on the pale sleeve of his jacket. She'd nicked him.

There was another shot, and a hole appeared in the side of the dirty graffiti-covered box truck Yu was passing. The round had landed right beside the Asian version of Usain Bolt's spiky head.

'Damn it! He's out of sight and range!' she said into the phone.

'It's okay. Get out, now! I got this,' he said, seeing the drips and lines of blood splatter on the asphalt as he picked up the pace.

CHAPTER 31

The assassin reached the end of the block just in time to see Yu dart under the shadowed base of the Manhattan Bridge. When he arrived at the other side, he saw Yu make a right onto Pike, and when he reached Pike, he saw Yu make a left onto Henry.

Damn, the little kid is fast, he thought as he ran down Pike Street. *I'll give him that.*

Two surprising things happened almost at once as the assassin turned at a run around the corner of Henry Street.

The first was a funeral procession coming out of a church right there, off the corner beside him. A crowd of mourners dressed in black stood on the corner, respectfully waiting as pallbearers brought a coffin down the steps.

The second and far more interesting thing was that Richard Yu was standing past them at the end of the short block by the subway entrance to the F train, pointing a gun at him.

He dove in front of the hearse as the gun went off. Several mourners in the crowd screamed as one of the elderly pallbearers fell and the coffin clattered down the steps.

He poked his head around the hearse just as Yu fled down into the subway.

'Hey! What you got? What you got?' yelled a jacked cop who appeared suddenly from the park across from the church.

'Ah, an armed robbery. In pursuit of an Asian male!' the assassin said as he took off. 'Just went into the subway!'

'Didn't hear nothing on the radio. You call it in?' the young eager cop said as he ran beside him, matching him step for step.

'Not yet. Just happened. Can you?' the assassin said as he took the subway stairs down two by two, trying to distance himself from the real cop.

Damn it! he thought as he arrived at the bottom of the rancid steps and saw that there was a train in the station. He heard the doors *bing bong* as he reached the turnstile and hopped it and dove into the car at the last second, through the closing doors.

'Yo, dude! Help!' said the cop, who was now wedged in the doors of the train car.

The assassin looked at him.

Then he lifted his foot and booted him square in the center of his muscular chest, knocking him sprawling onto the filthy East Broadway station platform. The doors rattled closed and the train pulled out.

He ran to his left down the train, through the cars, following the screams.

He ducked – there were more shots and the sound of breaking glass – as he pulled open the door to the last car.

He couldn't believe it. The window in the door at the end of the train was missing. The punk Asian kid had actually broken it somehow and escaped.

Or maybe not, he thought as he ran the length of

116

the car.

He arrived at the door and saw Yu rapidly disappearing in the distance in the glow of a tunnel bulb, his anime hair casting spiky shadows on the wall.

The assassin calmed himself. He cleared his mind and body with a breath and put the sights of the Glock 23 on the orange Knicks basketball on the back of the kid's jacket and unloaded.

He watched as Yu took two more steps and fell face-first between the tracks.

The assassin smiled as the train reached the next station and the doors opened.

Nice chase, Richard. You were just outclassed, son. Professionals never quit, he thought as he hurried for the exit.

CHAPTER 32

Paul Ernenwein was standing beside Chief Fabretti when I opened the door of the cramped observation closet on the third floor of One Police Plaza.

'Hey, Paul. What's up?' I said with mock cheeriness as I shook the middle-aged redheaded fed's hand.

As if I didn't know.

It was too bright and too warm in the tiny space. The overhead fluorescent buzzed like a trapped angry insect. You could smell and almost taste the frustration in the close air.

'This nut won't crack, huh?' Ernenwein said, cocking his chin at Pavel Levkov on the other side of the one-way mirror.

I looked over at him glumly. The muscular Russian was whistling as he drummed his fingers on the table he was sitting at. He had looked like that ever since I'd dragged him in. Like a hapless, lackadaisical guy with nothing to do, patiently waiting for a bus.

'That's an affirmative,' I said as I tried to roll the tension out of my neck. 'I tried three times, but our Russian friend here is about as communicative and cooperative as a cinder block. Any word on your informant that he scared away?'

'None,' said Paul. 'We're up on his wife's phone, but so far, jack. What's crazy is we have a crack Russian mob squad, and this Pavel here isn't on any of our lists. He doesn't go to any of the clubs out in Brighton Beach. We even checked his bona fides with our counterintel people on Russki spies, and he came back clean.'

'Exactly,' said Fabretti. 'Besides the parking tickets, he's never so much as gotten pulled over for speeding.'

'I mean, he looks mean enough,' said Paul, 'but he's not even remotely on our radar. I can't for the life of me think why our informant is so scared of him. Guy like this who seems so deeply connected pops out of the blue, makes me want to consider retirement, purchase some land in northern Wyoming, maybe.'

I checked my watch.

'Whatever it is, we can't hold him forever. What do you want to do?'

Paul yawned elaborately. Then he passed a hand through his thinning orange hair.

'Let him walk,' Paul said finally, taking out his phone. 'I have a team of my guys waiting downstairs to cover him. Let's put a little slack in this dog's leash. Who knows? Maybe he'll lead us to where he buried the bone.'

CHAPTER 33

After his release, Pavel went straight to the Bronx to the most secure of his several residences.

'Eat it, you stupid cops,' he mumbled as he hit a remote on the sun visor of his Jeep. He looked in the rearview mirror as the electronic security gate closed behind him, sealing off the driveway of his property on East 233rd Street.

He had noticed at once the three-car surveillance detail when he came out of the Brooklyn impound yard.

They wanted to watch him? They could do it far away, from the street. Maybe later, after dinner and a couple of drinks, he'd go to his window and give them something to look at – namely, a good long glimpse at the glowing white cheeks of his ass.

He came up the winding driveway toward the rambling old three-story Tudor house. Its six-acre wooded lot was completely sealed in by old rusting chain-link. He had bought the place in 2001 to build a housing development, but he never seemed to get around to it.

He got out into the circular drive. 'What the hell are you doing, eh? Sleeping on the job?' he said as he knelt and kissed his two Dobermans, Sasha and Natalya.

He kept them within a tight perimeter around the house with an electronic dog fence that he called his moat. The dogs whined at him hungrily now.

'Okay, fine, ladies. I'm a sucker for such pretty girls.'

He took the creaky front stairs two by two and opened the big oak door into the darkened, drafty front hall. The house had great bones, as they say. Like so many of the house's fine appointments, the elaborate mahogany staircase had been shipped over from a French château when it was built. But the house needed a couple million dollars of work.

Originally, at the turn of the century, it had been the compound of a paranoid, apocalyptic religious group, and though he kept it to himself, in the house at night, Pavel sometimes heard some wild, unexplainable shit. Footsteps. Doors slamming. A few times what sounded like screaming.

If he didn't sleep with his girls, a dead bolt lock on his door, and a fully loaded Armsel Striker street sweeper semiauto shotgun on his bedside table, he might have actually been scared.

'Hey, ghosts, I'm back. Miss me?' he said to the shadows as he headed to the butler's pantry to get the girls their dinner.

He was coming back into the kitchen when his knee exploded.

He didn't feel it at first – it happened so fast. He was just walking toward the drawer to get the can opener, and then he was collapsed on the yellow pine floor with a bloody ragged hole in the knee of his slacks.

'Pavel, hello down there,' said a voice.

Starting to hyperventilate at the growing pain, Pavel looked up at a distinctly unghostly-looking blue-eyed man who stepped out of the shadows with a smoking suppressed H & K Mark 23 in his right hand.

'You don't know me, Pavel, but my name is Matthew,' he said.

The sniper smiled as he squatted, getting down on his level.

'And I have a couple questions for you today.'

CHAPTER 34

'And the plot thickens,' said Paul Ernenwein as we stood by the nurses' desk at the second-floor ICU unit of Montefiore Hospital, in the Norwood section of the Bronx.

Pavel had been admitted at a little after two in the morning. A cab had come to his place, and the surveil team had followed it and Pavel to the emergency room.

He had some broken ribs and electrical burns on certain sensitive parts of him, and someone had put a .45 clean through his right kneecap. Apparently, he'd been worked over by someone who knew what they were doing. Who that someone was we didn't know, but we were very interested in finding out.

'We're obviously getting some promising results in the Pavel-seems-to-be-a-player hypothesis,' I said. 'Who do you think tuned him up?'

'All three of the Pep Boys, by the looks of him,' said Paul, pointing at the console's screen, which showed a bruised Pavel covered in cords, sleeping.

'The Russians? The Kremlin?' I said.

'You'd think, right?' said Paul. 'But why leave him alive?'

'What does the house look like?' I said.

'Clean. Too clean. He's got dogs. Plus there's no sign of entry. Someone picked the locks, it seems. There was water all over the kitchen floor. Either Pavel decided to do some bobbing for apples after he kneecapped himself, or he was waterboarded.'

'You think it was the president's shooter? Pavel was a middleman, and something got screwed up and the shooter needed to find out some information the hard way?'

'That's a good theory,' Paul said. 'We should use it.'

'You want me to go say hi?' I said.

'Can't,' said Paul. 'He's got some internal bleeding. Doctors said we need to wait until the morning.'

'Maybe this works to our advantage,' I said. 'If he spilled the borscht about something during his little inquisition, he might be in big trouble, right? We could offer him some sanctuary.'

Paul Ernenwein looked at the screen.

'Good night, Pavel. Sleep well. We'll more than likely flip you in the morning,' he said.

CHAPTER 35

At eleven fifteen that evening, Sophie, wearing a large camping backpack, walked east down East 20th Street, past the Gramercy Park neighborhood's charming Italianate and Greek Revival town houses.

She sighed as she passed the awning of the famous Players club, which had been founded by Edwin Booth, the brother of John Wilkes. Astors had lived in the famous neighborhood. Steinbeck, Thomas Edison, even Julia Roberts.

Though she lived in SoHo, she sometimes fantasized about moving onto the famously attractive historic block, with its exclusive, mysterious private park.

Too bad she wasn't here to house hunt. Her pick was already out as she got to the Irving Place entrance to the park. A moment later, its famous cast-iron gate briefly shrieked, and she was in.

She walked alongside snow-covered benches and hedges to the statue of Edwin Booth in the two-acre park's center. Walking past it, she panned her eyes left and right along the small park's straight and winding paths. But it was too cold and too late for anyone else to be there.

Good.

She cast a quick glance at the Gramercy Park Hotel, straight in front of her. Then she walked back to the statue and casually dropped the massive backpack she was carrying at its feet. She quickly zipped open the bag, making sure the flap was pulled all the way back. She scanned it. Everything looked good. Wired tight.

A moment later, sans backpack, she exited through the Irving Place gate and continued east down 20th, picking up her pace.

'It's in place. Are you?' she said into her Bluetooth.

CHAPTER 36

'Just a sec,' said Matthew up in the windy darkness above her, looking down at the park and the city lights.

The building he was on top of was a block behind her, on 19th, just in off Park Avenue South. It was a twelve-story prewar office building, uninhabited, with a sidewalk shed and black mesh wrapped around its edifice due to a major rehab.

His setup was pretty sweet. There was a brick structure atop the roof that housed the elevator equipment, and he was on top of that, belly down on the tar paper behind a tent made up of several sheets of the black construction cladding.

The rifle he lay beside was one of his favorites, a precision XM24 SWS with a long suppressor and five .300 Winchester mags in its detachable box magazine. Up on its bipod, it was pointed across the park on his target at the Gramercy Park Hotel. Suite 809, to be exact.

It had taken Matthew a long, busy, and messy two hours to persuade Pavel to tell him where he could locate the man he was looking for. No one knew the assassin's real name. Not even Pavel. The assassin was a hard old bastard who'd been around forever and whom they called the Brit. A true mercenary, he worked for the highest bidder.

And tonight, his long career was going to come to its inevitable end, Matthew thought, leaning into his rifle's fixed cheek piece.

Matthew blinked as he looked through the S & B nightscope. It was already dialed in on 809's floor-to-ceiling window, in off the corner of 21st and Lex. Beyond the curtain of the big window, the end of a low, dark leather couch and the edge of a huge, modern splatter painting on the wall were visible.

It was a joke of a shot, really. A little over two hundred yards on a slight left-to-right, four-story downward angle. He could have almost hit it with a pistol at that range, but it was windy. A steady ten-mile-an-hour wind was blowing out of the northwest; he needed the pop of the XM24 to compensate.

The setup was straightforward. Get him to come to the window with a distraction, then blow out the first visible, vital part of him with a .300 Winchester's supersonic boat tail.

Matthew wasn't the biggest fan of distractions. They worked far less often than people thought, and were just as likely to make your quarry alert as to trick them. But then again, everybody let their guard down sometimes.

'Okay, talk to me. On your call,' said Sophie in

his ear.

Matthew took some breaths, then closed his eyes, just listening, trying to still himself. After thirty seconds, he felt himself become one with the building beneath him. He felt the rush of the cold wind on his cheek, listened to the high shriek of a bus somewhere in the darkness below, a car horn.

He opened his right eye and dead-centered the reticle on the window.

'Ready. Hit it now,' he said.

CHAPTER 37

The Brit came awake to a pulsing flash of light on the wall of his hotel bedroom. There was a low boom, then light was shaking the room as a rattle of firecrackers went off close by.

'What in the world? Fireworks? Is it some Yank holiday?' his wife said, already sitting up and looking toward the pulsing window. 'Maybe it's the anniversary of that horrid little park. It's coming from that direction. Look.'

The assassin checked his Rolex on the bedside table.

'Maybe,' he said as another skyrocket popped softly outside the window, shivering the walls of the suite's living room with a pale-green light.

'Oh, it's pretty,' said his wife, who was still quite tipsy from all the wine they'd had that evening at the Four Seasons. 'Let's see if we can get a better look from the living room. Maybe the hotel is doing it. Call down and see what it is.'

'Just go back to sleep,' the Brit said. 'You know the amount of work we have to do.'

'You and your work. Please, for once, would you let us have a little fun?'

'Fine.'

The Brit got up and walked out the bedroom door. Two more rockets burst in the air as he crossed to the kitchenette's dark quartz island, where he'd left his phone.

Then two more exploded right at eye level, a yellow one and then another green. He smiled. He loved fireworks. Who didn't? It would be lovely to hug his wife and watch them. Enjoy one of those rare happenstances that entirely make a trip.

He found the concierge's number on his phone and thumbed it as he walked toward the window, the dark room glowing strangely in the billowing colored smoke and streaks of light.

CHAPTER 38

In the cold air rush, Matthew lay breathing evenly, watching the window through the nightscope.

There were other people now at the hotel windows, some of them taking pictures as Sophie's pack of skyrockets continued to streak at a slow and regular interval straight up from beside the park's central statue.

He could feel his heartbeat thump as he

watched 809's floor-to-ceiling window kill zone. The curtain. The end of the couch. The painting.

'C'mon,' he whispered. 'Come to Papa.'

'That's the last one. Any sign?' said Sophie as a big rocket burst into a yellow-and-red flower.

In its afterglow, Matthew watched, waiting, finger on the trigger.

No, damn it. Nothing, he thought. It wasn't going to happen.

'Tell me you have something,' said Sophie.

'Negative.'

'Maybe he's dead asleep or something,' she said. 'What do we do?'

'We go back to the drawing board,' he said, packing up.

Matthew was about to turn to go down the ladder when the round hit him. It caught him about four inches below his brain stem, just above the center of his shoulder blades. Its impact knocked him flat, facedown, as if somebody had yanked out his ankles from underneath him.

He came to a skidding stop halfway off the elevator housing, and he just let himself topple the rest of the way into space, just in time to get missed by the next suppressed shot that blasted brick bits and tar paper between his boots.

He smashed hard into the roof, bashing the shit out of his elbows and the top of his head and his ribs as he landed on the XM24 in the clunky kit bag. Knowing he was safe, he pulled his backplate out.

The indent in it! He shook his shirt and caught the big and still-hot mushroomed bullet that had been meant for his heart and just stared at it.

The bastard must have run up to the hotel's roof, which was level with Matthew's perch.

'Hey, I'm in the car. Are you coming?'

Fear hit him almost as hard as the bullet. He imagined himself running down the twelve flights of stairs just in time to see the prick lighting up Sophie.

But he calmed himself and calculated quickly. What would *he* do if he knew he was being ambushed? Attack or hold position? Hold position, definitely. The Brit might have spotted him, the sly bastard, but he didn't know what kind of operation he was up against. No way would he run from cover.

'Matthew, are you okay?'

'Fine,' he said after a few labored breaths.

He looked at the plate again and shivered.

'Fine, baby. Be there in a shake.'

CHAPTER 39

The telescoping stock of the rifle gave off a satisfying job-well-done snap as the Brit, crouching in the dark on the roof of the Gramercy Park Hotel, collapsed it with the callused heel of his palm.

He hid the new matte-black Belgian FN FAL with its suppressor and state-of-the-art night-vision scope under his fluffy white hotel robe. Then, still in a crouch, he slipped silently off the darkened hotel roof, back through the stairwell door.

Padding quietly down the hotel's back stairs in his bare feet, he thought he very well might have hit the prankster on the roof of the building on the other side of Gramercy Park.

And with a hefty 7.62 x 51 mm NATO round, he'd more than likely gotten his attention.

Who had it been? he wondered. Not the coppers. Company, then? Someone else? Definitely someone in the business, by the looks of the hardware they had. Whoever they were, they were a little sloppy. Fireworks?

Then he thought about it. Maybe not so sloppy. He had, after all, almost gone to the window.

Plus the fireworks were pretty. It was almost elegant, in a way. Like a birthday party. Only the opposite. A little light show before they cut his cake once and for all, the bastards.

When he got back to his room, he put the gun away in its case and called Pavel, who had hired him. It kicked into voice mail. Had Pavel turned on him for some reason? He pondered the implications of that.

Should he leave now? he thought as he went into the bedroom.

No. If it were company or anybody else in the game, they'd want him out on the street at night to keep it discreet. He took an OJ out of the minifridge beside the bed and cracked it and took a long sip. He nodded to himself. To heck with it. He'd check out in the morning, like a regular human being.

'Well?' said his wife when he got back into the bed. 'What was it?'

The Brit thought about who would want to kill

him. Then he laughed. He'd be up all night.

'I don't know,' he said as he snuggled in next to his wife. He kissed her above her camisole, right where he'd just shot whoever it was who thought he could pull a fast one on him.

'Aren't we so tender all of a sudden? What was that for?'

'Love, darling,' he said as he pinched her bottom. 'All we need is love, right?'

'And rockets,' she said after a moment, and they both began to crack up.

CHAPTER 40

'Now, finish up the rest and don't screw it up,' Flicka said, stabbing one of his long fingers in Marvin's face. 'I know what a gram looks like in my dreams, so you think about skimming, you think again. I'll go down and get the car. You be in the lobby waiting when I come around. Don't make me text your ass.'

Marvin waited for Flicka to leave before he let out a tense breath and looked around at the spare room.

The table. The electronic scale. The massive mound of rank marijuana.

'What the hell are you doing?' he whispered to himself.

The apartment was in Flushing, Queens, near LaGuardia Airport, with planes screaming overhead every five minutes. Flicka had taken him here three hours before and set him to work, busting down a couple of pounds of weed.

This whole thing was all over his stupid cousin. He just had to get into weed dealing with Flicka. But he messed up, stealing money or losing product, and got shot dead by Flicka. And now Marvin had to do Flicka's bidding to pay off his cousin's debt, like some sort of slave, or else his poor uncle down in North Carolina was going to get it, too, from the other guys in Flicka's crew.

Marvin had been trying to think of how to get out of the situation, but so far, he was coming up empty. What the hell could he do?

Maybe he could ask the family living here in the weed apartment for advice, he thought, shaking his head at the insanity of it all. The apartment belonged to some Asian people, apparently. A grandma, it looked like, and a three-year-old and a baby.

As he sat busting up the last of the weed, he watched as the grandma walked obliviously past the open bedroom door and headed into the hall bathroom.

Did Flicka have a deal with them or something? Marvin thought. Was the mama-san some sort of crook? He had no clue.

Marvin finished bagging the last gram and stuffed everything into the knapsack, along with the scale. When he came out into the hallway, he almost stepped on the three-year-old who was sitting there in a diaper, eating one of those long ices in a plastic sleeve. Which would have been way weirder than it already was had the apartment not been stiflingly hot. The ice was a blue one, and the stuff was stuck to the little guy's face and neck and chest. He was just covered in it.

Marvin winced as he stepped over him and headed out the door.

'What you waiting for? I should get out and hold the door open for you?' Flicka said as Marvin hit the sidewalk. 'Get in.'

Flicka was in his Escalade now. What he called his company car. The inside of it smelled more like weed than a lawn mower smells like cut grass. Marvin got in and put on his seat belt and looked around for cops.

About ten silent minutes of driving through the maze of Queens later, they pulled into the parking lot of a Stop & Shop supermarket and parked.

'Go out and get me one of them carts,' Flicka said with a jut of his chin.

'What?' Marvin said, staring at him.

'You deaf? Go get me one of those carts.'

'One of the shopping carts?'

'What other kind of carts you see, boy?' Flicka said. 'Get one and put it in the back. And flip it when you put it back there, too. I don't need it rollin' around, rippin' up my upholstery.'

What the hell now? Marvin thought.

After twenty more minutes of driving around, they pulled into a storage locker joint beside a U-Haul rental place. Flicka parked and ordered Marvin to take the shopping cart out of the back.

Marvin followed as Flicka rolled it inside the storage facility. They took an elevator up to the second floor and continued down a seemingly endless hallway lined with corrugated steel lockers.

'Two one six two. Here it is,' Flicka said, un-

133

doing the lock on one of the steel shutters and rattling it up.

Inside, it was jam-packed with moving boxes and kids' furniture and bicycles and clothes. Box after box after box.

'We gotta get all this out to my sister's new place in Camden,' Flicka said, handing Marvin the lock. 'Fill up the ride with as much as it can hold, and then come get me. I'll be in the diner across the street.'

Marvin stood there, staring at the boxes.

It's official. I'm a slave, he thought. *There's no way out of this.*

'Aw, don't look so sad, little Marvin. This here's what's called a character-building exercise,' Flicka said, grinning. 'If you get tired, don't worry. Just think of your uncle's smiling face, and everything will work out fine.'

CHAPTER 41

It was a little after nine o'clock at night, and Manhattan College's Draddy Gym was hot and bright and packed to the rafters.

The gym was an old seventies-era airplane-hangar-looking building that was sometimes criticized by visiting sports reporters. But when the Jaspers were playing their closest rival, Iona College, the fans' electricity in the joint could have outdone what you'd find at a Knicks game at Madison Square Garden.

Over the squeaks and squeals of sneakers on hardwood blasted the arena standard 'Get Ready for This,' as Manhattan's band and cheerleaders and dancers and student fan section Sixth Borough went batty.

They weren't the only ones. Myself and the rest of the Bennett bunch were at the top of the bleachers at half-court going berserk as we watched my son Trent compete in the halftime high jinks.

'Go, Trent, go!' we chanted.

He was trying to put on an oversize Manhattan uniform and complete a layup while a rival little kid fan tried to get on the gear of the Gaels.

Trent was in the huge green-and-white Manhattan uniform, half a step ahead of the Iona kid, when he got tripped up by the size 13 sneakers he was wearing and fell down in a heap.

'Nooooo!' we yelled.

But then the other kid tripped as well, as Trent got up and calmly banked it in.

'Yessssss!' we yelled.

'Wahoo!' Seamus yelled, and started handing out high fives as we jumped up and down.

I turned as Mary Catherine, wearing a Manhattan College hoodie, planted one on my lips.

We stared at each other.

'You look beautiful in green and white,' I said after a beat.

'I bleed green and white!' she yelled.

I was still laughing when Brian tapped me on the shoulder.

'Dad, look – it's him,' my son said.

'Who?' I said.

'With Marvin. Down there,' Brian said, pointing at the gym entrance. 'That scary guy I was telling you about.'

I looked over. There was a tall, older guy in an expensive goose down jacket talking to Marvin. The guy looked formidable both in size and attitude, and Marvin looked afraid of him.

I decided to take a walk down out of the stands to see what was going on. But by the time I got to the entrance, the guy was gone.

'Hey, Marvin. There you are. You made it,' I said as I stepped up. 'We were getting worried. How did your, um, after-school history project go?'

'Oh, hey, Mr. Bennett,' Marvin said. 'Yeah, it went great.'

I noticed that Marvin smelled like weed. Make that reeked.

He didn't seem high, though. If anything, he looked relieved to see me.

'Marvin, who is that guy? The guy you were just talking to.'

'Nobody. An old friend from my neighborhood.'

'You sure? He didn't look too friendly.'

'I'm all right. Really, Mr. Bennett,' Marvin said as he passed me, heading for the stands.

I decided to let it go.

For now.

136

CHAPTER 42

The private study down the hall from the Oval Office, where President Buckland held many of his more under-the-radar meetings, had a pale palette of cream walls and pastel high-backed chairs and yellow chintz sofas.

When the president walked in at 6:30 a.m. with his personal secretary, Maddy Holzer, his first thought was that Ellen Huxley-Laffer, his pale, Waspy national security adviser sitting on one of the yellow couches, fit right in with the decor.

'Good morning, Mr. President,' Ellen said, tucking away her smartphone as she stood.

'Morning, Ellen. Hope that wasn't a Snapchat,' the president joked as he sat on the couch across from her.

The president liked Ellen. Wearing an immaculate Saxon-gray blazer and skirt, the sandy-blond former captain of the Harvard Law debate team looked like a middle-aged Ralph Lauren model. But her stock soap actress looks aside, the fifty-four-year-old was about as well-rounded as one got in DC intelligence and Department of Defense circles. She was a National War College graduate and a former air attaché to the French embassy, as well as a CIA case officer.

'Can I get you anything? A bagel or a muffin?'

'No, I'm fine. So what's up, sir?' Huxley-Laffer said.

The president took a deep breath.

'Okay, Ellen. I heard from the others last night about the Ukrainian economic collapse. Are you up to speed on that?'

'The hryvnia, their currency, is collapsing in value, right?' Huxley-Laffer said. She had read about it on Bloomberg on her way in.

'Yes, it's completely tanking. Down twenty-four percent in the last three days. We have a friendly high up in their department of finance, as you well know. They've tapped us for a loan to stop the bleeding. I'd love to go forward with that, or anything else that will help the Ukraine stand up to the Russians after their annexation of Crimea. What's your take?'

Huxley-Laffer looked up in the air to her left and pursed her lips as she thought.

'I think, truthfully, that we need to back off a little, Mr. President. You know, calling them out on the false flag attempt last week was a really good move. It was very effective and needed to be done, but I think a loan or any other direct backing and involvement in the Ukraine on the heels of it is really going to be seen seriously as a threat to some of the hard-line higher-ups in Russia.'

'You think so?' the president said.

'Well, we know through our sources that they're already spooked by the increase in the military budget you made. And besides, we already have economic sanctions and help from our European friends to limit trade and especially credit to them. We have enough pressure already on them. It's time to let it do its work.'

The president squinted pensively at Huxley-Laffer.

'So let this one go?' he said.

'Yes, sir. I think you should let this one go.'

The president smiled.

'Slow and steady wins the race?'

'That's what they say,' Huxley-Laffer affirmed.

'On another topic, you think I should go to New York for this UN summit?'

'What does John say?'

The president rolled his eyes and smiled.

'The head of the Secret Service? What do you think?'

'They're still looking for the shooter?'

The president nodded.

'What do you want to do?'

'Go, of course.'

'I agree,' Huxley-Laffer said.

'Show of strength, Ellen.'

'Yes,' Huxley-Laffer said with a smile. Then she lifted a finger.

'But remember. Not too much.'

CHAPTER 43

With its old gray prewar tenement buildings and rusting fire escapes and garbage bags piled high at the curbs, Brighton Beach, Brooklyn, looked like a dilapidated chunk of inner-city blight plopped down beside the ocean.

Noon Tuesday, I was in a fed surveillance car in

the heart of the heavily Russian neighborhood on Ocean View Avenue. In the car with me was Paul Ernenwein and two of his best guys from the FBI New York office's Russian mob squad. A second car with two more agents sat around the block.

The object of our attention was the gaudy red-and-gold awning of a popular Russian restaurant called Sochi's that was a block to the north.

We'd finally gotten a decent lead. The feds had scoured Pavel Levkov's Riverdale place while he was still at the hospital. They'd found a cell phone in a false panel in the attic. And one of the numbers on it belonged to a well-known Russian mobster named Maxim Kuznetsov.

Kuznetsov, in addition to being a former professional heavyweight boxer, had been a suspect in over a dozen brutal murders of Russian nationals and Russian American immigrants in the last ten years. He had ties through his older brother to Russia's military intelligence organization, the GRU. He was also one of Sochi's owners.

As we sat there, staring at the restaurant, it started to lightly snow. You could see snow on the boardwalk down the side street and even a half-melted snowman on the beach, under the lead-colored sky.

'Call me crazy, but whenever I hear the word *beach,* it usually evokes images of sunshine and pastel-colored hotels and bikinis,' I said.

'Yeah, well, welcome to Siberia by the sea,' Paul mumbled as he looked through his binocs.

'Wait,' he said a moment later. 'There's a car slowing out in front. A BMW SUV.'

Paul's radio crackled.

'We see him. It's Kuznetsov,' said the feds in the other car.

Busboys were Windexing tabletops and a vacuum whirred loudly from somewhere as the five agents and I, in raid jackets, stormed into the restaurant ten minutes later.

There was gold everywhere. On the covers on the chairs, the brass railings, and the mirror frames. From the gilt ceiling hung massive, glittering chandeliers that were about as demure as Cleopatra's earrings.

We found Kuznetsov in the very clean and bright stainless steel kitchen. He was a tall man, about six foot four, in his fifties, wearing an apron over a stylish white dress shirt and gray silk suit pants. He was expertly chiffonading clusters of basil on a butcher block with a ten-inch chef's knife.

'Maxim Kuznetsov?' Paul Ernenwein said.

The beefy, gravely handsome dark-haired man glanced up at us, then slowly set down the huge knife. He blotted at his broad forehead with a paper napkin. Something good was cooking in a pan on the stove behind him. Some kind of chicken in a thick brown butter sauce.

'Yes. How can I help you?' he said in, surprisingly, completely unaccented English.

'We'd like to ask you a few questions about a national security matter,' Paul said. 'Could you come with us, please?'

He stared at us steadily with his dark eyes.

'Will I need a lawyer?' he said.

Paul smiled.

'I guess we'll just have to see,' he said.

141

CHAPTER 44

The next morning at around ten, Paul Ernenwein and I were walking south down bright and blustery Park Avenue, heading to a surprise meeting with the Secret Service at their forward team HQ.

The invite was quite sudden, and even more curious since this was the very same Secret Service who'd said they wanted to run their own separate departmental investigation in the search for the president's shooter instead of teaming up with us.

'So I heard our Russian friend, Kuznetsov, didn't bite,' I said to Paul as we crossed East 31st with steaming doughnut cart coffees.

'You heard right,' the stocky Boston FBI agent said as he pulled up the sleeve of his trench to check his watch. 'We released him around eleven p.m., when his lawyer showed. He maintains that he had no knowledge of Pavel Levkov and that his number on Pavel's phone could have been from any one of the patrons of his restaurant, to whom, he claims, he often loans his phone.'

'Oh, so that explains his connection to the attempted presidential assassination,' I said, rolling my eyes. 'Just a simple case of loaning out his cell phone. Our bad.'

'Don't worry,' the feisty redheaded agent said with a grin. 'Before we let him go, we let it be known that we were going to put full-court pressure on him and his entire organization until he decides to be more cooperative. He didn't exactly seem to be shaking in his boots, but we'll see what happens.'

Up the block, I followed Paul into the marble lobby of a prewar office building, and we badged our way past the desk. Through a buzzed-open and unmarked door on the eighth floor, I counted about two dozen stressed-out T-men among the laptops and file cabinets and paper shredders.

Paul said hello to one of the agents, who led us to the back of the office. Inside the briefing room, a dark-haired woman sat at a desk, biting on a pen as she stared alternately at the two laptops open in front of her.

'Paul, Mike – I'm Margaret Foley. Thanks for coming,' the tall, attractive, intense thirtysomething brunette said as she stood and smiled and shook our hands.

Paul had already told me that Foley was the Service's newly assigned agent in charge in New York. He'd heard she was supposed to be a pretty straight shooter, ambitious but fair. Her people seemed to like her.

Foley gestured at her laptops.

'I'll be blunt, fellas. We're getting absolutely nowhere in our own investigation on the president's shooter, and I was hoping we could maybe pool our resources in tracking him down. Does that sound like it makes sense?'

'Yes,' Paul said as he unbuttoned his coat. 'Finally.'

Foley laughed as she rolled up her shirtsleeves.

'Yeah, I heard my predecessor didn't play that

well with others. I'm hoping I can change that.'

She uncapped a marker with a sharp pop and brought us over to the whiteboard she had set up in the corner.

'Okay. Maybe you can help bring me up to speed on all of this,' she said, gesturing at the collage of printouts and photographs.

'Basically, the morning the president came to the UN, the FBI New York office got a call from a confidential informant,' Paul said as he sat down.

'Our counterintel division has had a pretty high-up guy in the Russian embassy for years who we trust. He told us six months ago that he had heard a rumor that a big hit was about to go down in the States and that it was being authorized by the Russian government. But he didn't know the target. Then, the morning of the president's visit, he called, frantically saying he had just found out it was the president.'

'That's insane. Just incredible,' Foley said. 'Do the Russians want a world war? Who's the shooter supposed to be? A Russian?'

'No, we think the Russians probably opted for a professional killer for hire,' Paul said. 'Why bring one of your own people in when you can use a world-class sniper turned mercenary?'

'Where did you come into all this, Mike?' Foley said, turning toward me.

'I was put on a task force with Paul's guys on the morning of the president's arrival to find the shooter. It didn't take long. I was part of the aerial countersniper surveillance covering the presidential motorcade coming in from Kennedy, and as we came into Manhattan with the motorcade, I spotted something under the lip of the MetLife Building.'

'The sniper's blind,' Foley said, tapping the crime scene photos on her board that showed the blind. 'Okay. So you crash-land on the roof and attempt an arrest, but the assassin shoots the cop with you and escapes. Then what happened?'

'Our Russian confidential informant from the embassy went missing,' Paul said. 'But not before he gave us a lead on a guy named Pavel Levkov.'

'Levkov,' Foley said, pointing to a picture of him. 'That's the guy who was shot in the kneecap?'

'One and the same,' I said. 'We think he was the shooter's handler. We also think that we're not the only ones looking for the shooter.'

'Who's the guy, Kuznetsov, that you picked up yesterday? How does he fit in?'

'Kuznetsov's the head of the Russian mob in New York,' I said. 'We found his number on Levkov's phone. What makes things even more interesting is that Kuznetsov also has ties to Russian intelligence. He has an older brother in the GRU, the Russian army's military intelligence.'

'So more Russians again,' Foley said, shaking her head.

'We figure maybe that Kuznetsov got the order from the Kremlin to do the hit, then hired Levkov as a middleman to hire an assassin,' I said.

'It's a theory, at least,' Paul said with a shrug. 'We actually had a talk with Kuznetsov last night, but his lawyer sprung him after ten minutes of getting nowhere. We have surveillance on him and Levkov, so hopefully something will break.'

'What's the deal with the president?' I said,

peeking out the meeting room's blinds.

I looked up at a jaw-dropping view of the Empire State Building two blocks northwest, then back at Foley. It was getting cloudy now, darker, threatening to snow.

'Is he actually coming back for this next round of UN meetings?' I said.

Margaret Foley popped the cap back on the marker.

'We advised against it, of course, since this shooter might very well still be around,' she said.

She clicked the marker to the magnetic whiteboard and crossed her arms.

'But the president insists. He's stubborn,' she said.

'Stubborn,' Paul said as he drummed his fingers on the table.

'Sounds like our job just got a whole lot harder,' I said.

CHAPTER 45

The British assassin entered the Holland Tunnel from Manhattan to New Jersey at a little after twelve noon.

It began to snow lightly when he came out of the tunnel. He turned up the heat in the rental car, a Chevy Camaro LS, which he thought would be crap, but it was actually surprisingly nice, fast, comfortable, and quiet.

He drove through Jersey City and got off I-78

before the Newark Bay Bridge. At a Shell station on the opposite side of the exit ramp, he stopped and went in and bought a cold bottle of raspberry-lime seltzer that he drank as he checked the address again on his phone.

After he had his bearings, he sat patiently, sipping his refreshing beverage as he looked out at the traffic on the exit ramp for another few minutes. He'd already made several maneuvers to deter surveillance, but you couldn't be too careful.

Things were looking positive, for a change. He'd been able to establish contact with a new representative for the client last night, and everything was full speed ahead again. Regrettably, someone had tortured the information regarding his whereabouts out of his handler, Pavel. They didn't know who this inquisitive person was, but they were thinking perhaps a member of the CIA, as the torturer seemed to know a lot about what was going on and was an American.

He thought about what had happened at Gramercy Park. Whoever was after him, he was confident he could handle it.

The client apologized profusely for such an unfortunate incident and, in addition to getting him a new handler, offered compensation for the screwup on their end in the form of a 50 percent increase in fee upon completion of the job.

Being a good sport, the British assassin had readily accepted the apology. And, of course, the money. It was the least he could do. One never wanted to disappoint so gracious a client.

Drink and thoughts finished, he pulled out of the gas station. Ten miles and minutes later, he pulled off 440 onto Pulaski Street near Port Jersey Boulevard. He passed along a couple of football field lengths of chain-link fence with shipping containers stacked behind it before turning into a parking lot.

The low, ugly brown brick building he parked in front of had the words FLEET LINE RENTALS above the door. There was a security camera bolted to the brick beside the sign, so he pulled a bloodred Washington Nationals ball cap low over his eyes before he got out of the car.

Spa music was playing softly in the small reception area inside. The office was quite dingy, but in one wall sat a plate glass window with an open view of the Manhattan skyline across New York Bay.

'Can I help you?' said a middle-aged woman from a windowed slot in the scuffed Sheetrock wall after a couple of moments.

'Yes. I spoke to Mr. Rodriguez this morning. My name is Peters,' the British assassin said with a perfect Midwestern American accent. 'Is he around?'

'He's on the phone. If you have a seat, he'll be more than happy to help you when he's done.'

As he waited, he took out his phone but decided not to fiddle with it. He was trying to quit that nasty modern habit. He turned it in his hand as another atrocious spa song began. He stared out at the distant lower Manhattan skyline, the ugly new Freedom Tower standing out like a broken tooth. As he watched, two tugs appeared close offshore, pulling a bulk freighter through the Claremont Terminal Channel.

'Mr. Peters?' said Rodriguez, suddenly standing beside him. He was a heavy, very pale, bald Hispanic man with striking hazel eyes.

'Mr. Rodriguez. Thanks for meeting with me,' the British assassin said, shaking Rodriguez's soft, gold-ringed hand.

'Thank you for waiting,' Rodriguez said, swiping away sweat from his forehead as he nodded rapidly with a little smile. 'I had one of my guys bring her up this morning so you could take a look right away. If you'll follow me.'

They went out back. Parked in front of a five-vehicle bay of garage doors was a fifty-thousand-pound tri-axle Caterpillar dump truck, blue in color. It looked far bigger than it had in the on-line ad, the British assassin thought, concerned. A real monster. Maybe it was too big.

He took a slow walk around it.

'How old?'

'Two thousand eleven. But it runs perfectly,' Rodriguez said. 'Listen.' He nimbly climbed up and turned it over. It coughed once, and again, and then snarled to throaty, rumbling life.

'Sounds great,' the assassin said.

'You need it for a month?'

'Yes,' the assassin said. 'Tell me: off the top of your head, how wide is it?'

'Did you say *wide?*' Rodriguez said, squinting at him.

The British assassin smiled, nodded.

'Um, standard width,' Rodriguez said with a shrug. 'Eight and a half feet, same as a tractor-trailer.'

Excellent, the British assassin thought. It would

be snug, but it would fit.

'Shall we start the paperwork?' asked Rodriguez hopefully.

The British assassin smiled again.

'Yes,' he said. 'Let's.'

CHAPTER 46

Around two on Wednesday, Doyle called with news on the Rafael Arruda drug hit that he needed to share with me in person.

Thirty minutes later, I found him and my other protégé, Detective Lopez, in Washington Heights' Thirty-Third Precinct's second-floor break room.

With a grand flourish, I placed on the table, between the Styrofoam cups of wretched coffee they were nursing, the plastic bag I was holding and removed the two huge waxed paper soda cups and perfectly greasy white paper bags that I'd just brought them from Shake Shack.

'Eat, gentlemen,' I said. 'And talk.'

'We'd hit a brick wall in the investigation, Mike,' Doyle said between bites of his double cheese with bacon. 'No witnesses, no nothing. So we decided to go back and look at all our video that faced the street near the drug building two weeks prior. I mean, it was just hours and hours of nothing. I was thinking maybe we could market the tape as the breakthrough cure for insomnia when we saw him.'

'Who?' I said.

'This neighborhood guy,' said Arturo, smiling. 'His name is Sol. Sol Badillo. But everybody calls him Jinete, which means, like, *jockey* in Spanish, on account of he used to be a horse trainer or something when he was younger.'

'Sol's one of these hang-around guys you often see in an inner-city hood,' Doyle said. 'Divorced, late fifties, lives with his grown daughter. He's sort of a super's helper, runs errands in the local stores, deals a little weed on the side. He's in and out of the barbershop every five minutes. He patrols the block the way a beat cop does, but instead of enforcing the law, he more likely helps the friendly neighborhood crooks break it.'

'Exactly,' Arturo said. 'In medieval times, this guy would be, like, the town crier or fool. He shuffles around twenty-four/seven and acts like he's half homeless or crazy, but meanwhile, he knows everything and everyone on the block. He's like the block's memory. Its underground eye-witness news anchor.'

'Go on,' I said, smiling. I liked the sound of this.

'Jinete was actually one of the first guys we canvassed,' said Doyle. 'Of course, he said he didn't know anything, but then we saw him in the video. Two weeks prior to the hit, plain as day, he puts a camera in a car parked across the street from the drug building.'

'The camera was pointing right at the building?' I said.

Doyle nodded, sipping his shake.

'So you're thinking he was working for whoever killed Arruda?' I said.

'Not thinking,' said Doyle with a wink. 'We're

knowing he was involved. We spoke to Jinete again two days ago. We showed him the video, and he finally broke down and told us everything.'

'So who hired him?' I said excitedly.

Doyle took a printout from a folder. It was a blown-up photocopy of a driver's license. Some blond guy on it. Matthew Leroux, it said, with an address in SoHo.

'Jinete said this guy, Leroux, gave him money to rent a car and the camera and five grand.'

'The guy gave Jinete his name?'

'No,' Arturo said. 'Jinete said Leroux called himself Bill. He said he was a slick guy. Spoke fluent Spanish. They met several times. But like I said, Jinete is no fool. He likes to know who the hell he's working with, so he actually had his daughter secretly follow the guy after one of their meetings. She followed him all the way back to Chelsea.'

'Chelsea,' I said. 'I thought the address on the license was in SoHo.'

'Chelsea is where this guy, Leroux, has an art gallery,' said Arturo, wide-eyed. 'He must have gotten bored perusing the canvases, so he decided to up and slaughter a drug gang.'

I looked at the photo, a tingle beginning in my stomach. This was good. Damn good. We were finally getting a break.

'Did you speak to Leroux?'

'No, we wanted to talk to you first, of course, Mr. National Security,' Arturo said.

'We do good or what, Mike?' said Doyle, smiling.

'No,' I said, taking out my phone to call Paul Ernenwein. 'You did amazing.'

CHAPTER 47

A reporter was doing a cutaway to get the United Nations in the background when Matthew and Sophie came up the steps on Ralph Bunche Park onto East 43rd.

It was morning, just after rush hour, on Thursday, and the pair was on the hunt.

They didn't look like it, of course.

Idly wandering around on the sidewalk in front of the flag-draped United Nations Plaza on First Avenue, clutching maps and a zoom lens Nikon, they looked like a young, stylish, maybe European couple touring the Big Apple for the first time.

As they walked west on 43rd, a street cleaner came down the street, churning a cloud of dust onto a rack of Citi Bikes before it made a U-turn. In the distant haze to the west, the green copper cathedral-like roof of Grand Central Terminal could be made out, and above it, the lip of the MetLife Building, where their target had set up his blind.

This morning's question was, where would he set up his next one? Matthew thought, frustrated.

After their first attempt at taking out the British sniper had failed, it was all about outthinking the assassin now. And outmaneuvering him.

They needed to find this bastard, Matthew thought.

Find him and put him down once and for all.

Sophie bought a half-pint of blueberries and some almonds and dates from a fruit seller on the corner of Second Avenue. They crossed the street and stopped and stood, chewing, beside a pay phone kiosk, silently watching the passing pedestrians and traffic on the avenue.

'Okay. What are the motorcade routes again?' Matthew said after he finished his nuts and berries.

'All right,' Sophie said. 'From the Waldorf to the UN, you have four avenue blocks and seven cross streets. Because of the length of the motorcade, they hate making turns, so usually they cordon off Fiftieth or Forty-Eighth and take it all the way to blocked-off First Avenue and down several blocks south to the UN's entrance.'

'That's the most direct route, but they have to have alternatives,' Matthew said.

'They could do Park to Forty-Sixth to First, but that's about it. They have several dozen vehicles, Matthew, and they need to get crosstown as quickly as possible.'

'It'll be Fiftieth, Forty-Eighth, or Forty-Sixth, then, where the next attack will come,' Matthew said, nodding. 'That's where the motorcade is most vulnerable. Where it can be boxed in.'

'Do you still think it'll be an attack on the motorcade itself?'

'Yes. He's tried the long shot. It didn't work out. He'll want to be closer this time. Point-blank range, maybe, or ambush with the use of some sort of explosives. He needs to change tactics. That's what I would do.'

'You're right,' said Sophie. 'He's got everyone

thinking long-range shot now, so it's time to switch up the script. Go for an up-close, in-your-face surprise. But how? The president's car is impenetrable.'

'So we're told,' said Matthew, looking at her bleakly. 'Remember that they said the *Titanic* was unsinkable. We need to expect the unexpected.'

'What do you mean?'

'Call it a hunch, Sophie. Intuition. I know this guy. He's a perfectionist. Winning is everything to him. War inspires artistry, and this guy truly thinks he's Michelangelo. If he can't do this with pizzazz, he won't do it at all.'

'But from where, Matthew?' Sophie said, looking up at the millions of windows. 'Where will it come from?'

Matthew smiled and put his arm around his wife's waist and kissed her.

'That's what we're here for, baby. We're the dream team. We're the hunters who hunt hunters. We'll find him.'

'I don't know, Matthew. Maybe we're in too far this time.'

'We take it the whole way, babe,' Matthew said. 'Just like we decided in the beginning. We have to find this fool. We have no choice.'

But what if he finds us first? Sophie thought, but didn't say.

CHAPTER 48

My just-popped can of Diet Coke hissed along with the old radiator in the corner of the small, dark room as Paul Ernenwein and I sat in a too-warm, windowless, secure comm room in a non-descript FBI building on East 56th.

We were on the fourth floor, just down the hall from Paul's office, sitting on metal folding chairs and watching a flat screen.

On it was a live feed of a blond couple walking west up East 43rd Street.

The two were an attractive pair: a weather-beaten blond guy in his late thirties and his pretty platinum-blond wife, probably five years younger. The guy reminded me of that laid-back dude on the HGTV show *Fixer Upper*, only he had a ridiculously muscular Olympic gymnast's body, a slim waist with broad shoulders, and huge forearms and hands.

The couple was being videotaped with a zoom lens from over a block away by one of Paul's guys in a state-of-the-art surveillance car that looked like a taxi minivan. The van and feds had been on them since I'd sent in the lead the afternoon before. They were also up on their house and cell phones.

'Despite the tourist getup, they look like professionals, don't they, Paul?' I said. 'Just the way they move, heads up, relaxed yet alert. Also the way they keep a lot of space between themselves, almost as if they don't want to reveal to anyone watching if they're actually together or not.'

'They're operators, all right,' Paul said, nodding. 'Who leaves their primary cell phone at home in the middle of the day? That's trade-craft.'

'As was the superslick way Matthew hired Jinete in Hamilton Heights,' I said. 'Intelligence service asset recruitment one oh one.'

'Though they're trying to appear to be tourists,' Paul said, 'watch how even as they look up at buildings, they don't stumble or bump into people. You can tell they're familiar with the area. These guys are analyzing, fact-finding. They're in mission mode.'

'You think they're scoping out the motorcade route?'

'Could be. Mike, you saw the shooter. Could this guy be him?'

I stared at Matthew Leroux as he walked with his wife.

'Maybe,' I said after a bit. 'Same athleticism. Same build.'

I'd already read through the extensive info folders Paul and his team had put together on Matthew and Sophie Leroux from the fed data-bases.

It turned out they weren't your regular art gallery owners.

In fact, they were both ex-CIA.

They'd met in 2005 in Iraq, where Matthew, a former Navy SEAL turned Special Operations Group team leader, and Sophie, a CIA analyst, both cycled into the Joint Special Operations Command.

What they had worked on together there was classified, but Paul had spoken to some people at State and speculated that they had both been ground zero in the insurgent terrorist-hunting business. For four years, they had worked side by side, gathering intel and finding and fixating and terminating jihadi bomb makers in and around Falluja and Mosul.

When Matthew was a SEAL, he'd actually earned the Distinguished Service Cross, one medal below the Congressional Medal of Honor, for almost single-handedly suppressing a truck bomb attack on a forward operating base in Bagram.

He and Sophie had married in '07 and had put in their papers at the same time in 2011, when she had gotten pregnant with their now four-year-old daughter, Victoria. Matthew was a hick from rural Indiana, so it was Sophie who was wearing the pants in their somewhat successful art gallery biz. Sophie was a born-and-bred Manhattanite with a father who had apparently been a famous gallery owner.

They didn't seem like assassins, but then again, we had every indication that they had been involved in the hit in Hamilton Heights.

And now they looked like they were casing the streets between the Waldorf and the UN, where the president would be driving around in less than a week's time. It was concerning, not to mention scary as hell.

'Is this even possible, Paul?' I said as I watched

them. 'This can't be what it looks like. Two former distinguished and dedicated patriots now working for some unknown enemy actually setting up our own president?'

I watched the good-looking couple on the screen as they took another picture.

'It seems weird to me, too, Mike, but anything is possible,' Paul said. 'Maybe they've got money problems or a drug habit, if you consider how wackadoo the art world can be. Or maybe they picked up a crazy ideology. Couples do go nuts sometimes, and these guys were deep in the shit over there in Iraq. For years, all they did was eat, drink, hunt and kill people, and sleep. These people are definitely persons of interest.'

CHAPTER 49

At a minute before five o'clock that evening, I found myself at Riverbank State Park in Harlem, listening to Katy Perry sing about fireworks from the cranked-up ice rink speakers over my head.

'Dad, what do you think of my moves?' said my son Ricky, excited as he wobbled past, almost falling three times.

'They're persistent, son. Real persistent,' I said, wondering if I should fetch him a bike helmet from the van.

A moment later, Fiona and Julia and Jane sailed past on their skates quite gracefully, their elbows locked as they sang along with Katy at the top of their lungs. I joined them for a few bars from the sidelines, until for some reason they told me to stop.

'What's the problem?' I called after them with mock concern. 'Wrong pitch? No, wait. It's my key, right? Where are you going? Wait, I can go higher.'

The annual skate-athon fund-raiser for my kids' school, Holy Name, was officially under way. As an official rinkside lap counter, I was freezing, but it could have been worse, I knew. Instead of my kids, it could have actually been me out there, falling and scraping and clunking against the boards over the Zamboni-freshened ice.

Though I was dog-tired from our all-day surveillance, I couldn't pass up the chance to spend some time with the kids. I'd been working too much lately on the joint task force. Way too much, if you considered how little there was to show for it.

And the fund-raiser really couldn't have been for a better cause. Catholic schools were truly hurting due to low enrollment, closing all over New York as they were all over the country. The thought of Holy Name actually closing was too depressing to even think about. Everybody at the school and the parish was like family to us.

Speaking of the saints, I busted Mary Catherine, beside me, staring at me as I put down my clipboard and lifted my not-so-hot cocoa. I smiled at her warily as Katy died out and the All-American Rejects started up.

'What?' I said as she continued to stare without saying anything.

'Nothing,' she finally said, with a small grin.

160

'It's just nice to see you like this.'

'See me like how?' I said. 'Dry and on solid ground instead of out there, sitting on the ice with a wet, red, sore frozen butt?'

'No, that actually might be cute,' she said with a wink. 'I meant happy, relaxed, and, as a bonus, actually here.'

'I'm here, all right. Mike Bennett in the frost-bitten flesh,' I said, blowing on my hands. 'Too bad we can't say the same for Brian and Marvin. Where are those two? It can't take that long to get here from Fordham. They should be here by now.'

I saw Mary Catherine wince with worry as I said this. I knew she was already quite attached to our new houseguest and considered him to be family. Besides, she was no dummy. Like me, she knew full well there was something up with Marvin. Something that for all intents and purposes seemed to be heading from bad to worse.

'How do these damn kids become such experts at worrying parents to death, anyhow?' I said as I took out my phone to text Brian yet again. 'The second they outgrow the playpen, it's over.'

CHAPTER 50

Brian Bennett took a quick peek at his vibrating phone as he stood at the greasy window inside a Chinese takeout dump called New Dragon Palace on Westchester Avenue in some misbegotten, run-down section of the Bronx.

He looked up from his dad's latest freak-out of a text and put his eyes back on the car underneath the elevated track across the street.

It was a Mercedes, a two-door glossy silver E320 ghettoed out with big silver rims and dark tinted windows. He'd been doing nothing but stare at it for the last ten minutes.

It was because of Marvin.

Marvin was now in the car doing who knew what with that old psycho gangbanger dude who seemed to be stalking him.

This wasn't supposed to be happening, Brian thought. What was supposed to be happening was Brian and Marvin attending the Holy Name skate-athon with everybody at the rink in Harlem.

But after school, Marvin said he had something to do and would meet him later. Brian knew what that meant, so, on an impulse, he decided to follow him.

It was quite the odyssey. The B train at Fordham Road to Yankee Stadium. The 4 train from there to 125th, where Marvin got a third train, an uptown 6 that had taken them back into the Bronx here, to a place called St. Lawrence Avenue.

He didn't know what St. Lawrence was the patron saint of, but his street was one of the sketchiest blocks Brian had ever set foot on. Coming from the stairs of the subway, he'd passed an auto glass store that looked like it had been torched beside a bodega with a bulletproof glass sidewalk kiosk. The only light on the dilapidated block seemed to be from the blood-red neon PETEY'S DISCOUNT LIQUORS, in front of which the Merc was parked.

162

It didn't make sense, Brian thought, shaking his head. Marvin was the coolest dude. Enthusiastic and humble and nice to everybody – parents, even freshmen. A solid B student, with his athletics he was a shoo-in for a good college scholarship.

He even talked about his future plans all the time. He said he knew he probably wasn't good enough for the pros, and that he was going to major in management. He had an uncle who owned a bunch of tire stores down south, and he wanted to do something like that: manage a franchise or something and work with colleagues and customers.

At sixteen, he was by far the most mature of all their friends, Brian knew.

And yet in spite of all that, he was here in Fort Apache, the Bronx, doing some ... sinister drug deal or something.

It just didn't make sense.

CHAPTER 51

What would Dad do? Brian wondered as he continued to stare at the car.

That was easy. He'd probably walk on over across the street, tap on the tinted window, and demand to know what the hell was happening.

But Dad was a cop, wasn't he? He had a gun and a badge and twenty years' experience in crazy, dangerous, drug-infested places like this.

What did *he* have? Brian thought. A book bag

and a friendly smile?

Brian winced as he listened to the steel drum rattle of a passing 6 on the elevated track overhead.

What the hell would happen next? he wondered as Marvin suddenly got out of the car with a small duffel bag.

Brian immediately bolted out of the restaurant and crossed the street, tailing Marvin north under the El toward the intersection of St. Lawrence. As he got to the corner, he watched as Marvin made a beeline toward a tenement on the north side of the street. The run-down structure had an NYPD SAFE HALLWAYS sign above its main door that even Brian knew meant it was a hard-core drug building. Just then, three people – two jacked gangster-looking black guys and a tough-seeming, probably Hispanic chick with cornrows – came out of the building's front door and sat on its stoop. The girl lit a cigarette, and then one of the cold-eyed black guys snatched it out of her mouth as the other guy laughed.

Brian ran up as Marvin was about to cross the street.

'Marvin! Yo, Marvin!' he cried.

'Brian?!' Marvin said, staring at him in shock. 'What the hell are you doing? Following me? You shouldn't be here, man. What are you doing? Didn't I tell you to leave me alone?'

'What am I doing?' Brian cried. 'What are *you* doing? You have to stop all this crazy stuff, Marvin. I saw you in that car with that crazy dude. Are you out of your frickin' mind? You're gonna get arrested or killed. Why are you throwing your

164

life away?'

Instead of answering, Marvin turned and watched over Brian's shoulder as a car passed by back on Westchester Avenue. It was a beat-up maroon Chevy. It slowed and stopped on the corner. The three street toughs on the tenement stoop immediately scattered as some chubby white guys climbed out of the car.

'Oh, damn! It's cops! C'mon!' Marvin said, tugging at Brian's jacket.

Before he could stop and think about it, Brian was moving quickly with Marvin down St. Lawrence. They took a left on an even worse disaster of a street called Gleason and started running. They hooked another left on a street called Beach. Halfway down Beach, Brian watched as Marvin threw the duffel bag over a graffiti-covered wood fence into an abandoned lot. Then they ran all the way back to the elevated subway station on Westchester.

'C'mon, Marvin. Let's just get the hell out of here,' said Brian as they huffed and puffed on the stairs for the El. Brian looked over by PETEY'S DISCOUNT LIQUORS, but the Merc was gone.

Marvin shook his head.

'No, man. We just need to wait a few minutes. I have to go back.'

'Go back?' Brian said, disbelieving.

'I have to go back for that bag,' Marvin said.

'Why? What the hell is in it, anyway?'

Marvin gave him a fierce look.

'Don't you worry about that. Just wait here,' Marvin said, pointing at him. 'I'll be ten minutes, tops, okay? Just wait.'

Brian's phone went off again as he helplessly watched Marvin run back across the street the way they'd come.

Where the hell are you guys? Dad wanted to know. *I'm not kidding, Brian. You should have been here an hour ago. Where the hell are you? Tell me now.*

Brian looked around as another train arrived above, its violent, industrial rattle like a death metal drum solo.

As if I know, he thought

Sorry, Dad. We were stuck in a tunnel. Just got out. Train's stuck again though, Brian lied, typing quickly. *But we should be on our way any minute.*

If we're both still alive, Brian thought, shaking his head again as he hit Send.

PART THREE

CATCH ME IF YOU CAN

CHAPTER 52

Paul Ernenwein and I were called to a surprise lunch meeting with Secret Service special agent in charge Margaret Foley, at the famous Bull and Bear Prime Steakhouse at the Waldorf Astoria.

We found Agent Foley at a black leather banquette in the corner, sitting with a boyish dark-haired fortysomething gentleman in a tailored navy suit.

'Guys, I'd like you to meet Mark Evrard,' she said. 'Mark's with the DSS.'

DSS was the Diplomatic Security Service, I knew, the security and law enforcement service of the State Department. They were the guys who protected US ambassadors and embassies all around the world.

'After you brought up the Russian angle at our last meeting, I asked around, and a friend got me in touch with Mark,' Agent Foley said as we sat. 'He's been with the DSS for the last fifteen years at the American embassy in Moscow. He also teaches a Russian foreign relations seminar at Johns Hopkins and is considered one of the most knowledgeable people about Russia in all of Washington. If anyone could broaden our understanding about the Russians and the way they think, it's Mark.'

'Well, I don't know about all that,' Evrard said in a down-to-earth Chicago accent after a sip of his whiskey sour. 'But maybe I can help. What kind of Russki info are you guys looking for?'

'Well, I guess the first question is, how credible do you think it is that Grekov or anybody else in the Russian government would actually try to kill President Buckland?' I said.

'Exactly,' said Paul Ernenwein. 'I mean, I know some of these Russian mobsters are nuts, but is it also true of officials in the Russian government? Of people that high up?'

Evrard took another sip of his drink.

'You're actually talking about the same people,' he said, smoothing his tie. 'Along with the oligarchs who seized control of the Russian industries after the fall of the Berlin Wall, the Russian mafia and the Russian government are all part of the same power structure.'

I shook my head as that sunk in.

'It's that bad? I mean, it's obvious Russia has some corruption issues, but that's nuts, isn't it?'

'Yep, it is nuts, and tragically true,' Evrard said, looking at me calmly. 'They all work together. The Russian mafia provides security and muscle for Russian industry bigwigs. Russian industry bigwigs pay off corrupt politicians and bureaucrats and cops.

'You actually have corrupt Moscow cops who have multimillion-dollar properties in places like Switzerland and Dubai. Politically connected oligarchs have vacation mansions built on protected public land. They say Grekov himself had a billion-dollar summer palace built for himself on the Black Sea with Russian tax money.'

'How can that be? How can they get away with

that?' I said.

'Easy. When asked about it, the spokespeople at the Kremlin all have the same standard Russian answer: 'We are not authorized to speak on this issue.' Reporters who push harder have a funny way of ending up dying under mysterious circumstances. Everybody scratches everybody else's back. It's all one big rotten family.'

'With Grekov as the daddy,' Paul said.

'Yep. He's the top of the pyramid, the shot caller. He was KGB in the old days, and ruthlessly worked his way up to prime minister, and then president. Some say he put the squeeze on all the oligarchs during his first two presidential terms for a hefty slice of Russia's entire economy. All its oil, mining, logging, fleet fishing, telecommunications – everything. Because of this, the same people say that Grekov is probably the richest guy in the entire world.'

'Does that make him crazy enough to go after Buckland?' I said.

'Have you ever heard of the Russian apartment building bombings of 1999?'

I shook my head.

'In 1999, apartment buildings in three Russian cities suddenly blew up, causing upwards of three hundred deaths. Grekov and the Russian government quickly blamed it on Chechen terrorists, despite the fact that massive amounts of highly sophisticated RDX Russian military explosives were used. Then Grekov, who was prime minister, ramped up the Chechen war and then rode the war's popularity into the presidency.'

'You're saying it might have been a false flag?' I

said. 'That he might have killed three hundred of his own citizens to get his poll numbers up?'

Evrard nodded.

'And it's not just in Russia that he's not afraid to take off the gloves,' he said. 'In 2006, Vladimir Sayanski, a Russian ex-FSB agent and Grekov critic who emigrated, was actually poisoned and assassinated with radioactive material *in London.*'

'Okay, that answers that,' Paul said. 'Grekov apparently has no qualms about anything.'

'Which brings me to the other reason why I wanted to have this meeting,' Foley cut in. 'Grekov is coming. Grekov is coming here to New York to join the UN talks.'

'Grekov is coming here?' I said. 'But I thought Buckland was coming.'

'He is!' Foley said. 'As if we need another ball to juggle. They're both coming. Grekov and Buckland will be in town at the same time.'

CHAPTER 53

With no traffic, it took the British assassin two hours flat to get to East Hampton, Long Island, in the Camaro.

It was the first time he had ever been there. He'd read that it was supposed to be a big deal, a tony artist colony and summer playground for the rich. But driving down Montauk Highway, its main street, and passing a lousy Starbucks and a CVS pharmacy, he wasn't seeing it. Billionaires

172

were attracted to this dump?

What a grubby, horrid country America was, he thought, not for the first time. He couldn't wait until this job was finally done so he could get back to civilization.

His final destination was east of Montauk Highway near Two Mile Hollow Beach. Behind the chain-link, the address was more wood-shingled shack than house. There was a broken surfboard propped beside the front door and the rusting shell of an old Jaguar coupe under a listing carport. As he stood there, an old filthy dog that might have been a German shepherd came out from behind the ruined sports car and began barking.

A moment later, a man in faded blue coveralls opened the hovel's front door. He took off a pair of oil-covered black rubber gloves as he came out into the yard.

'Down, Airplane,' Billy Dee said to the dog as he gave it a soft kick. 'Manners, now, girl. We have a visitor.'

Billy Dee was a tall, lanky Australian with dirty-blond hair, dark-brown eyes, and a netlike crisscross of fine lines up and down his long, weather-beaten face. He had a reputation as a highly competent and discreet mechanic and designer who'd work for anyone for the right price. He'd worked for the cartels. Wall Street hustlers. Even Hollywood.

The back of the house was one big studiolike workroom piled with tools and spare parts. The British assassin couldn't make out what half the stuff was. There was a drill press beside a 3-D printer. An engine crankshaft on a blue rag-covered workbench. Wired circuits on an elaborate breadboard hanging from the far wall.

'It's a big job, is it?' the Aussie wanted to know. 'I only ask because you came with the highest of recommendations.'

'Where is it?' the British assassin said, ignoring him.

'Straight to business, eh? No problem, friend. I got your baby right over here,' Billy Dee said as he brought over a milk crate from a corner and placed it down beside the crankshaft.

Inside the plastic crate was what looked like a mix between a metal skeleton of a robot and a bagpipe. It was a jumble of hydraulic cylinders and pistons and clamps and wires, all jutting from the torso of a large electric motor box.

'How does it work?' the British assassin said.

'Okay,' Billy Dee said excitedly as he lifted one of the pistons. 'The signal opens the float switch in the control box here, which engages the magnetic contact over here, and–'

'I don't give a fuck how it works technically, monkey wrench,' the assassin said coldly. 'I meant, how do I work it?'

The Aussie looked hurt.

'Install the hardware, then hit that app I already e-mailed you. Everything pops up on your phone screen, the video feed, the whole shebang, and Bob's your uncle, you're in control.'

'What's the range?'

Even more lines appeared on Billy Dee's *Old Man and the Sea* face when he smiled. His crooked yellow teeth were sickening.

174

'What's the range of a wireless cell phone signal? Infinite?' the Australian said, and began laughing. 'That's the real beauty here. You could be anywhere, mate. You could work her from the other side of the world.'

The British assassin smiled himself as he looked at the contraption, picturing it. It just might work after all.

He took out the large manila envelope with the hundred thousand in it and placed it next to the crankshaft.

'I'll see myself out,' the British assassin said as he lifted the crate.

'Pleasure doing business with you,' said the Australian, already thumbing hundreds.

A moment later, the big Aussie made less noise than expected as he dropped to the workshop floor with the back of his head blown open.

The British assassin stepped over Billy Dee, straddling his waist, as he put two more in the bigmouthed grease monkey – this time in his temple – with his suppressed .22.

There was no way he could have let him live. Not at this point. The risk was too great.

The man had actually been right. This was a big job. The biggest probably of all time.

Too big to fail, he thought with a smile.

'Pleasure's all mine, mate,' the British assassin finally said as he aimed his gun to take care of the dog.

CHAPTER 54

There were over a hundred people in the West Chelsea gallery that night for the opening.

You could tell right away that these were not the PBS tote bag-schlepping bridge-and-tunnelers you sometimes saw at MoMA and the Met. Quite the contrary. With the amount of Botox and Hermès Birkin bags and bespoke tailoring on display, it was obvious that some of the most serious players in the multibillion-dollar downtown NYC art world were on the scene.

In front of the mixed-media installations and huge paintings, you could hear exotic languages being spoken: Portuguese, Chinese, Russian. The art market, like the real estate market, in New York was red-hot right now with the new influx of foreign billionaire money. One had to have something *just so* to hang on the wall of one's new twenty-million-dollar sky-view apartment, after all.

Since I wasn't a foreign oligarch and my art collection consisted mostly of finger paintings on my fridge, I was there because I was on the job, of course. In the Chanel-scented crowded gallery behind me, about twenty feet away, over my right shoulder, stood Matthew and Sophie Leroux, the ex-CIA art dealers who for some unknown reason seemed to want to pull a Lee Harvey Oswald on President Buckland. They were under 24/7 surveillance now, and we'd been on them from the second they left their SoHo town house an hour before.

In his sleek black suit and expensively simple white shirt, Mr. Leroux certainly looked the part of the rich art dealer. And could act it as well, given the expert way he and his pretty and slim wife, Sophie, air-kissed and backslapped with all the globally loaded folks in attendance.

As I watched them, I couldn't help sensing how tight they seemed. The way they held hands and conferred with each other between meet and greets when no one was looking. They were attractive and sociable, but their relationship seemed quite real. They seemed like serious, committed people.

Which was more than a little troubling, I thought, considering the two highly trained ex-spies seemed very much to be plotting to blow the president of the United States' head off in less than a week's time.

I turned as my old buddy Brooklyn Kale arrived in a cocktail dress and handed me a club soda. I noticed that my head wasn't the only one turning at the sight of my tall and lovely partner in her little black undercover dress.

I'd actually pulled some strings and had several of my old Harlem crew buddies reassigned to the anti-assassination task force. In addition to Brooklyn, I had Arturo Lopez and Jimmy Doyle in an unmarked Chevy parked outside, across West 24th.

With the president and now Grekov due in town, and still having really no clue what was up, we definitely needed all the help we could get.

'What are these paintings supposed to be about again?' Brooklyn said, staring up at the immense dark-toned abstract canvas in front of us.

'"With their never obvious inert compressions,"' I read off a pamphlet some pretty blond waif had handed me at the door, '"Scheermesje's latest work possesses a fragmented rawness that is at once a departure from, but also a profound echo of, his earlier work's often gummy tactile resonances."'

'Oh, I'm feeling those compressions,' Brooklyn said, shaking her head. 'Every time I look up at it, I want to pop a couple of Tylenol.'

When I glanced over my shoulder, I saw that Leroux and his wife were suddenly moving through the crush of people.

'Maybe they're heading for the bar,' Brooklyn said hopefully.

But they weren't.

We stood there watching as Matthew and Sophie reached the gallery steps near the entrance and went up them and straight out the front door.

CHAPTER 55

'Arturo, Doyle. Look lively. They're coming out,' I called into my hastily dialed phone as we made a not-so-subtle beeline after the couple through the dense crowd.

When we finally climbed the steps and hit the

street, I could see a gaggle of models oohing and aahing at one of those Mercedes six-wheeler super-SUVs that had pulled up on the cobble-stones out in front. What I wasn't seeing was the Lerouxes.

'Where are they?' I asked Arturo.

'Down the block. On your left,' he told me.

Damn it! Half a block away, on the corner of Eleventh Avenue, I could see the Lerouxes already getting into a taxi. No, wait: it was only one of them. Sophie Leroux sat in the cab while Matthew closed its door and quickly jogged east across dark Eleventh Avenue.

'What the...? Splitting up?' Brooklyn said.

Had they made us? I wondered.

'Arturo, you guys stay on the wife in the taxi,' I said into my phone as I hurried east with Brooklyn. 'We'll stay with the husband on foot.'

On the other side of Eleventh Avenue, Brooklyn and I picked up the pace as we watched Leroux moving quickly along West 24th Street's shadows and steel shutters. He was on his phone now, I saw. He definitely seemed purposeful, which was weird since the entire industrial area was completely deserted.

Where was he going now? I wondered as I rushed to keep up. To meet his contact?

He was about halfway to Tenth Avenue when it happened. Leroux put his phone back into his pocket. Then he hooked a sudden left off the sidewalk and dropped completely out of sight.

No! Had he ducked into a building? An alley-way? I wondered in a panic as I started running. What now? What the hell was up with this guy?

179

He had just suddenly disappeared.

Brooklyn and I groaned in unison when we got to the spot where Leroux had left the block.

Because it wasn't a building. It was a parking lot. An empty one that ran the whole block north to 25th Street.

Leroux was gone.

I threw up my hands as I stared at the lonely expanse of asphalt. He must have booked the second he was out of our sight. We'd lost him.

'You gotta be kidding me with this James Bond routine,' Brooklyn said.

We'd broken into a jog and were halfway across the lot toward 25th when the headlights of a vehicle suddenly swung off 25th Street into the driveway of the lot.

It was a truck, a dark new Chevy Suburban SUV with black-tinted windows. It was moving fast – too fast. I reached back and palmed the undercover Glock at the small of my back as the truck roared straight at us.

I could feel my heart pounding hard in my chest as the vehicle came to a quick tire-barking stop a foot in front of us. Then I was moving around the side of the truck with my Glock pulled.

'NYPD! Hands where I can see them!' I yelled as the front passenger window began to zip down.

As the dark glass fell, I held my breath with my finger on the trigger, thinking that in a split second I would see the face of ex-SEAL turned assassin Matthew Leroux, and a lot of lead would start flying.

But I was wrong.

It wasn't Leroux.

Instead, a dark-haired boyish man was sitting there. He was wearing a nice pin-striped suit with a two-tone banker's collar, minus the power tie. Like a Wall Streeter out for fun after work. There was a stupid smile on his face.

'Hey, Mike. How's it going?' he said.

I didn't recognize him. Then I did. It was Mark Evrard, the State Department's expert and adviser on Russia from the restaurant meeting with Secret Service SAC Margaret Foley.

What the...?

'It's fine, Mike,' he said. 'You can put away the gun. Honestly. We're all friends here. I can explain everything.'

Still in shock, I looked in at the driver beside him, a mean-looking, stocky middle-aged guy with thick forearms and hands.

'Mike, who the hell are these jerks?' Brooklyn said, still training her own Glock at the truck.

'I don't know,' I said. 'Who are you jerks?'

'Mike, we didn't mean to spook you like that. I think it's time we should talk,' Evrard said. 'High time, in fact.'

'About what?' I said as I finally holstered my gun.

Instead of answering, Evrard climbed out of the truck and opened the back door.

That's when the real shocker of the night happened. Actually, there were two of them.

My redheaded buddy Paul Ernenwein was sitting in the back of the truck.

And beside him, sitting there calm as a picnic in the park, was none other than Matthew Leroux.

'You got me, Officer. I give up. Don't shoot,' the blond ex–Navy SEAL said, smiling as he held up his empty hands.

CHAPTER 56

'Hey, my apologies again, Mike,' Mark Evrard said. 'I know we caught you off guard.'

We were heading downtown now, through the meatpacking district, the tires of the Suburban changing pitch as we crossed at the cobbled intersections.

Doyle and Arturo had picked up Brooklyn, and it was just Paul and me riding along with Leroux and Evrard and the driver. I didn't know what was going to happen next. But I was dying to find out.

'Like I was saying to Paul, it seems like we've gotten our lines crossed here, Mike,' Evrard said smoothly, turning from his front passenger seat.

I stared at him. There was something smug about him that I couldn't put my finger on that really drove me nuts. The strong cologne he wore reminded me of the big-bucks crowd back at the gallery.

'That's why I wanted to finally meet up,' the slick bastard said, nodding at me. 'To bring some clarity. Lay out what we're doing before we trip each other up. First of all, know that everything I'm going to reveal is top secret, okay? It stays in this truck.'

'Is this guy for real, Paul?' I said to Ernenwein,

182

sitting beside me.

'I was at dinner when my boss called and told me to meet up with him,' Ernenwein said with a shrug. 'He checks out, Mike. Believe it or not.'

'Top secret?' I said, still mighty pissed at Evrard, or whoever the hell he was, and his stupid spy versus spy head games. 'So, I guess this means you're not in State Department protective security, huh? Let me take a wild guess. You're CIA?'

'Technically, I'm a retired CIA officer turned rehired contractor currently working out of the CIA's Counterterrorism Center,' Evrard said, smoothing his lapel. 'But it's all semantics these days, Mike. For example, last year I worked for the Office of the Director of National Intelligence in conjunction with the Department of Defense's National Reconnaissance Office, doing the same exact stuff. It doesn't matter whose budget my paycheck comes out of. We're all the good guys here. We're all on the same team.'

'And you?' I said over at Leroux, on the other side of Paul. 'You CIA, too? I mean when you're not selling Picassos or murdering Hamilton Heights drug dealers.'

Leroux winked at me with a cold blue eye. There was an unsettling palpable stillness to him as he sat there, the tension of something fast unnaturally at rest.

'What can I say, Mike?' he said with a slight Western cowboy twang in his voice. 'Murderers like me? We gotta stay busy.'

'Enough, Matt,' Evrard said as he took a folder out from somewhere up front and handed it to me. 'You're mistaken, Detective,' he continued.

183

'That wasn't murder up in Hamilton Heights. Rafael Arruda's termination was an action authorized at the highest level.'

Inside the folder was a document printed on thick stationery with an embossed presidential insignia at the top.

There was some legalese gobbledygook after the heading, but at the bottom I read:

Mr. Rafael Arruda poses a current and ongoing threat to the United States and therefore meets the legal criteria for lethal action pursuant to the Presidential Finding.

It ended with the previous president's signature in bright-blue ink.

'The president is whacking out ecstasy dealers without a trial now? On American soil, no less?' I said as Evrard took the folder back. 'Does CNN know about this?'

'Ecstasy wasn't the only thing Arruda had his hands in,' Matthew Leroux said calmly as he looked out the window. 'For the last few months, after a hard day's teach at Columbia, that slime spent his nights online lending his chemical expertise to an offshoot of ISIS in their quest to develop sarin gas. The members of his drug crew were actually trained by Islamic militants overseas.'

'Bullshit,' I said. 'Just bullshit. Arruda was a jihadist?!'

'No,' said Evrard. 'Just a worthless scumbag who didn't give a shit who paid him a lot of money for his weapon-of-mass-destruction recipes.'

'Okay, fine,' I said as we rolled. 'Let's say I

believe you. You're CIA. And Arruda was an enemy combatant in the global war on terror. How does that explain you guys surveilling the president's UN route in midtown? Is the prez staying up late Skyping with the bad guys as well? Does he, too, now somehow meet the legal criteria for lethal action pursuant to the "Presidential Finding"? Is it time to pull his plug, too?'

Leroux laughed at that. Hard. I'd really tickled his cowboy funny bone, apparently.

'No,' Evrard said. 'Matthew was doing what's known as countersniping surveillance. If the shooter is after the president, we need to see where he would set up in order to find him.'

'Exactly,' Leroux said. 'I'm not out to snuff Buckland. My wife and I were actually doing what you're doing: looking for the guy who actually is. We know him. Or at least of him.'

'What?' I said, completely stunned. 'What the hell are you talking about? You know the shooter?'

'We think so, Mike. We think it's this man,' Evrard said as he reached out and gave me another folder.

CHAPTER 57

I flipped open the folder and looked at the photograph inside.

It wasn't a very good one. A blurry black-and-white blown-up still of a dark-haired white guy on a sidewalk, taken from a not-very-good surveillance video. It could have been anyone, I thought. It could have been a picture of me.

'So you think this is the shooter I saw at the MetLife Building?' I said.

Evrard nodded.

'We don't know his name,' he said. 'We just call him the Brit because about all we know about him is a snatch of his northern England accent in a brief phone conversation we recorded in oh nine. We assume he's ex-British Special Air Service, but who knows? Their Royal Marines are pretty damn good killers as well.

'We also know that he's one of the most sought-after work-for-hire assassins in the world. The troubling thing is, like Arruda, he doesn't care in the slightest who he works for as long as the price is right. He's killed for the Japanese yakuza, the North Koreans, the Taliban, ISIS.'

'And he's not just any old gun for hire, either,' said Leroux. 'He's an amazing shot. He took down three of our guys from a high ridge outside of a firebase in Kamdesh in oh seven. I ranged it myself after we came in to get the bodies. He scored three kills at twenty-five hundred yards. That's one point four miles. One kill you could chalk up to luck, but three head shot hits at that distance when you account for the wind and the Coriolis effect is just insanity. Gandalf the wizard stuff. You wouldn't think it was possible.'

'Who hired the wizard? Was it the Russians? Do you know? Is Grekov actually behind this?'

'We're as in the dark about that as you are,' said Evrard. 'It's either Grekov or somebody who hates Grekov and wants to make it look like Grekov, perhaps one of the Russian oligarchs. It's definitely somebody out of Russia. That's where the tip came from, right, Paul? You guys got a guy at the embassy, right?'

'Why haven't you guys let us local law enforcement know about your information on the Brit until now?' Paul Ernenwein said.

'It wouldn't have helped,' Evrard said. 'He uses disguises and aliases. This guy is an apex predator. You're not going to catch him with an APB.'

'So what?' I yelled. 'He's out to kill the fricking president. To heck with the FBI and NYPD. This photo should be on the news!'

'Also, how do you know it's this Brit guy?' Paul wanted to know.

'We have access to more databases than you,' Evrard said. 'Our analysts plugged in the numbers. Eighty percent it's him. There are very few people in the world with that expertise. It's a process of elimination.'

I watched Evrard and Leroux exchange a quick look.

'No, wait. I get it,' I said. 'You're not out to protect the president. You're just hunting this guy. He's on your hit list as well, isn't he? Like Arruda. You didn't tell us because you don't want him arrested, do you? Like Arruda, you want him dead.'

'Well, now that you mention it,' Evrard said after a beat. 'He is on the Presidential Finding list as well.'

'Didn't you hear what I just said?' Leroux said over to me. 'He killed three of our guys. Three Navy SEALs in Afghanistan. Not only that, but he trained a bunch of those savages to kill who knows how many more Americans. He's a real scumbag, Mike. He needs to be removed from the battlefield yesterday.'

'Battlefield,' I said with a laugh of my own. I noticed that it had started to snow again as I tapped at the window. 'That's not a battlefield out there, Matt,' I said. 'That's just West Broadway.'

'Mike, grow up, huh?' Leroux replied. 'Wise up. The war is everywhere now. The enemy, too. There are no more neat little definitions and borders.'

'I get it,' Paul finally piped up, staring at Evrard. 'You're bringing us into it now because we were investigating Mattie over here. We were getting too close to blowing your little hunting party.'

'Guys, come on,' Evrard said. 'What difference does it make if our interests are the same or just run parallel? We're on the same team. We thought we could take care of the Brit by now, but he's been more elusive than we had hoped. We need your help, or should I say, we need to team up officially to nail him.'

'Dead or alive, huh?' I said. 'Only without the poster? Or the chance of a reward. Maybe we can string him up from a traffic light in Times Square. Any word on stringing people up in the Pre-sidential Finding?'

'Hell, Detective,' said Leroux with another laugh and wink. 'We don't need him dead necessarily. We're so desperate, even a couple of bloodthirsty murderers like us might let you bring him in alive, just this once.'

CHAPTER 58

It was five minutes to one in the afternoon on Tuesday when the British assassin double-parked the Home Depot rental truck in front of an ugly white brick high-rise on Second Avenue near the southwest corner of East 67th.

He could hear kids hollering and carrying on in the yard of the public school across the street as he slid the heavy rectilinear box out over the tailgate and slipped it onto a hand truck.

'Doing a little painting, are we, sir?' one of the high-rise's maintenance men asked in the basement as the British assassin rolled past with the box, toward the freight elevator.

'Work, work, work,' the Brit said with a smile.

He took the elevator to nineteen and rolled the box to the end of the hallway and took out his key. He had rented the two-bedroom on a popular apartment share website a month before, when he was in the planning stage. As he rolled the box inside, he chuckled to himself as he remembered the website's new age mission statement: *Trust. It's what makes the world go round.*

After he cut open the box, it took twenty minutes to assemble the steel painting scaffold in the apartment's living room. It had caster wheels for easy moving, and its plywood deck could be adjusted up to six feet. He moved the couch into the corner and then rolled the high portable platform into position across from the west-facing window.

After he locked the scaffold's wheels in place, he went into the bedroom. A moment later, he returned with a comforter and laid it on the plywood platform and climbed up and lay prone.

He smiled as he faced the curtained window with an imaginary rifle in front of him. The apartment was warm. Clean. Comfortable. In other words, about as far from his usual blind setups as you could possibly get.

As he lay there, he recalled a particularly nasty blind he'd been in in Syria six months prior. In a downtown section of a small city he'd already forgotten the name of, he had lain in the deep interior recesses of a shattered shopping mall. For three days, in the stench of an open sewer, from a hole in the structure's wall, he watched the sepia desert light on the mall's ruined plaza as the government forces drove their dirt-caked, chirping, clanking Russian T-80 tanks around, playing cat and mouse with the jihadi rebels who had hired him.

On the third morning, as one of the tank's 125mm rounds punched yet another hole in the already chewed-up building's northern end, he finally laid eyes on his target with his hunting scope. The Russian tank adviser's name was Alexandrov, and through the blackened, jagged stumps of some palm trees beyond the plaza, he could see him sitting in a white Ford pickup truck, coordinating maneuvers from just under two thousand yards away.

Even through the 10x Unertl scope of the KSVK Russian anti-matériel rifle, his target was not very big. No matter. He calculated calmly, made his clicks on the scope for distance and wind. Then he resighted the reticle and calmly let loose with a massive 12.7mm round.

He would have missed by a hair if Alexandrov hadn't leaned forward at the exact right moment. Had he been about to open the truck's glove compartment? the British assassin wondered, not for the first time. Was he moving to answer his phone on the dash? To tie his shoe?

The British assassin tsked. He would never know, and for a man of precision such as himself, to never know stung.

Oh well. Enough strolling down memory lane. Back to work, he thought as he pushed himself up off the platform and climbed down the scaffold.

He walked to the window, where his hunting scope was already set up on its tripod, and parted the curtains.

There was a blur in the eyepiece as he tilted and panned and zoomed the scope over the city buildings and cell sites and water towers. When he was done, a sidewalk-level doorway was directly centered in the viewfinder.

The door was a much-scuffed black steel one outlined by blocks of pale dressed granite, set in a building wall of dull red brick. Lacking a handle or knob, it looked like the back egress door one might see at a theater.

The British assassin smiled again as his mind made the obvious associations.

Presidents and theaters and assassins, oh my! he thought.

191

CHAPTER 59

At five minutes after four o'clock, Mary Catherine put on the water for the ziti and then took out the mix for the cupcakes that Bridget and Fiona needed for their class trip bake sale fund-raiser. A Blake Shelton song came on the country-western station as she was getting out the eggs, and she turned it up and began humming along as she stood at the island cracking the eggs into a mixing bowl.

From the dining room, Eddie Bennett watched all this in his peripheral vision as he pretended to do his homework.

'How is it going in there, Eddie?' Mary Catherine called out as she chucked the eggshells into the can behind her without looking.

'Never better,' Eddie lied.

Eddie had been relegated to the dining room table, under Mary Catherine's watchful eye, until further notice because he'd come home with another C in math.

Quite unfairly, in his opinion. To his thinking, a C was actually more than acceptable because, as everyone knew, math was idiotic and pointless. What the heck was algebra for, anyway? Would he one day find himself pinned in a car wreck, struggling for his life, and at the last second save himself by remembering that $x = 7 + y$ (5r)? The answer to that one was no. Numbers and equations were inherently evil, as was his cruel and unusual imprisonment here at the table of pain.

No doubt about it, instead of doing extra math problems, what he really needed at this juncture was the iPad that Mary Catherine had hidden on him. Or, more specifically, he needed what was on the tablet. The utterly amazing and cool Zombie Highway Squish, his new favorite video game.

That's why when the whir of Mary Catherine's mixer started up a minute later, he made his move. Tiptoeing into the living room as stealthily as the ninja he one day hoped to become, he quickly searched all of Mary Catherine's favorite hiding spots for banned items. On top of the bookshelf, under the couch, behind Dad's chair.

'What are you up to now, you little sneak?' Brian said around the yellow highlighter jutting from his mouth as he sat on the couch, squinting at some paperback Shakespeare. 'Aren't you supposed to be doing your homework?'

'Looking for my, eh, workbook,' Eddie said innocently.

Now where would she hide it? Eddie thought. He snapped his fingers. Precisely. The last place it was allowed to be. In the boys' room!

He hurried into their darkened room and had just peeked in the closet when he saw the sheets hanging loose at the side of Marvin's bunk.

Eddie went over immediately and lifted the mattress.

And just stood there staring.

And staring.

At the gun sitting there on the box spring.

It was a subcompact. A small, semiauto black

193

metal pistol with a light-green crosshatched synthetic rubber side panel on the grip.

Eddie, who may have played very realistic first-person-shooter video games at a friend's house, didn't have to read the P-32 KEL-TEC stamped into the scuffed black steel of the pistol's barrel to know that it was real. He even knew at a glance that it was loaded – by the little metal comma of the magazine sticking out at the bottom of the grip.

What he didn't know was what it was doing there. Nor did he care. His young brain was too mesmerized by the sight of the sleek L-shaped hunk of dark metal that lay there, practically glowing with coolness.

He suddenly longed to feel it in his hand. Just once. Just for a second.

'What the hell are you doing?' Brian said, suddenly at his back.

Eddie, spasming as if he'd been Tasered, dropped the mattress.

'I'm sorry! I'm sorry! I was looking for the iPad. I swear!' he said, backing up with his hands raised.

Brian went to the bed and lifted the mattress and then removed the gun, mindful of the trigger. He stared at it with a furious look on his face.

'I can't believe this. He'd bring this here? Here! Into our room?' Brian said in outrage. He quickly left the room with the gun.

'Hey, where are you going, Brian? Dinner won't be long,' Eddie heard Mary Catherine call from the kitchen.

'To the library. Be back quick. Promise,' Brian said.

'Oh, no,' Eddie whispered to himself as he heard the apartment door slam shut with a loud bang.

'What did I do now?'

CHAPTER 60

'Hello. Do you sell Barretts?' I said into the phone.

'The .50-caliber sniper rifle?' asked the dealer at Harry's Guns for the Good Guys, of Dublin, Pennsylvania, the seventeenth gun dealer I had spoken to in the last hour.

'Yes,' I said.

'Is this a joke?' he said.

'No,' I said.

'You are aware that the rifle you're talking about costs in excess of ten thousand dollars?' he said. 'I also believe the going rate of each round is four or five bucks.'

'Yes, I heard it's expensive. Do you have one?'

'Money's no object, huh? Lucky you,' the guy on the phone said. 'Well, no, I don't have the gun in stock per se. But what we can do is have you order it online and then purchase it through me. See, they won't just ship it to your house unless you have a federal firearms dealer's license. You have to have it shipped to my store so we can do the background paperwork and whatnot. Provided you don't live in New York, New Jersey, or Connecticut, which all have a ban on large-caliber sniper rifles.'

195

Too bad no one told the guy who had almost blown away President Buckland from the Met-Life Building, I thought.

'Wow, that's interesting,' I said to the dealer. Then I asked him what I really wanted to know. 'Have you actually bought any Barretts for any-one recently?'

'Don't I wish,' he said with a sigh. 'Dealers get a tidy cut of the Barrett's price for their trouble.'

A moment later, I racked the phone after another dead end and rubbed my eyes and stared up into the dusty ceiling of our task force's new work space at the FBI's midtown building at 56th Street. The first office had been drab, but this one was even more so: a small windowless cell in one of the subbasements. It had a striking resemblance to a boiler room.

Was it because we were working with the CIA now that we had to be in some secure bombproof location? I kept wondering. Would we be issued shoe phones?

This new tack in our search for the shooter – talking to gun dealers – had come from our suspect turned partner CIA soldier, Matthew Leroux. He said if *he* was in town to take some-body out, he'd buy all his hardware locally, if possible. It wouldn't be that difficult, he said, if you had the proper fake ID.

That was just the thing with the task before us. We had to find a guy whose name we didn't know. A guy who was most likely moving around a lot, paying in cash, and using fake IDs.

And find him discreetly, too. We were told by the Secret Service that in no way could we use the media in our manhunt. It would make Buck-land look weak. As if dead looked strong.

No bones about it, even with the spy agency's help, the case was still in bang-your-head-against-the-wall mode. We'd reinterviewed all the MetLife Building people. Did another forensic sweep through the blind and the MetLife Building's roof. I'd even put out feelers to every former cop and detective I knew in Jersey and upstate New York and Long Island for anything, any oddball incidents that might give us a lead, especially incidents involving people with British accents.

After another minute of brooding, I sat back up straight and picked up my clipboard and dialed the number for the next gun dealer, a store called Benny's Gun Coliseum, located in an upstate town with the unlikely name of Butternuts, New York.

'Yeah, hi. Do you sell Barretts?' I said.

CHAPTER 61

'Look, everyone It's five o'clock, also known as vitamin C time,' said Paul Ernenwein as he came over with two red Solo cups of water and those little orange-flavored packets.

I don't know if it was due to his FBI training, but Paul, I had learned, was very particular in his workday habits. Coffee precisely at nine and then eleven. Lunch at one. Another coffee at three. Vitamin C packet time at five. In a red Solo cup.

We had been spending a lot of time together.

'Paul, tell me. How does the CIA even know it's the Brit?' I said, flicking at the terribly vague photo stuck to the whiteboard beside our desks. 'And don't say you can tell me but then you'd have to kill me, because at this point, I'd say okay, just to figure out anything at all about what's going on with all this puzzle palace stuff.'

'I don't know, Mike,' Paul said. 'We just have to trust them, remember?'

'Trust them. Sure,' I said. 'But they're leaving something out.'

'A lot of somethings, more likely,' said Paul as he ripped open and then poured out his packet into his cup. 'But think about it. These spooks have been asked to do some real questionable stuff since nine eleven. Stuff that might make a new administration go "Egads! 'What's this?" and start looking for goats to scape.'

'So they're covering their ass?' I said.

Paul nodded as he lifted his Solo cup. 'They pretty much have to,' he said as my personal phone rang.

'Hey, Mike. Sorry to bother you,' Mary Catherine said.

'No bother, Mary Catherine. What is it?'

'It's Brian, Mike. He said he was heading to the library, but he didn't come back. I texted him and tried to Find My Friends him, but his phone is off or something.'

'Do any of the kids know where he is?'

'Eddie seems to know something. He seems nervous. I'll keep working on him. Do you think you could swing by? I'm actually getting a little nervous myself. Also, Marvin hasn't come home yet, either.'

'Same old story, huh?' I said, shaking my head.

More mysteries, I thought. When it rained, it poured.

'On my way,' I said.

CHAPTER 62

A cold wind blew in Brian Bennett's face as he sat on a stone wall in the now dark Riverside Park, near the Soldiers and Sailors Monument.

He was facing west, and down through the leafless trees, he watched the streaming red lights on the West Side Highway. There were some blinking red lights out on the black plain of the Hudson itself, he noticed. Some big ship, a tanker or something, looming out there on all that water, just chilling.

Chilling was the word, he thought, tightening the drawstrings on his hoodie before thrusting his hands back into his coat pockets. He checked his phone again. Nothing. What was up with this joker? he thought. He had said to be there in twenty a whole hour ago.

Brian sighed as he noticed he had 7 percent battery left. 'Just great,' he mumbled as he glanced over his shoulder, up the empty stairs toward the monument.

After finding the gun, he'd walked around in a panic, trying for the life of him to figure out what to do. He wanted to tell his dad, of course, but what would happen then? Would Dad have to arrest Marvin?

All the while thinking that any second, a cop would notice the suspicious look on his face and ask to search his backpack. Then, as he was about to head into the Starbucks on Broadway to warm up, it dawned on him.

How to end this whole crazy thing once and for all.

'Hey,' said a voice from behind him.

Brian turned up to the dark figure standing at the top of the monument stairs. Then he swallowed as Big Flicka, Marvin's crazy drug-dealing tormentor, started slowly walking down.

A week ago, Brian had secretly gotten the dealer's number from Marvin's phone to give to his dad in case Marvin didn't make it home. An hour before, he had called Big Flicka and told him that he had found Marvin's gun in the room just before his parents were about to rearrange the furniture. He said that he was panicked and didn't know what to do with it, said that he had called Marvin and couldn't get in contact with him, and could Flicka come get it?

And here he was, Brian thought as the huge drug dealer halted in front of him, practically as big as the monument above.

Be careful what you wish for.

CHAPTER 63

'So you got it? Flicka said, scanning the park.

'Yep. Here it is,' Brian said quickly, reaching into his bag.

'Easy now. You watch that shit,' Flicka said, tilting his head as he reached into his own pocket.

'It's okay. I unloaded it,' he said as he handed over the racked semiauto and its magazine.

'Tell me why you giving this to me again,' Flicka said, immediately tucking the items into the pockets of his enormous goose down jacket

'My nanny was about to clean the room. I didn't know what to do, so I thought I could give it to you since you and Marvin work together or whatever.'

Flicka eyed him, his glance icier than the wind off the Hudson.

'Marvin tell you that?' he said. 'We workin' together?'

'No, I just figured.'

'How you got my number, then?'

Oh, shit, Brian thought. He hadn't anticipated that question. What should he say?

'I found it in one of Marvin's notebooks,' he finally pulled out of thin air.

'You a real nanny boy, huh? Couldn't just leave it in your book bag? You think it gonna bite you? Gonna explode? Guns don't kill people, boy. How stupid can you be?'

201

'I didn't know what to do, man. I thought this would help you out. I'm sorry to bother you. I was just trying to help. Honestly.'

'Yeah, you better be sorry. And Marvin's gonna be real sorry, I guarantee you, after I get through teaching him about how to properly stash my precious belongings.'

Big Flicka suddenly leaned in close to where Brian sat on the wall. Brian held his breath. He was one big, big dude.

'Now, you listen up because I'm only gonna tell you once, you nosy little nanny boy,' Flicka said in his ear. 'Don't you be concernin' yourself anymore about me and Marvin. Do I need to illustrate how bad that would turn out for you, for your family?'

'No. I got it. Honestly,' Brian said. 'Please. I'm sorry.'

Flicka tsked as he slowly backed of. Then he laughed and smiled. Like intimidating people was the funniest joke in the world. He actually had a really nice smile. He could sell things on TV.

'I believe you are,' he finally said, and Brian let out his breath as Flicka headed for the stairs.

Brian watched as Flicka made it to the top of the stairs, and he immediately got up off the wall and started booking north along one of the park paths.

Just as he saw the kiosk around the bend in the path up ahead, he looked at his phone to see that Marvin was calling him.

'What the hell are you doing, Brian?' Marvin said. 'Is it true you met with Flicka? What the hell?'

'I'm ending this, dude,' Brian said as he ran.

'What do you mean?'

'You can't do it, so I am. That's what friends are for, right? I'll call you back.'

Brian dropped his cell into his pocket as he arrived at the battered pay phone. He lifted the receiver and heard a dial tone. It had to be one of the last working pay phones in all of Manhattan. Maybe the world.

He quickly dialed.

'Nine one one. What's your emergency?' asked a female operator.

'I just saw a guy with a gun in his hand in Riverside Park. A tall black guy in a black goose down jacket. He's getting into a Mercedes on Riverside Drive. Plate number 347-WRT. He's near the Soldiers and Sailors Monument. Hurry.'

'Do you want to leave your name?' the operator wanted to know.

Brian thought about the dealer again, the sheer horrendous size of him.

'Not in any way, shape, or frickin' form, ma'am,' Brian Bennett said before he hung up the phone with a sharp clang and continued running.

CHAPTER 64

At seven that night, I was in the company Impala with Seamus, scanning the empty, dark streets around my building, looking for Brian.

I was starting to get nervous. Actually, if you wanted to get truly technical, I was on the brink of a massive panic attack.

The tires squealed as we came off 89th onto Amsterdam Avenue with some speed. We zipped past a Thai restaurant, a pizza parlor, a dive bar.

'Wait – maybe he went into that bar back there, Seamus,' I said. 'Do you think we should stop?'

'No, I don't,' Seamus said calmly. 'He's sixteen. He's just walking around. It's going to be fine. We'll find him, Michael. Soon.'

'Why do kids do this, Father?' I said. 'Drive their parents so sick with worry?'

'I remember when you were young,' Seamus said. 'Your parents beamed as you shined your shoes and whistled as you made your way back and forth from choir to altar boy practice. You never worried anyone to death with all your wild hooligan carryings-on.'

'It was a different time back then,' I said in my defense. 'Everything wasn't so nuts.'

'Right you are,' Seamus said. 'In the seventies and eighties, this city was a moral paradise. If you recall, Michael, it's only natural for a boy to gravitate toward shenanigans. Why, it was only yesterday your father and I were out looking for you! When ya went to – what was it called? – Laser something in Central Park, and blind my eyes if we weren't in his squad car then as well!'

'Laser Zeppelin,' I said, laughing. 'At the Hayden Planetarium. Give me a break, Seamus. That was … educational!'

I remembered it vaguely. It was a laser light show across the dome of a huge dark room where the immortal Zep was blasted at an unbelievable volume. Teens would tailgate, sipping tequila and beer in the park outside every Friday night, and my friends and I would go join the festivities, trying to get girls' phone numbers. As I strolled down memory lane, I suddenly remembered my own father, murder in his eyes, by a park bench when I came back from upchucking in the bushes.

'Not fair, Seamus,' I said as I continued cruising down Amsterdam, my head on a swivel. 'How dare you bring up, at a time like this, the fact that I, too, was sixteen once.'

We did another circuit around the apartment and onto Riverside Drive, and I spotted blue and red spinning lights somewhere in the high eighties. As I zoomed up, I could see that cops had cuffed a big figure in a goose down jacket and were putting him up over the hood of a Mercedes. Thank God it wasn't Brian, I thought, driving past.

Then, a minute later, there he was. On the corner of 96th, waiting to cross at the light.

'Hey, Dad. Hey, Seamus,' he said casually as I screeched up in front of him.

'Get your butt in this car now!'

I twisted around toward the back as he sat, and I looked deep into his eyes.

'One chance. What are you on?' I said.

He gaped at me.

'Nothing, Dad, I swear. I went out for a walk. My phone died. I must have lost track of time. Jeez.'

'Better your phone than you, you idiot,' I said. 'You're up to something. Your brother is sick with whatever it is. What the hell is going on in my house? I want answers.'

'It was nothing. I went to the library, and I met

my friend. We just started walking and talking.'

'Which friend?'

'Rob from the football team. He came down to the city from Westchester, and we were just chilling. He just hopped in a cab the second you showed up.'

I squinted at him.

'Brian, people lie to me all day. I need to get it at home, too?'

'I swear, Dad. Please. Call him if you don't believe me.'

'And listen to what? What you told him to say? No, thanks.'

'Leave it for now,' Seamus whispered, leaning over toward me. 'Remember the lasers, Michael.'

I rolled my eyes as I ripped the tranny into drive and hit the gas.

Seamus was right. And not for the first time.

CHAPTER 65

President Buckland heard the trill of the Sikorsky VH-60N White Hawk's rotor lower in pitch as the two Secret Service agents on the midnight shift softly closed the Rose Garden doors behind him.

As he cleaned his shoes on the mat and walked down the warm carpeted corridor, he thought about the Secret Service and the two young full-dress marines who had just popped the double doors of Marine One for him. Thought about all the Americans out there in the cold and dark, around the world, manning their posts.

In the beginning, it had been difficult to accept all the fuss and ceremony of the job, but then he realized it wasn't about him. The fact that spit-shined marines would greet him with a salute at three o'clock in the cold morning was just a small symbol of the extraordinary lengths they would go to to protect their country. The dedication and full commitment of America's first responders never failed to humble and inspire him.

He made a right at the end of the corridor and found the basement stairs. His chief of staff had texted during his late meeting at Langley that Buckland's presence was requested in the White House kitchen.

Which could mean only one thing.

Some trick his wife was pulling, of course. Forty-three years of age, and she still loved tricks and pranks. Even here in the White House. Upstairs in their personal quarters, she would hide on him from time to time, like an overgrown three-year-old.

As he approached the kitchen, he looked around for Danny, the workaholic head chef. Even at 3:00 a.m., he probably wasn't too far away, waiting for the president and his wife's little 'moment' to be over so he could have his kitchen back.

The kitchen was dark but for one pendant light shining down on his wife, who was sitting at one of the stainless steel prep counters, smiling and beautiful in her robe and slippers.

He watched as she quickly slipped her rosary beads back into her pocket. She had always been a woman of faith, but ever since he'd gotten the big job, she'd become even more so. He prayed from time to time, but it was a constant with her.

He sat beside her and kicked off his shoes.

'And what the heck is this, now?' Buckland said to his wife. 'It's the middle of the night.'

'Don't tell me you forgot,' she said.

'Forgot what?'

'Our anniversary.'

'That's in June!' Buckland said, throwing up his hands.

'Not that one,' she said. 'The other one, silly.' She pushed over the covered silver tray beside her.

He took off the cover and his mouth fell open as he saw the two Klondike bars on the tray.

'Oh. *That* one,' he said, laughing.

He remembered it like it was yesterday. He had prepared a special dinner for the two of them – loin lamb chops and garlic mashed potatoes – on a plastic table on the balcony of his crummy first apartment, near his first post in Tucson. The balcony overlooked the parking lot of a Goodwill store, but it had looked like the Champs-Elysées seen from the window of the nicest hotel in Paris when she sat down across from him, done up in the little black dress she'd worn for the occasion.

Dessert, which they had only gotten around to the morning after, had been two Klondike bars melted to mush on the kitchen counter.

Buckland smiled. How long ago had that been? He suddenly thought about all of it, the summers and Christmases and dozens of birthdays, first together and then with their kids. All that fun and joy. The fullness of the life they had had because they had somehow found each other.

People talked about his heroic accomplishments, but no one knew that every one of them had been because of her. She was the one who had fulfilled his potential. He had simply been lucky enough to have found someone to be a hero for.

'I was going to use this as a way to beg you not to go to New York,' his wife said, 'but that would be useless. In fact, selfish. Our country needs you to go. The world does. Grekov is a wolf. It's time he learns what a sheepdog is all about. Somebody has to do it, and it's you.'

She took his hand and led him through the darkened kitchen toward the elevator.

'But wait. What about the Klondike bars?' he said.

'Tomorrow morning, Mr. President. We have to do this right, remember?'

CHAPTER 66

The bright white rectangle of the TV screen lit up in the darkness and then the video was rolling.

The footage opened up on the long gray carpet of a downward-sloping New York City cross street near the United Nations in the Turtle Bay neighborhood, east of Madison Avenue. The Midtown South side street was unnaturally clear of traffic and parked cars, and there were steel pedestrian barriers, as one would see at a parade, completely lining the curbs in both directions.

By the gold tinge to the light and the short

sleeves and summer dresses of the handful of pedestrians behind the barriers, it appeared to be a summer evening. At the top of Madison Avenue in the distance, through the suffused light, appeared the silhouette of a uniformed cop with his arms folded, his back to the street.

Then the vehicles came over the rise.

A blue-and-white marked NYPD cop car came first, its flashing and blinking lights barely perceptible in the twilight. It moved by quickly – forty-five, maybe fifty miles an hour. It was followed by an equally rapidly moving black Chevy Suburban, then a blue-and-white marked NYPD SUV, and then an NYPD tow truck. Behind the tow truck came another black speeding Suburban SUV, and then another, and then another.

'How many bloody cars are there again?' the British assassin's wife said as they watched in the dark of the old office.

'Altogether, fifty-four,' the assassin said. 'Shh. Watch.'

There was a break in the motorcade for nearly a minute and then a rumble began. Seconds later, in a phalanx of blinking red and blue, there were NYPD motorcycle cops, half a dozen in a loose V, followed by more and more cop cars and vans and SUVs.

Finally, a full four minutes into the video, down the slope came what everyone was waiting for. Pedestrians at the curb began lofting phones and waving plastic American flags as what was referred to as the Beast – the first of two massive presidential Cadillac limousines – barreled over the rise.

The assassin hit the Pause button on the remote.

'Right there. You see?' the assassin said, pointing behind the barrier, to the right of the limo. 'It happens right there.'

'Oh ... I see. That's brilliant! You've outdone yourself. I can picture it now. Out of nowhere like that. When it happens, it's just gonna be...'

'Bedlam,' the assassin agreed.

He got off the couch and went to the small washroom and clicked on the light and began scrubbing out the oil beneath his fingernails with Lava soap and a brush.

They were at the rented workshop in Brooklyn, and they'd just finished all the final adjustments on the dump truck. Everything was ready. Everything was in place. Disguises. Equipment. Distances. Now vehicles. Done, done, done, and done.

'And the route is confirmed?' his wife said at his back.

'Our contact is in the Secret Service, love,' he said, glancing at his fingernails and switching the brush to his other hand. 'They know before the president himself does.'

'It can't be stopped, then. It's done. We've done it.'

The British assassin rinsed his hands and smiled at his reflection, then came back into the room. He finished the Gatorade he'd been drinking and bank-shot the bottle into the wastebasket along the old office's brick wall.

'The toy soldier has been wound, doll. Now it's just a matter of pushing the button.'

In the glow of the paused screen image, the assassin's wife pulled off her shirt. She wasn't

211

wearing a bra. She lay back on the couch, staring at him with her feline-gray eyes.

As he watched her slip out of her jeans, the British assassin imagined the new Italian Racing Red Jag XFR-S he was going to buy when the final payment came. The rumble of its five-hundred-plus horsepower under his palm. The way it would drift on the hairpins above the Mediterranean.

'Then what are you waiting for?' his wife said in the glow. 'Push away.'

CHAPTER 67

It was Saturday, and down on the field, a bunch of thin dudes in baby-blue uniforms milled around another crew of skinny guys wearing all-white uniforms.

The crowd around me suddenly roared as a light-blue guy with girlie hair booted the ball with a loud champagne-cork-popping sound. The spinning ball made a surprisingly sharp curve through the air as it streaked for the top right corner of the goal. Then the crowd groaned as the ball banged off the goal's top bar and spun out-of-bounds.

As I watched the slo-mo replay of the corner kick up on the massive Jumbotron above Yankee Stadium's center-field wall, I couldn't decide which was more surprising: that I was actually at a professional soccer game or that the soccer game was sacrilegiously occurring down on the hallowed outfield grass of my beloved Bronx Bombers.

'Gee, get out of here. There wasn't a goal made?' I said sarcastically to Arturo, beside me.

We were standing in the cold of the open terrace-level seating, just below the stadium's upper deck on the third base side. Around us, a crowd of about thirty thousand surrounded the improvised soccer field, set up foul pole to foul pole in the baseball stadium's outfield.

'Tell me, is there ever a goal in soccer?' I said. 'Or is zip-zip the point? Is it, like, a Zen thing?'

'Soccer no longer exists, Mike,' Arturo said as he lifted his binoculars. 'It's called football now, and it's the world's sport, so get into it.'

'Oh, I do, Arturo,' I said, lifting my own binocs. 'But only when it's played properly, on Sundays by men with upper body strength who wear helmets.'

I was on my way home from another fruitless day of not finding the assassin the night before when Arturo had called me. Arturo, a soccer fan, had heard on the radio about the Saturday exhibition match between the new New York City Football Club and a team from England called Leeds United.

Leeds United, as it turned out, was a team from *northern* England.

Precisely where our shooter was supposed to be from.

Coming here this afternoon with Arturo to look for him was a long shot, I knew. Under normal circumstances, I'd say there was probably no chance in hell that a public enemy number one on the run would do something as nuts as pop by and cheer on his home team.

But then again, this was no normal crook.

I'd been studying up on these warrior sniper types, and the thing about them was, although they were extremely precise and patient, they truly had no problem with risk. Things like grenades without pins, tightropes with no nets, and jumping out of perfectly good aircraft were for some reason incredibly alluring to them. Risk was how they got their rocks off.

Also a plus point – probably the only one – was that the CIA had actually dug up another, slightly better photo of the Brit, standing in the crowd at some Middle Eastern market. He was wearing aviator sunglasses, but the shape of his nose and ears and jaw were clear. Better than that, the smug frown on his face and the way he held himself, with a kind of shoulders-back, arrogant swagger, were quite distinctive.

I studied the photo for the thousandth time, the features, the demeanor and carriage. Then I lifted my binoculars and went back to scanning the crowd. If he was here, we could find him.

Maybe.

I panned over the sea of baby blue. Though the mostly male crowd jumped up and down a lot and did weird chants as they drank beer, they struck me as, rather than violent Euro hooligans, clean-cut fellows who had probably played soccer in high school and college. Good-natured enough. Well, except for the idiots who insisted on constantly blowing those stupid head-splitting vuvuzela horns that sounded like bees buzzing.

After another minute of not finding the needle in the haystack, an air horn went off near us at an eardrum-perforating volume as another baby-blue guy failed to kick the ball into the goal.

'Take me out to a *real* ball game,' I sang under my breath as I put my Nikon binocs back up on my eyes.

I saw it a nanosecond later. I aimed the glasses down on the main level almost directly by first base and kept them there.

'No,' I said, spinning the target into focus. 'No.'

'What is it, Mike?'

'C'mon,' I said as I jogged up the stairs for the concourse. 'Hurry up!'

CHAPTER 68

The British assassin smiled at the curvy brunette waitress with big black-rimmed eyes as she stopped before him with a tray filled with bottles of Budweiser and champagne in flutes.

He was going to grab a few lagers, but then his wife elbowed him, and he thought again. A second later, another chesty serving wench brought caviar and hot dogs. This one was a no-brainer. He liberally sprinkled beluga onto two franks.

'Welcome to America,' he said to his wife after a surprisingly tasty bite.

They were in luxury suite 321 on Yankee Stadium's private level, and it actually fit its ridiculous billing. It had leather seats and couches, flat screens everywhere, a pine-scented private loo. The suite even had a heated balcony overlooking the field, which was coming in quite handy now, this far into November.

Leeds United's American debut was a true to-do of the old school, so it was filled with posh expat Brits, and even richer real Brits from the other side of the pond, in the Northern Territories.

There were obnoxious Brit big oil crooks and obnoxious Brit big media crooks and obnoxious Brit too-big-to-fail central banking crooks who lent them other people's money. Coming in, they'd almost knocked down a former Brit super-model famous for getting busted snorting heroin on the prime minister's plane. There was even an old rock star from the early eighties drunk off his ass in one corner, slurring into the ear of a bitchy Brit magazine publisher who talked on the news shows from time to time.

It was the wife's idea, of course. An old friend of hers from boarding school had married a Leeds boy who'd stepped in it and was actually a minor owner of Leeds United. So here they were. His wife was all about status, social networking, moving up the ladder. He couldn't care less. Whatever she wanted. He was no dummy. As it turned out, 'Happy wife, happy life' applied even to hired killers.

Besides, he was in a fairly good disguise, having dyed his hair silver gray to go along with his fake goatee. With some artfully placed stage makeup, he easily looked ten years older than his thirty-nine years.

They had done their homework. They could

squeeze in a quick drink or two now that everything was set up. Especially for the one and only Leeds United.

Then the lady of the private suite came by and grabbed his wife, and he stepped out onto the field balcony, from which he saw that Leeds U was inexplicably still tied up with the American hacks. He had to say, the stadium was impressive. The vastness of it, the scope, and yet everything clean and crisp and polished, no expense spared. He looked out at the white scalloped frieze that rimmed the top of the venue, down the bowl of the terraced seating that increased in price the closer you got to the field.

Something Ancient Rome about it. All the different classes in separated seating. Senators and knights in the front row, sweaty plebes and slaves back in the bleachers. Come one and all to cheer the bloody circus.

'We might be scum, but we never run! Leeds, Leeds, Leeds!' said the wife's friend's boorish ass of a hubby, Terry Rich Jerk, as he came out onto the terrace in his smart tailored jacket and posh jeans.

'You know, I haven't been this pumped up since me and the boys sent a manhole cover through a pub window in Millwall,' he said, reeking of Scotch as he clapped the British assassin on the back.

He was referring, as so many others liked to do, to the legendary brawl between Leeds and Millwall fans in 2007. Only problem was that Terry, like so many others, hadn't been there, the assassin knew.

217

As one of the top head breakers in the Leeds service crew – the gang of hooligans who had supported Leeds U since the midnineties – he never missed a game when he wasn't abroad.

There'd been no manhole covers through pub windows that day, but he and a few chums had set a chip van alight when things started getting interesting. Come to think of it, he'd actually broken a K-9 cop's arm with a length of black pipe when her evil bloody dog bit his friend.

The British assassin smiled as he lifted his flute.

'The good ol' days,' he said.

'Sally was saying you were in the Royal Marines, was it?'

The British assassin nodded vaguely.

Terry peered at him with his red face.

'What are you in now? Corporate security?'

'Executive protection, they call it these days,' the assassin said. 'Ya need an armored S-Class? Tell Sally I know a guy.'

The British assassin looked at Terry as he laughed. He was an upper VP at the Bank of England. The Bank of bloody England! Who the fat sot had had to strangle in order to finagle his way into the upper realms of finance – where the real players pulled the strings, loaning to governments and setting the currency rates as they saw fit, out of thin fucking air – was beyond him. And the whole government-approved scam run for everyone in the small exclusive club getting richer and richer 24/7/365, year in, year out, no matter if rain fell from the sky or buckets of burning lava.

'It's shit, New York,' Terry mused as he drunkenly looked out at the crowd. 'Innit? I mean,

London is shit, too, but this is worse. Now they're playing football like it's some kind of progress. Don't they know bloody Liberia has football? It's like they actually want to become a third world craphole. Anyway, where'd you grow up? In Leeds proper?'

'Off the York Road in Seacroft. You?'

'The other side. In Bramley. You're in Brighton now, Sally said?'

'Yep,' he lied.

'Well, you'll have to come by the place in town some Friday night and reminisce.'

The place in town, the assassin knew, being a town house mansion in the Boltons in Chelsea, where the gated piles started at about twenty million quid.

'That sounds like it might be nice, Terry,' he said as he gave another smile.

'Who knows? Maybe we could do a little business,' Terry said with a wink. 'You never know when the merc might be in the market for a new machine gun.'

CHAPTER 69

Some inebriated young woman sloshed half a microbrew onto my shoes as I made my way through row C near the first base side of the main seating level.

At the end of the row, I came down two steps and knelt in the aisle and tapped the shoulder of a light-blue-clad gentleman sitting at the end of row A.

'Hey, how's it going, buddy?' I said.

CIA operative Matthew Leroux smiled broadly as he looked at me. Beside him, his blond wife, Sophie, also clad in blue, rolled her eyes. They, like Arturo and me, were both sporting some pretty expensive-looking binoculars, I noticed.

'Mike, buddy! Small world!' Leroux said. 'You a big New York City soccer fanatic, too?'

'Oh, the biggest,' I said. 'I still have my Pelé Cosmos lunch box from second grade.'

'No way. Original owner, huh? I had to buy mine on eBay,' Leroux said. 'But I just bought this nifty supporter blue scarf. What do you think?'

'Stylish. It goes with your eyes,' I said. 'I see you've brought your wife, Leroux.' I turned to her. 'I'm Mike. Detective Mike Bennett.'

'Oh, I remember you, Detective,' the pretty blond woman said, peering at me. I peered back at the intelligence in her green eyes. There was something else there, too, I could see. Something still and cold and dangerous.

I suddenly remembered the blood-splattered Hamilton Heights crime scene, and how this petite, friendly woman had more than likely done some of the splattering.

Were all CIA couples this nuts? I thought.

'All in the family, huh?' I said.

'All in every day, Mike,' Leroux said, taking a sip from his Bud Light.

'I hear that the family that watches soccer to-gether stays together.'

Leroux smiled. 'Couldn't agree more,' he said,

looking around.

'Think the visiting team has a chance?' I said.

'Overconfidence will get you every time,' Leroux said.

'You would know,' I said.

Sophie, still scanning with her field glasses, suddenly tapped Leroux on the arm.

'Third base side under the upper deck. The luxury booth. Twelve o'clock.'

I lifted my own glasses along with Leroux. I looked over at third base, then panned up. There were half a dozen men standing on a railed balcony. I scanned their faces, then looked at the photo. Then looked back.

'Third from the left?' I said. 'Isn't he a bit old?'

'Same nose and jaw,' Sophie said.

'Same cocky bearing and frown, too,' I said. 'What do you think, Matt?'

Leroux focused his glasses, then stood.

'I say close enough for government work, Mike,' he said. 'Give me your phone.'

He quickly typed his number into my contacts.

'We'll take the right flank, you take the left. Call me when you get on the luxury level. And don't call for backup yet. This guy's slippery. He'll know if something's up with security.'

'Hold up a second,' I said. 'What are you going to stop him with? Your new scarf?'

'Don't you worry about us,' Leroux said, patting his wife's bag as they moved out of the row, into the aisle. 'Let's just get up into position before he figures it out.'

CHAPTER 70

From the deck of the luxury balcony, they heard the Yanks down in the section beneath cheering as one of the Leeds players got a yellow card for a hard tackle.

'Oh, I hope he didn't rip his panties,' the drunken has-been rock star yelled as he hurled a plastic cup of beer at the blue-clad crowd beneath. 'Piss off, ya useless lot of bearded hipster wankers.'

All the men out on the now crowded balcony started laughing at that. Then Terry's arm was around the British assassin's shoulder, and he put his over the shoulder of the rock star, and it was like a time machine. As if they were all seventeen again, jumping up and down with a 'Leeds, Leeds, Leeds!' chant.

Terry pinched the waitress's ass as he grabbed another bubbly. The British assassin drained his champagne and took a breath and drank it all in, there in the cold above the crowd.

This was the life. One more trigger pull, and he'd get the sour he'd been sucking all his life out of his mouth, once and for all.

He felt it a second later, right as he placed his empty on the tart's tray. It was like a tingle along the nape of his neck, a sixth sense.

He glanced around left and right, down into the crowd below, without moving his head.

There were eyes on him.

Of all those eyes, someone was watching him. It was impossible that he knew it, but it was true. He was a watcher, and he knew. He could feel it. He'd seen it happen often enough to targets. The glass would come on them, and they'd suddenly run, dive, duck. There was something psychic between a hunter and his prey.

Now he was the one being spotted.

He looked down to the left, on the stairs two sections below. A guy was heading up them. A guy in a suit, cop all over him.

He sucked in a breath. Felt the hard beat of his heart in his chest as he held the breath.

He'd screwed up. Big-time. They shouldn't have come here. He needed to get out.

Now.

He slowly stepped back inside. He got his wife's attention, and then he touched his ear, giving her the bug out signal. They had planned contingencies to split up and regarding where to meet later. At least they weren't looking for her.

Her eyes widened with a rare expression of fear, and then he was moving for the door.

There was no one yet out in the luxury level hall. The level had its own private elevator on the left, but that would be the first thing they'd be onto.

On his right, he saw a waitress go through a staff-only door. Following her, he saw that there was a small kitchen and wet bar behind it and another door on the other side of the room.

'Sir, can I help you?' the waitress said by the sink as he crossed the room.

He kept going. The new door led to a narrow,

slightly curving back corridor. There were garbage bags in a gray plastic rolling bin on the right. As he hurried toward it, he saw the stainless steel threshold of a freight elevator just beyond it.

He poked his head in. Except for a mop and a yellow rolling bucket, the elevator was empty. Better yet, the car's security key was in the console. He stepped in and turned the key and hit the Main Level button.

The elevator spilled him out into the great hall by gate 6, where he had come in. He faced the cavernous space and headed for the gate, walking steadily toward the dozen stadium security guards standing there.

He swallowed as he got closer and saw that there were two NYPD uniformed cops standing with the guards. He took a breath as he approached and forced himself to glance at them. They weren't on their radios. They didn't seem any more alert than usual.

A sudden roar from the crowd boomed out low and muffled in the high-ceilinged concourse.

It's okay, he mentally coached himself. *Just walk out. They don't know yet. Fifty meters. You can do this. Just calmly walk past them.*

He was outside in the plaza, fifty meters on the other side of the ratcheting turnstile, when he heard the yell at his back.

'Stop that guy in the white hoodie! Stop him!'

He didn't turn around. Instead, he just moved north quickly, yet still passably casually. There were a hundred or so people moving around souvenir vendors and hot dog carts to hide among.

Then, as he reached the corner of 161st Street and River Avenue, where the elevated track was, he suddenly bolted beneath it.

He'd made it across River Avenue and was booking around the corner of the stair entrance for the uptown side of the subway when he almost ran straight into the uniformed beat cop coming at a run from the other side with his partner.

'Hey, yo! Stop!' the beefy Asian cop said, reaching out with his palm.

Instead of stopping, the Brit kept coming, and seized the cop's hand and yanked hard, breaking two of his fingers. Then he reached and grabbed the baton out of his belt and cracked the other cop, a short Hispanic-looking woman, across the bridge of her nose. He brought the baton whistling back across at the first cop, breaking his wrist, as the Glock the guy was in the process of trying to pull from his holster clattered across the concrete.

The assassin scooped up the semiauto as he ran north up the incline of 161st. He needed to make the corner, he thought, as he flat out sprinted toward it, past shocked pedestrians out in front of the small, ugly run-down stores.

Just the first corner, he thought, his thighs and lungs beginning to burn.

The supersonic crackle of a bullet suddenly passed less than an inch to the left of his ear.

No! They were going to shoot him down in the back as he was running, the bastards!

The first bullet was followed by another that shattered the glass side of the phone kiosk on his left as he passed it.

Then he was around the corner, pulling off his hoodie, sweat flying and arms pumping in the cold as he ran for his life.

CHAPTER 71

Racing out of the stadium, I ran under the El on River Avenue and was twenty feet behind Matthew Leroux when he suddenly hopped up on the grass median between the lanes on 161st Street.

A woman across the street screamed as he produced a suppressed pistol and began firing right there in broad daylight at the sprinting Brit up the block.

'Are you crazy? Put that damn thing away! You're going to kill someone!' I yelled, smacking the barrel of his gun down as I arrived.

'You're right! I am! The president's assassin!' he yelled back as he hopped off the median and started running north, after the Brit.

'Arturo,' I said as he and Sophie caught up to me. 'The Brit just turned the corner and is heading south. You guys head south down River in case he tries to come around the block.'

People were coming out of the stores to gape as I ran up the north side of 161st Street behind Leroux. I thought I was pretty fast for my age, but Leroux was incredible. The commando was pulling away at an embarrassing clip.

I finally followed around the first corner onto Gerard Avenue and spotted Leroux in the middle of the street, already halfway down the block. Then he suddenly turned into an alleyway between two buildings on the right.

As I got to the entrance of the alley, I heard a clatter of metal and looked up. On the third-floor fire escape, I locked eyes with the gray-haired guy I'd just seen on the luxury balcony in Yankee Stadium.

For a split second.

I reared back in a kneeling dive to the asphalt as he pointed the Glock he was clutching. As the passenger window of a parked moving truck I'd just been standing beside exploded glass in my face, I scrambled out of the line of fire, to the right.

When the shock wore off enough for me to get my own gun out and hazard another peek upward into the alley, the Brit was gone. Instead, I saw Leroux booking up the fourth-floor stairs of the brown, rusted zigzag of the tenement fire escape like it was an Olympic event, and he was going for the gold.

Instead of taking the fire escape, I ran inside the building, through its lobby to its east side stairwell, and began running up.

An emergency alarm went off when I banged open the roof door, huffing and puffing, a minute later. Gasping for breath, I looked around the roof for Leroux or the Brit. To my right, ten feet away, was the edge of the building's roof, the gap over a narrow alleyway, and then the edge of the roof of another building, to the north.

Had they hopped the gap? I wondered as I went to the edge, searching the next roof for any sign of either man.

I knew the answer to that was affirmative when I heard a gun pop twice on the other side of some huge AC units on the north building's rooftop.

My phone rang a second later.

'I got him, Mike!' Leroux screamed. 'He's pinned on top of the building to the north! He's cornered around the housing for the building's elevator. Northwest corner. There are no more fire escapes, no more nothing. Call for backup, the cavalry, air strikes – everything you got! I'll sit tight so he doesn't go anywhere. Hurry! We finally got him!'

CHAPTER 72

No, no, bloody no!

The British assassin had come around the housing of the elevator equipment on the roof, hoping for a fire escape. But there was none. Over the edge of the north side of the building was a sheer four-story drop onto the roofs of the buildings on 161st that he'd run past. Worse, at the rear west side of the building, there was a five-story drop down into a concrete alley behind the building.

He crouched down in the corner, gripping the Glock as he stared at the brick edge of the elevator structure. He was going to die here. In one second, the professional who was chasing him was going to pop his gun around that corner and rake half a dozen 9mms into his chest and blow him away.

228

He just had to see the bloody game, didn't he? Idiot. Now this was it. The place of his death, he thought, staring up at the gray sky. This rooftop on some crumbling wasteland of a filthy Bronx block that was the color of burned charcoal.

It wasn't supposed to happen like this. It really wasn't. It just wasn't … fair.

He peeked out over the rim of the roof to his right as a train went by on the rusted elevated track far below on River Avenue. Then he shot a quick glance farther right, up over the elevator housing, where some ugly cell site antennas were mounted. He peeked out again at the back of the building and saw that the thin fiber-optic cabling and electrical cords of the antennas dropped straight down, all the way to the concrete alley.

It was possible that if he hung down off the building's rim with his hands, he could hang, swing, and jump and just be able to grab the cables. Possible. The question was, would they hold his weight? Would his one hundred and seventy pounds rip the cables free from wherever they were attached on the antennas? He pictured himself falling to his death, trailing the antennas.

Then he paused.

He closed his eyes, envisioning himself actually doing it.

Edging over. Jumping. Grabbing the cables.

There was no more time. He had no other choice.

He got up and tucked the Glock into his waistband.

Then he straddled the terra-cotta rim of the building and hung down off the back of it, with his belly against the brick.

The sensation of hanging out there in the breeze, being held by only his palms, was a very, very bad one. It didn't improve an iota as he began to move. Right hand first, then left hand, then right.

When he ran out of room where the roof edge met the wall of the elevator house, he commenced swinging his legs to his left and back to build up some momentum. When he did it the third time, as he swung to the right, he pushed sideways with all his might off the rim.

And let go.

He'd never felt his adrenaline spike higher as he free-fell in midair, with dirty old bricks scraping at the tip of his nose. There was air and air and then his hands were in the vinelike cluster of black plastic cables. His fingers were squeezing and his palms were burning as the vinyl cables sizzled through them. He gasped as a cable tie took the skin clean off his entire right pinkie, but he didn't let go.

He was able to hook his right boot down into the cable cluster, and he was suddenly slowing.

And then, a miraculous second later, he was no longer falling at all.

The now swinging cable made a creaking sound under his weight.

He began laughing uncontrollably as he descended hand over bloody hand down the length of the building like the world's largest, happiest monkey.

He scrambled down toward the alleyway and whatever else was going to happen next.

CHAPTER 73

I heard Leroux moaning as I finally arrived on the roof of the north building with three uniforms.

'Where is he?' I said, hurrying around the corner of the elevator housing.

'He's gone!' Leroux said, crazed, bent out over the edge, looking north and then west.

'Gone? How?' I said. 'Where?'

He continued to stare out at the buildings.

'The cables there! Look!' he said, pointing at some cell site tower cables hanging down the back of the building, behind the elevator house.

'That's impossible,' I said. 'He's dead, then.' I looked down at the shadowed alley far beneath. 'The cables are too far off this edge. Spider-Man couldn't do it!'

'Well, *he* did it. We need to get someone down there now. What's that low building there, between us and the train track?'

'Stan's Sports Bar. Don't worry. If he's down there, we got him,' I said as an NYPD Aviation Bell helicopter came in low from the south. 'We're surrounding the block. He's not–'

I wasn't able to finish the sentence because the *boom boom boom* of a gun started below, to the west by the River Avenue side of the sports bar. I couldn't see what was happening because of the elevated track. The initial shots were followed by two more and then there was the high shriek of

231

tire rubber.

It took us just over two minutes to fly down the stairs and come out onto River Avenue, under the giant rusting jungle gym of the elevated track. This close to the stadium, the whole low block was sports bars and souvenir shops. Everything red, white, and blue, with Budweiser signs and Yankees billboards everywhere.

We came upon Arturo first. He was across from the front entrance of the bar, down on his butt in the gutter, surrounded by half a dozen people. As I ran up, I saw that he was clutching an apron to his blood-soaked leg.

'Forget me. Help Sophie! Over there!' he said, pointing farther north, where three people were kneeling beside someone propped up on one of the elevated track's steel legs.

Leroux ran over and knelt by his wife. A second later, he had her down on the asphalt and was doing chest compressions on her. When her head lolled to the side, I could see blood, stark and wet, in the white blond of her hair.

I knelt down and helped Arturo shimmy over and sit back against the tire of a parked car. He looked pale. Too pale. A train clattered past overhead.

Job one was keeping him from going into shock. I held down his hand when he tried to lift the apron to look at his leg.

'Talk to me, brother. What happened?'

Arturo took a breath. 'Just as we were running up to surround the block like you said, he comes out the front door of Stan's here.'

'The Brit?'

He nodded.

'He walks out almost right into us with the Glock in his hand. Sophie, who was a little bit ahead of me, got the drop on him before he spotted us. She put her gun to his head, got him on his knees. I'm coming up behind him with the cuffs and then *pop pop pop* behind us. It was some bitch in a car shooting from the open driver's window.'

'What kind of car was it?' I said, motioning to one of the cops behind me to call it in.

'A silver Ford. A Focus or something. Maybe a rental. It went south down River,' Arturo said. 'It was some kind of submachine gun or something, Mike. After I took one in the leg, I was able to drop down behind the pillar, but Sophie got caught out. She tried to run, but the bitch just lit her up.'

I patted his back as he started crying.

'It was so brutal. So messed up,' he said.

'Hang in there, pal. They're coming. It's going to be fine.'

I looked over at Leroux, ten feet away on the street, pressing against his wife in the El's tattered shadow.

'They're coming,' I said.

CHAPTER 74

Eleven o'clock that night, I found a parking spot on the corner in front of my West End Avenue building. After I shut the engine, I sat for a moment and looked out through the windshield at the traffic and buildings and the stoplight down on 96th swaying in the cold wind. Just as I was about to push open the door, I tensed up and smacked at the steering wheel with the palm of my hand half a dozen times as hard as I could.

I guess you could say I was a tad frustrated.

I'd just left the Bronx's Montefiore Hospital's intensive care unit, where Sophie Leroux was in a coma. She'd been shot four times in the lower abdomen, and they had to take out half of her pancreas. There had been complications with the surgery, and she'd lost a ton of blood and was now clinging to life by a thread.

The look on Matthew Leroux's face when I left was terrible to behold. Having lost my own wife, Maeve, to cancer, I actually knew how it felt to helplessly watch a person you deeply love hover between life and death. How the inconsolable pain of it buries you to the point where the thought of your own death is actually a hope and a comfort.

I felt incredibly bad for the both of them. Since 9/11, so many heroes in the military and intelligence services, like the Lerouxes, were out there

234

on the front lines taking the hits for all of us. And did anyone even notice anymore? Or care?

Speaking of hopelessness, we hadn't found the Brit. I'd gone back to the stadium to the luxury booth, where we had spotted him. But the man who had rented it, some British banker by the name of David Chester, had left. I traced him to the Carlyle hotel and then out to Teterboro Airport, only to find he had just taken off for London in his private jet.

Dear holy Pete, did it piss me off that some rich English jackwad actually knew the assassin!

Matthew Leroux's boss, Evrard, said he was putting pressure on the State Department, which was putting pressure on the Brits to talk to Chester and figure out who the assassin was. But I knew what a load of hooey that was. If Chester had the kind of connections that a transatlantic private jet suggested, there was no way he would ever admit to knowing or consorting with an assassin. None. His lawyers would drag their asses on this like there was no tomorrow. While for Sophie Leroux, there actually might not be one.

I couldn't believe this assassin had slipped away from me for the second time. He'd reached out and almost killed another one of us, and we still were no closer to finding him.

I was staring out at the lonely street when there was a knock on the passenger window.

I smiled as I turned to see that it was Mary Catherine. I reached over and opened the door.

'Where are you off to on this cold bitter night?' I said as she sat next to me and closed the door. 'Back to Ireland? I wouldn't blame you, you know. Heck, maybe I'll go with you. It's getting dangerous around here.'

'I saw the car. When you didn't get out, I got worried,' she said.

I squeezed her hand.

'Rough day?' she said.

'Yep. Situation normal there,' I said. 'How about upstairs? About the same? How's Brian's grounding going?'

'About what you'd expect. The surly level is even higher than usual. I think he's got his headphones actually Krazy Glued to his ears now. But he's home, at least. No more mysterious late-night library runs.'

'Thank God for small mercies,' I said as I reached over her and opened the car door and slid out after her.

'Did you eat?' she said as we headed for the front door of the building.

'I thought about it.'

'Well, you're in luck,' she said with a smile. 'I made fried chicken.'

'You don't understand precisely how good that sounds right now,' I said. 'Have you eaten already?'

'No,' she said. 'I was waiting for you.'

She'd wait for me forever, I realized as I watched her walk ahead of me to the door.

Are you actually going to make her? asked a voice in my head.

PART FOUR

NOWHERE TO HIDE

CHAPTER 75

Noon two days later found me on Queens Boulevard, staring up at a building that was twelve tall stories of ugly.

It was a dirty beige brick seventies-style residential high-rise that looked pretty much exactly like a giant cardboard box with windows. There were lots and lots of windows. Eighty-four of them, to be exact. I'd counted them with my spotting scope three times already, looking for a rifle barrel.

Alexander Grekov had finally come to New York for the UN summit, and Paul and I and the rest of our task force were following him around. He'd just come in from Kennedy and his first stop was here on Queens Boulevard, in Kew Gardens, Queens, of all places. There was a restaurant of a long-lost cousin of his or something, and he'd just gone in with his brutish personal security detail for some backslaps and vodka shots.

It had fallen on us to stand watch and make sure that he didn't get any of the nonvodka kind of shots to his head. Which was ironic, since we still didn't know if he was behind the ongoing stalking of our own president by the still-missing assassin, the Brit.

'Paul, I gotta say, this international relations shit is truly pissing me off,' I said as we sat in an FBI van parked in the greasy alleyway between the Russian restaurant and a run-down funeral home. 'I mean, here we are, busting our horns protecting this jackwad from getting taken out, when what we probably should be doing is slapping cuffs on him for trying to take out President Buckland. I mean, how the hell does this make even the slightest bit of common sense?'

'Mike, please. Where've you been?' Paul said from behind me, where he was sitting with some of the FBI's Hostage Rescue commando guys, who'd recently been assigned to our detail. 'Do you honestly believe that the bigwigs above us who run these things would deign to use something as common as common sense in making decisions? Our elite leaders, of course, use only Ivy League sense, which has had all the seedy lowborn common sense bred out of it for years now.'

'Honestly, Paul. You ask me, the whole thing – Grekov being here, all of it – is a distraction, a head fake,' I said. 'He wants to be as close to Buckland as possible if something goes down. "But, Officer, how could I be responsible? I was right beside him. It wasn't me."'

'Well, we can't let that happen, then, can we?' Paul said. 'We bag the Brit beforehand, Grekov loses.'

'If it even is Grekov,' I said with an exasperated sigh. 'Do you really think it is? That it is actually Grekov, and this is all some Deep Blue chess move he's making that only Garry Kasparov could figure out?'

'I don't know,' Paul said. 'As usual, we have lots of questions but, unfortunately also as usual, no answers.'

'I'm getting sick of those.'

'The questions or the fact that there are no answers?' Paul said.

'Yep,' I said as I started counting windows again.

CHAPTER 76

Several hours later, coming on seven that evening, after Grekov was in for the night upstairs at the Waldorf, we were downstairs in a back room off its ornate lobby, in one of its conference rooms.

The beautiful varnished boardroom table we were sitting at was done up with the Waldorf's signature A1 high style. There were sumptuous flower arrangements running down the middle of the table, and tissues in intricately carved decorative boxes. At each of the twenty or so seats were china coffee cups and water bottles and crystal water glasses set up on little doilies.

We were there to have our own little international summit between us and Grekov's Russian security forces.

'This spread is fit for a king, isn't it, Paul?' I said to Agent Ernenwein as a pleasant middle-aged waitress filled my coffee cup for the third time. 'So this is what it feels like to be a central banker. I must say, I'm impressed.'

'Now, Mike, it's not fair to denigrate the wizards behind the curtain,' Paul said. 'They deserve every luxury we can provide for them. Do you actually think it's easy to conjure up trillions of dollars of global debt with a wave of your manicured fingers over a keyboard?'

I was still chuckling when the Russian security guys came in. There were six of them – six big thick-necked guys in tailored suits. Think Brute Squad by way of Savile Row.

'Enough of your lies,' the lead brute, a pale bald guy, said without preamble or sitting down. 'Why do you think that Grekov is out to kill your president? Do you think we are so stupid that we cannot see that this is some plot you have set up to discredit him? You wish for a premise for war? Yes? Of course you do. For without Russia, the US can just take whatever it pleases, such as Iraq. You will find very painfully we are not the Iraqis, I assure you. Russia will defy you, then defeat you faster than you will believe.'

After ten seconds of unbelievably dead silence following this verbal crowbar to the back of the head, I stood, holding a crystal water glass aloft.

'Hi. My name is Mike. Welcome to America,' I said. 'Please sit down so we can discuss how to be friends with one another.'

'You stupid American,' baldy said. 'If anything happens to our president, you will not be laughing, I can assure you. The joke will be on you and the smoldering little of what's left of your decadent country.'

'Did somebody wake up on the wrong side of the bed this morning or what?' I whispered a little too loudly to Paul.

'Please, gentlemen. There's no need to speak in such a way,' said Agent Margaret Foley, giving me a look like she wanted to turn me into something smoldering. 'As you may have heard, Mr. Stasevich, our president was almost shot.'

'And we have very good reason,' Paul jumped in, 'to believe that the shooter was hired by someone in Russia. But we have never stated that we thought it was your president. Not once. So I don't know where you're getting that from.'

'Would any of these reasons have something to do with one of our agricultural attachés, who seems to be missing?' Stasevich inquired with a roll of his eyes. 'Tell us, how long did it take for your CIA interrogators to waterboard this false information out of him that we are involved?'

'Enough, please, gentlemen,' said Agent Foley. 'These outrageous accusations get us nowhere. As with all visiting dignitaries, we will be doing everything we can to ensure your leader's protection while he is in our country.'

'And to imply that we are not is a flat-out insult,' Paul said, feisty now.

'Please accept our deepest apologies,' said Stasevich. 'And listen to me very closely. We deny any and all involvement. And to show you that our only wish is for global stability, like a true partner of all nations, our president is willing to appear with your president out in front of the UN as the dignitaries arrive. Alexander Grekov is willing to put himself in the line of fire.'

'I will pass along your generous offer to the president,' said Agent Foley. 'Thank you for meeting with us.'

'It's just like I told you,' I said to Paul as the Russkies left. 'The Brit can shoot the nose hair

243

out of a flying mosquito at four thousand yards. This is it. When Grekov and the president are out in front of the UN, waving to the crowd, that's when the shooting will happen.'

Paul shook his head, then let out a breath.

'I don't know, Mike. Maybe these guys are on the level. They look genuinely pissed off.'

'Which means what? They're not involved? Grekov's not involved?'

Paul shook his head again, then shrugged.

'Maybe not. Maybe it's one of the oligarchs who want to take Buckland out. Heck, maybe the oligarchs want to take Grekov himself out. Every time you think you're getting a bead on this, something new pops up that makes it impossible to say what the hell is going on.'

'It's like those Russian dolls. What are they called?' I said.

'Matryoshkas,' said Paul, nodding.

'Exactly, Paul. You nailed it. From day one, this whole case has been one big mind-screwing matryoshka. The doll within the doll within the doll.'

CHAPTER 77

The British assassin thumbed away his well-cleaned dessert plate, took out his blue pack of Gitanes, and lit one for himself and his wife off the linen-draped table's candle.

What a meal! he thought as he flicked ash onto

his coffee saucer and blew smoke up toward the ceiling.

There had been beef tongue carpaccio, roasted quail, risotto with shaved pecorino, smoked eel on black truffle toast, jowl of pork. Each dish perfectly cooked and washed down with bottle after bottle of 2007 François Lamarche La Grande Rue.

He'd caught the foodie bug back when he was a teenager and worked in kitchens all over London. He'd actually been a line chef at Le Gavroche for three months, as a fill-in, and was prepping at the Fat Duck, in Bray, when he got his call from the marines.

When this was over, first order of celebration was going to be eating their way across the continent, starting in France, he thought as he looked out the window beside him at the city lights. He glanced over at his sexy wife and pictured them cruising through Burgundy's quiet villages in something unconscionable, like an Aston Vantage or a Bentley Continental GT, her blond hair flying as they ripped around the vineyards and hills and gravel bends.

'Everything okay?' asked Jill, the Culinary Institute-trained chef and apartment owner as she came in to clear the plates.

They had jumped with both feet when they saw the Asian thirtysomething's ad on an underground dining website for a farm-to-table, cooked-to-perfection gourmet feast. They were actually seated in the glassed-in balcony of her twentieth-floor apartment in a high-rise in northern Manhattan, of all places.

It couldn't have worked out better. With the shooting still fresh in the news, they had to stay out of the public eye until the job was over.

'Perfect, really,' said the assassin's wife. 'How rude of us. We forgot to ask if it is okay to smoke. It's been ages since I actually had a postmeal smoke at the table.'

Jill, who'd already been paid the fee of eight hundred dollars in cash, smiled.

'Please – you're my guests. *Mi casa es su casa,*' she said as she left with the plates.

He was stubbing out the Gitane in the glass ashtray Jill had brought them when his disposable phone rang.

'Are you this stupid?' was the first question he was asked by the client's electronically disguised voice when he answered the phone in the bathroom.

'It's fine,' he said.

'It's not fine. You shot a cop and a spook. The spook's at death's door.'

'That's the way the cookie crumbles,' the British assassin said. 'Playing for keeps isn't for the squeamish. Have you the final route? I've been waiting.'

'I just sent it to your e-mail.'

'I see it,' the British assassin said, looking at his smartphone. 'No changes, then?'

'No. They're going with the original route. It's a lock.'

'Good, then. I'll expect the last of it by close of business tomorrow.'

'Close of business?' the client said. 'That's not in the contract. The second after he's confirmed dead, the escrow will be released to you. Be it an hour later or a year. That's the deal. Killing him. That's the important part here. Finishing the job.'

'No problem,' the British assassin said with a yawn as he looked at himself in the mirror.

'So you're good to go now, right? You don't have to deal with Levkov anymore, do you?'

'No, I haven't spoken to him since I started dealing with you.'

'Good. We can start the housecleaning on our end, then, tonight.'

'Whatever you need to do,' said the Brit. 'That's none of my concern.'

'Get some sleep. The weather looks good to-morrow. Crisp and clear.'

'I like the sound of that,' the British assassin said, thumbing the cheap phone off.

CHAPTER 78

After he buzzed the Chinese food guy out, Pavel Levkov carefully arrayed his dinner of beef with broccoli, fried wontons, and egg drop soup on his cleared desk.

He was in his office at the meat warehouse in Brooklyn now, where he'd just finished up the mountain of payroll and inventory paperwork that had piled up during his hospital stay and detention by the feds.

He was in an electric wheelchair, his kneecapped leg in a bulky aluminum and resin brace. The rented chair was costing him a fortune since he had a high-deductible plan, but he needed it, as walking was a no-no since the pain in his knee was unlike anything he'd ever felt. The doctors had told him it had something to do with all the bones in the knee that the American bastard's bullet had smashed to jelly.

All in all, he was lucky, he knew. He'd paid back all his debts and was out of all of it. Though he had been kneecapped, his duty as middleman between the British assassin and the Russian mobster had been completed.

A bullet to the knee and a couple of phone calls were actually a pretty fair price to pay to erase the massive poker debt he had with the mobster. He'd run with the devil and was still alive. That was winning, in his book. It was time to retire now, sell his businesses, get out of New York altogether. Quit while he was ahead.

Meal over, he was dry-swallowing a Percocet when his new dog, a boxer-rottweiler mix he'd named Sweetie, began growling at the locked office door.

Immediately, he took his fully loaded and cocked SIG Sauer P220 Match Elite .45 out of the knapsack on the side of the wheelchair. The dog began barking like mad a few seconds later, and then he smelled it. Smoke. As he watched, a wisp of it floated in under the door.

Then, over the dog's bark, he heard it. Out in the hallway, there was beeping from the ceiling smoke alarm.

Somebody had set his place on fire.

Gun in his right hand, he zipped the wheelchair over to the door and unlocked it and pulled it open. He coughed in the gray smoke that poured in as the dog shot out into the hall like a missile. Panicking, Pavel Levkov stared at the smoke, waiting to hear something. The dog barking, a struggle – anything. But even after a minute, he heard nothing.

He'd just made it out into the hall, braced leg first, when the shadow fell over him and something smashed into his outstretched knee.

It was an aluminum softball bat, he saw, as it smacked again, into his torso this time, sending the .45 flying away.

'I didn't talk, I swear,' he said in Russian. 'I did everything you said.'

'We shall see about that,' the Russian voice replied as he was lifted bodily out of the chair.

CHAPTER 79

Five the next morning, I was in Yonkers, just over the border of the Bronx. On my right was the Hudson River, and on my left were the Metro-North train tracks, and in front of me, beside an old rusted-out Ford flatbed truck, was our Russian suspect, Pavel Levkov, lying facedown in the gravel, dead.

The Russian, who was in a leg brace from his kneecapping, had been shot in the back of the head a couple of times. His wrists and ankles were bound in wire hangers twisted together really tight with a pair of side cutters or something. It was a neat job. There was no blood at the scene, which probably meant he'd been dumped.

'Who found him?' said Paul as he came up along the railroad tracks with a couple of coffees.

'Guy walking his dog,' I said. 'Yonkers PD got him in a car back in the station lot. He's a local kid. Didn't see anyone.'

There was a small stand of leafless trees beside the crime scene atop of which some crows were cawing up at the gray sky. I suddenly picked up a rock and chucked it at them, sending them flapping.

'Bird lover, I see,' said Paul.

'No. A peace and quiet one,' I said.

'You know,' Paul said, 'the old-timey houses back there and the water and trees here remind me of a sad book I once read. It's set in the thirties or something, and it's about an upstate New York Irish bum who'd been a ballplayer and goes back to see his family in Albany for Thanksgiving.'

'I remember. Nicholson played him in the depressing movie.'

'Yeah, he did. What's the name of it?'

'*Ironweed*,' I said. 'Now how about our friend here. If our Russian buddy were a depressing novel, which one would he be, you think? *War and Peace? Crime and Punishment?*'

Paul looked at me pensively, then snapped his fingers.

'*The Death of Ivan Ilyich*,' he said.

'You're good,' I said. 'So what does this mean,

250

Paul? Levkov was the link to the Brit. The middle-man. And now he's dead.'

'He's the cutout, so they cut him out.'

'Meaning?'

'The Brit doesn't need him. Or, I should say, the people who hired him to hire the Brit. Even if we catch the Brit, he can only lead us back to this gentleman, and the dead tell no tales.'

'Everything is set, then,' I said. 'This thing really is going down.'

'The fuse is lit, Mike. We need to find the bomb.'

'How many hours till touchdown?'

Paul checked his watch.

'Ten,' he said.

I shook my head as the crows came back, their caws skipping out over the gray water.

'It's official,' I said. 'We're going to have to make our own luck now.'

CHAPTER 80

The bright white light gradually grew larger in the dark predawn sky until suddenly Air Force One materialized above the JFK runway lights, its big jets screaming.

I held my breath as it came in right over the Port Authority airport command center beside me. I actually didn't let the breath out until the plane touched down safely on the tarmac.

This was going to be one long day.

The idling vehicle in whose front passenger seat

251

I was sitting was a military personnel carrier called a BAE Caiman MRAP. Behind me, in the bank vault-like rear of the truck, Paul Ernenwein and a half dozen members of the FBI's Hostage Rescue Team were doing last-minute coordination over the radio with the Secret Service's tactical CAT agents.

The massive presidential motorcade was beside us, on the left. But because our bulky composite armored vehicle looked like something fresh off the battlefield, it wasn't going to be in the motorcade itself, but always nearby. There were actually going to be two of them present for the entirety of the president's stay in New York.

As I glanced out at the taxiing plane through the bullet-and blast-proof windshield, I remembered what CIA sniper Matthew Leroux had said about the battlefield being everywhere now.

He was actually with us, there in the back, dressed in the same black body armor and gear as the Hostage Rescue guys. It was a last-second thing. His wife, Sophie, was in stable condition now, thank God, and he had pulled some strings to get put onto the protection detail as a special adviser. Though obviously emotionally involved, Leroux was actually considered one of the top five snipers in the country, so the New York FBI SAC had finally reluctantly agreed.

'Poor son of a bitch,' said Paul Ernenwein, pointing a chin to where Leroux knelt in the back, doing a meticulous equipment check. 'You see the look in his eyes? Jeez.'

'Mike!' Leroux called up to the front of the truck.

'What is it?' I said as I arrived beside him.

'I was wondering if you could do me a favor,' he said.

'What's up?'

He stared at me intently with his blue eyes.

'Somebody told me you used to be a spotter. I want you to be mine.'

'These other FBI guys are far better trained, Matt. I–'

He held up a hand.

'I'm sure they are, but I don't know them. I know you. You're old-school like me, Mike. I need someone beside me who knows that quit ain't ever an option.'

He held out the spotting scope in its case carefully, with both hands.

'Will you do it?' he asked.

I stared at the case, at the terrible look in his blue eyes.

'Of course,' I said as I took the case.

CHAPTER 81

As the President's motorcade made its long, slow loop out of JFK miles to the east, the British assassin and his wife burst out of the southeast end of Central Park at a run, caught the green, and crossed Fifth Avenue.

They were layered up in the latest cold weather running clothes: black North Face skullcaps, Capilene shirts and pants, neon-yellow Brooks running jackets that matched their flying ASICS. Coming east in the street down 58th, past midtown's early morning delivery and garbage trucks, they looked just like they wanted to look. Like another high-flying yuppie couple getting in their essential morning run before work.

They arrived at Madison and crossed it and then hooked a right a block down, onto Park.

The British assassin looked up at the MetLife Building looming now in front of them as they ran toward it. Then he forced himself to stop looking at it, and shook his head.

No thoughts about past failures. No room for that. Not today, of all days.

As they came across 57th Street, they could see the security already amassed around the Waldorf.

They hooked a left, east down 56th, to Lexington, and then crossed that, and then, after another block, crossed Third. Between Third and Second Avenues, they paused for the briefest of moments to scan the dump truck.

They had parked the monster the night before, and it was just as they had left it. Nothing awry.

They exchanged a quick tense glance as they made the corner of Second Avenue. It was almost impossible to consider what they were about to do today. History was literally in the making, and they were the ones making it. All systems were go.

They did their stretches out in front of the Starbucks on Second, noting their progress on their Fitbits like good yuppies. Once inside, she waited at a couch by the window while he arrived with their Venti blacks and the *Times*. They sat reading

254

for twenty minutes.

He took a breath before he folded the Metro section and placed it on the table. He stood and looked at her.

She looked back then, leaned forward, and grabbed his hand fiercely.

He squeezed back. Then he was back out in the cold, and a taxi was pulling up.

'Yeah?' said the hack as the British assassin sat.

He could see his wife through the window. His heart faltered, then fluttered. A bad feeling came over him. A premonition? Or was it just nerves?

Maybe they didn't have to. Maybe...

'Yo! Where to?' said the driver.

The Brit looked at his wife again.

'Sixty-Ninth and Second,' he said, and then he closed his eyes and his wife was gone.

CHAPTER 82

Brian Bennett was in fourth period Latin class when he smelled the french fries.

At the front of the classroom, Mr. Swanson (the kids called him Swansonius Maximus among themselves) was fervently trying to explain the subtle difference between hortatory and jussive subjunctive independent clauses. But this close to lunch, and now with the smell of the cafeteria fries wafting in through the open door, he had about as much of a chance as Carthage during the Third Punic War.

Undeterred, Swansonius continued on, and Brian suddenly remembered the honey-nut clusters Mary Catherine always stuck in the side pocket of his knapsack. He could ask for a bathroom break and then do a quick drive-by to his locker, down the hall, around the corner, he thought. Going to your locker during classes was technically a detention offense, but he was Starvin' Marvin.

Speaking of which, Brian thought, turning around to glance hopefully at Marvin, in the next row. But Big Marv only looked away. Still pissed at him.

Marvin still wasn't talking to him after what he had pulled in the park with Big Flicka. Marvin had assured him it wasn't over. That he didn't know what he was doing. That Flicka wasn't stupid. That he knew when someone had set him up, and that he would kill him if he got out on bail.

Brian hadn't known what to say to that, except that Marvin was the one who had started it, bringing a damn gun into their house. He raised his hand and asked to be excused.

Five minutes later, Brian had scarfed down both honey-nut clusters from his locker and had just finished washing them down at a hall water fountain when he heard the shoe squeak down the deserted hall to his right. He tensed at first, before he looked, thinking it was the dreaded Brother Rob, the dean of discipline, about to crack him for being out of class. Then he looked up, and boy, was he wrong.

Brian's eyes opened to their outer limits.

Guess Big Flicka made bail after all, came a tiny

scared voice from somewhere far off inside his head.

He didn't know how. He didn't know why. All he knew was that the crazy-ass drug dealer he'd pulled a fast one on was marching down the middle of the hall!

Their eyes met. Flicka's were going wide, lighting up with recognition.

Then he was reaching into the pocket of his big black goose down parka.

Brian didn't wait to see what he was reaching for. He just bolted, made the hall corner, saw the outside emergency exit door, and hit its push bar at a run.

Out in the cold, he ran across the dead hard grass of the football field behind the school in his black dress shoes faster than he ever had in cleats. A moment later, the emergency siren blaring in the distance behind him was interrupted by a flat, hard fire-crackerlike pop.

He started zigzagging then, past the twenty, the ten, and then into and out of the end zone, not breaking his sprinting and dodging until he hit the stand of trees on the other side of the field's chest-high fence.

Past the trees, he came upon the busy four-lane road of Southern Boulevard. With no time to look, he ran right out into traffic. He almost got hit, first by a brown Mustang, then by a white Euro delivery van. Then he was on the other side, running alongside a tall hedge.

The hedge ended suddenly and opened onto a parking lot with a sign beside its driveway that said THE NEW YORK BOTANICAL GAR-

DEN. There had to be a cop or something, he thought as he saw a guard booth.

Please, God. Please help me, he prayed as he ran. *I don't want to die.*

CHAPTER 83

Twenty feet up the park road, past the empty guard booth, Brian Bennett spotted a long set of cement steps on his left-hand side and pounded up them with everything he had.

The worn concrete treads flew past under his shoes. In twos, sometimes threes. He hardly felt them. He could feel only one thing. The massive power of his sixteen-year desire to live, boosting adrenaline into his bloodstream like nitro into a funny car's engine.

He topped the steps without breaking stride and hit a path that skirted the base of a vast grass hill. He looked about frantically. The empty path. The empty hill. Dead gray trees. The dead gray sky. No cops. No security. Nobody at all. It was like the entire park was abandoned, the entire Bronx, the entire planet.

It was just him and Big Flicka now, he thought as sweat began to sting his eyes. He and his own personal psycho killer, left all alone in this calming urban nature oasis to play the deadliest game of tag in world history.

The botanical garden's famous and immense domed greenhouse appeared as the path crested a rise. He'd been to the garden a few times with his family when he was a kid, but he'd never looked at the greenhouse before. It looked Victorian and somehow futuristic at the same time. Like something out of an H. G. Wells novel.

Twenty flat-out running seconds later, he reached it and ripped open its door.

And stopped and stood blinking.

The building was even weirder inside than out, an *Alice in Wonderland* indoor forest world of stone paths meandering in multiple directions among green grass and bushes and trees and wildflowers. You could smell the sweetness of the flowers in the suddenly warm air. As the door clicked behind him, he waited to hear bird chirps or maybe crickets. Instead, it was dead silent.

Outside inside upside down, he thought as he hurried left down an interior woodland path.

'Hello? Is there anybody here? Hello? Help!' he called.

Another twenty yards down the path, beyond a huge weeping willow, he pulled a French door. This even curiouser room of the enclosed English garden had an actual pond on its other side, with lily pads and a bronze fountain gurgling in its center.

'Please, someone! Hello? Is there anyone here?' he yelled up at the glass ceiling as he began to jog.

Odd structures began to appear in the underbrush beyond the pond as he kept going. It was a wicker world New York City. A wicker St. Patrick's Cathedral, a wicker Grand Central Terminal, little wicker skaters holding hands on an ice rink before a towering wicker 30 Rock.

Around a little bend in the path, beyond this frivolous insanity, he spotted another door, marked EXIT.

'Hey! What are you doing here? The garden's closed today. You're not supposed to be in here.'

Brian shot a look up to his left. There was a little white-bearded man in maintenance blues atop a high ladder. There was a set of Christmas lights in his little hands, a bunch of twist ties between his little white teeth. He was in the process of stringing the lights around the trunk of an enormous palm tree.

Garden gnome, Brian thought, opening his mouth to ask for help.

Then a pistol cracked behind him, and he was past the ladder and out the exit door in a panicked bolt, running and zigzagging again in the cold.

CHAPTER 84

Less than a minute later, Brian crashed through a thick hedge that put him outside the botanical garden, back onto Southern Boulevard. Its four lanes were empty this time as he ran across them and ducked behind a parked car, gasping and gulping for breath.

Not fair, he thought, down on his knees, dripping sweat, his hands shaking. His hands were actually bleeding now, he could see, scratched all to hell from tearing a hole for himself through the hedge.

260

Where were the cops? he thought, wiping blood on his khakis. On strike? Would no one help him? Did everyone actually want Flicka to kill him?

He swiped his drenched face with his shirt-sleeve and desperately looked around. Down at the bottom of the little descending grass embankment, something caught his eye. It was a gleam, a thin flash of light off metal, coming through the underbrush. And then Brian jumped up as he remembered.

Crashing through the bushes at the incline's bottom a split second later, Brian looked south down the long straight lines of the train tracks and raised third rail. He could see it was only a hundred or so yards down the tracks to the platform of the Fordham Road Metro-North station.

Having used the train plenty of times, he knew that the long open-air platform abutted the fence for the Fordham campus. He also knew that there was actually a hole in its fence that all the Fordham Prep kids used to avoid going all the way around to the campus's main gate.

Brian sprinted over the trestles and had just pulled himself up onto the Westchester-bound concrete platform when he saw that the train was coming in at its far end. It had slowed to a stop by the time he was about to cut through the hole in the fence.

That's when he remembered. The Metro-North trains had conductors. They could call the cops!

When he hopped through the opening doors of the train car and moved left down the car's aisle, he saw that the seats were more than half empty. He passed a middle-aged white woman. Then an old Hispanic-looking man.

Since both were glued to their phones, they were completely and utterly oblivious to the apparition that walked past. The world's most panicked Catholic school white boy, dripping sweat and blood like a lost young medieval saint sent running through the countryside after being visited with the stigmata.

He was all the way down the car, about to head into the next, when he heard the woman scream.

Brian turned.

And froze.

Flicka, sweat dripping off his terrible face, stepped into the car in his big black parka.

The huge dude had to actually duck a little to clear the opening. Brian's eyes darted immediately to the gun the big man held. It was a little silver-and-black semiauto.

This was it, Brian thought as he helplessly watched the gun rise toward him in slo-mo. He'd tried with all his might for it not to be it, but he had failed. He was going to die now. He couldn't believe it. After all that.

He glanced around helplessly. A sunset on an ad placard promising cheap flights to Miami. An abandoned newspaper on a pleather seat.

He wiped at his nose with the back of his bloody hand.

Before he even graduated from high school, he was actually going to violently die on some stupid damned commuter train.

CHAPTER 85

Just as he thought this, from beyond the still-open train door to Flicka's right, there was a sound and movement.

Brian watched, immobilized, as Marvin bounded into the car, already off his feet, Superman-style, as if shot out of a cannon. He hit Big Flicka high, blindsiding him, actually taking him off his big feet sideways and crunching him against the opposite, closed door of the train.

Brian shook off his shock and ran forward as Marvin straddled Big Flicka and started pounding him, screaming and screeching like a wild animal as he clubbed the drug dealer again and again in the face.

Brian spotted the pistol on the scuffed train floor beside them, and he kicked it out of the door of the train, and then gloriously joined in on the beating of Big Flicka, kicking at the guy's long legs, his stomach, the side of his head. More passengers arrived out of nowhere, yelling and screaming as the three gasped and growled as they fought for their lives there on the dirty train floor.

Then suddenly, after he didn't know how long – a minute, an hour – a big uniformed cop was pulling Brian from the back, up onto his feet, and he was outside on the platform getting handcuffed.

A second later, Marvin was handcuffed beside him, and they both watched as Big Flicka was dragged out.

Brian couldn't believe the state of him. There was blood pouring out of his broken nose and out of a huge gash on the side of his head, which was swelled up like a pumpkin.

He was out cold, or maybe dead, hopefully, Brian thought as he realized he was crying.

He wasn't the only one, he saw, as he turned to Marvin. Big Marv was flat out bawling on the platform next to him, just helplessly weeping. Brian leaned over and nudged him with his cuffed hands.

'It's over, Marvin. It's okay, dude. It's over. We got him. You saved me, man. You saved me.'

That's when it really hit Brian. When he looked at the number of cops around them. The crowd of commuters standing outside the stopped train. The EMTs rattling a stretcher over the platform's cement.

How close they had come to not making it.

'No, man,' Marvin said in an almost whisper through his weeping. 'You did it. You saved me, bro. It was you.'

CHAPTER 86

Yellow and white sparks pinwheeled off the Black Hawk helicopter's windshield glass as we ascended out of the shadow of the Chrysler Building, into the bright, late morning sunlight above the canyons of midtown Manhattan.

From my perch on a none-too-comfortable bench in the rear of the FBI's big black military-style helicopter, I stared out a side door window at midtown Manhattan's east side. Next to me was CIA sniper Matthew Leroux, and we, along with another helicopter team that was now hovering over the East River near the UN, had been assigned countersniper air cover for Buckland's motorcade.

I had tried to beg off being Leroux's spotter several times as we rolled into the city behind the motorcade in the MRAP. I'd cited my lack of qualifications, that it had been years since I'd held a spotting scope.

Leroux had ended the discussion at the 59th Street heliport, where the FBI Black Hawks were waiting, by holding up some fingers.

'How many you see, Mike?' he had said.

'Two,' I told him.

'Then by the powers vested in me by the gods of war, I here now dub you officially qualified,' he had said. 'Stop worrying. I got you covered. It's just like riding a bike.'

Some bike, I thought, feeling the hard, high turbine thrum of the five-ton military aircraft through my back and butt and shoe soles.

Leroux was busy kneeling on the deck of the cabin, putting the final touches on some bulky piece of military hardware called a gyroscopic shooting platform. It was a gun bench, an extremely expensive, high-tech, rotating adjustable gun sling that was underhung with the same pill-shaped gyroscopic motors that Hollywood steady cams use to counter vibration.

But instead of a camera chocked into the gyroscopic mount, there was a huge bolt-action sniper rifle called a CheyTac M300 Intervention. Leroux had explained to me that the long, futuristic-looking steel and carbon fiber gun could actually shoot sub-minute of angle. Sub-minute of angle precision basically meant the big rifle could consistently put bullet after bullet into a circle the size of a human head at preposterous distances.

And what a bullet it shot. Leroux had said its .408 CheyTac round, though smaller and lighter than a .50 BMG, could easily drop personnel targets at two miles. That kind of range in narrow Manhattan was actually very comforting. It meant we were providing air cover from the East River to the Hudson at any given point.

Leroux had been throwing around tons of superassassin lingo from the moment I'd decided to be his spotter. He spoke of yaw and linear air drag and spin rates and ballistic coefficients. Speed and altitude and angular motion of the aircraft. Slant distances.

Since it was all pretty much Greek to me, I just nodded along. He was Jordan Spieth getting his game face on. I was just his caddy.

Actually, as we were strapping into the aircraft twenty minutes before, at the heliport, I'd learned that we'd caught somewhat of a break in the case.

Doyle, who was working the Pavel Levkov murder, had sent me a text. He said a witness from one of the houses near the drop site in Yonkers had come forward. The witness had said he saw our departed Russian friend dumped by two men in a large black SUV. Apparently, the witness even got a partial on the plate that Doyle was frantically trying to run down.

Since we already knew that Levkov was the liaison who had hired the Brit, a line on whoever had killed him would point us directly to whoever the hell was behind all this.

At long last, it looked like we might finally have a substantial lead.

I looked down at the city below, the red and blue bubbling police lights of the presidential motorcade already starting to form over by the Waldorf.

I just hoped it wasn't too little too late.

CHAPTER 87

After Matthew Leroux finished the final touches of the gyroscopic rig, he stood and checked both of our safety harnesses.

Wow, was this guy a pro, I thought as I watched him triple-check everything. A truly topflight operator. Whatever else he was, Leroux was a good guy to have in a foxhole, I thought. Especially one that was hovering at five hundred feet.

Then I realized *why* he had checked our safety harnesses.

'Opening the doors,' Leroux called over the intercom headset.

Holy moly. *Is that such a great idea?* I wanted to ask as my eyes went wide.

I didn't get a chance. The bass hum of the craft's

turboshaft engine suddenly became molar-loosening as Leroux rolled open the doors on both sides of the Black Hawk's cabin. My stomach did a little rolling as well as I suddenly looked out at the sharp edges of stone and glass buildings down there in the open air below my shoe tips.

With the brisk wind ripping in through the now open door, I could see we were at a low hover over Bryant Park, where the famous NYC library was. On the ground way down below, I could see lucky people safely and obliviously walking to and fro in front of the marble lions.

It's hard to describe how peculiar it felt to be sitting there with the aircraft's doors open. The enclosed cabin, which a second before had felt sort of safe, like being inside a car or something, now made me feel like we were sitting in a kid's hastily built clubhouse, precariously perched on the tip of the Empire State Building.

'Give us a three sixty, Cap,' Leroux called smoothly up to the pilot as he hunkered down on his little hunter's chair beside the other open door and placed an eye to the CheyTac's scope.

There was a subtle change in the whine of the rotors, and we started slowly rotating counter-clockwise. Manhattan began to pan across my spotting scope, the east side replaced by Central Park replaced by the bright – even in the daytime – glow of Times Square off the high-rise hotels.

When it had just about done a full turn, the chopper suddenly did a heart attack-inducing tilt sideways, to the left, snapping my harness line taut.

'Whoa, Nelly,' the pilot said calmly as he tilted

us back level. 'Those darn wind gusts. Thank goodness this baby has good drink holders.'

When I looked over at Leroux to see if he had maybe fallen out, I saw that he was sitting as before, completely still and relaxed. The calm, slightly concerned expression on his face as he sat at the door's edge, above the tips of the skyscrapers, was that of a mailman sorting letters or a carpenter screwing up some Sheetrock. What did this guy have for blood? I wondered. Freon?

He turned and looked at me and grinned.

'Feel that wind, Mike? Don't you love it? That's game temperature, baby.'

'Oh, yeah. Nothing like it in the world,' I lied as my saliva evaporated.

To take my mind off my terror, I glanced at my phone and saw that it was eleven thirty.

I glanced down, over the building tops, at the bubbling roof lights by the Waldorf again.

We were thirty minutes away from President Buckland's ride to the United Nations.

Thirty minutes away from seeing what in the loving green world of God would happen next.

CHAPTER 88

In the middle of blocked-off Park Avenue, in front of the Waldorf Astoria, the assassin's wife held up her phone, snapping pictures along with the rest of the fifty or so looky-loos.

She could already see, past the pedestrian

barrier set up along the median, a large portion of the motorcade formed and waiting along blocked-off East 50th. She could actually see the rear of one of the two presidential limousines between two SUVs.

In front of the limo, there was a thick, white cloth tent stretched from the Waldorf's 50th Street side entrance awning halfway into the street. The tent was to conceal President Buckland's entry into the vehicle, she knew.

As she watched, several business-suited men – undercover cops, or maybe Secret Service agents – came out from around the tent and began milling about. There were more than usual, which was saying something. She'd heard on the radio that they'd even brought in some military-style MRAPs to bolster this visit.

She stifled a laugh. What would be next? An M1 Abrams tank? An aircraft carrier? All because they were afraid of one measly little man.

Well, one man and his wife.

She checked her phone. Eleven forty-five. It was getting close now.

They've absolutely no idea what is about to hit them.

The smoky, bitter roasted-coffee smell of a pretzel cart hit her as she walked closer to the corner of 50th.

The scent, surprisingly strong, halted her for a moment as memories even stronger than the aroma instantly flooded in. Ever since she was a kid, that simple yet of its own essence pretzel smell was New York for her. Midtown and Times Square and yellow taxis. The gigantic Christmas tree in Rockefeller Center, Broadway musicals, and Eloise at the Plaza.

How many of her dad's business trips from England had she been on back then? A dozen, perhaps? They had taken the Concorde more than a few times. How wonderfully NYC storybook it had been. How wonderfully, royally, let-them-eat-cake. For how many other little girls in the history of the world had ever had breakfast in London, lunch in New York, and then dinner in London?

But what did kiddie memories matter now? she thought, shoving them quickly down a mental dustbin. She needed to focus now, really focus, and do the final checks.

If she got this right, she'd be letting everyone eat cake again for the rest of her life.

CHAPTER 89

The business-suited cops behind the barriers began getting into their armored vehicles as she arrived on the northeast corner. She watched as the NYPD tow truck that would be the tip of the motorcade arrived at the 50th Street barrier and was let through.

She swallowed as she felt a butterfly swirl of tension begin to corkscrew in her stomach.

Now. She gripped her iPhone, turned it in her hand. It was happening right now.

'Don't you just love Buckland?' said a voice close by as she was about to leave.

She turned to her left, a little startled. A boyish

man, tall, handsome, and preppy in a Brooks Brothers overcoat, stood there on the corner beside her, his arms crossed, smiling.

She looked at him, warily checking his hands, trying to place his American accent. Chicago, maybe.

A cop? she thought. No. Too well dressed. Too ... prissy. But who knew? She expected the feds to have agents in the crowd. They were all on high alert now. Just how many agents she didn't know. It unnerved her, though, that they were perhaps being called in from as far away as the Midwest.

Was it the look on her face? she wondered quickly. *Did she appear too keyed up? Too off in some way? Was her cover blown?*

'He's awesome,' she finally said, giving him her dumb-blonde act along with her best American accent.

'I know, right?' the guy said, gesturing at the motorcade with a little fist pump. 'He's bringing our country back, and not a moment too soon, if you ask me.'

This fool was actually just being patriotic, she realized. He was just as he appeared: some overgrown American frat boy finance type with a massive preponderance of bone between his ears. He was just flirting with her.

'I'm Jimmy, by the way,' the man said, giving her his Division I quarterback smile. 'I'm supposed to be at my trading desk across the street, but what the hell, I slipped out. Be a fool to miss all this.'

'You said it,' she said, winking as she turned on her heel. 'So long, now.'

It was nothing. The guy was nothing, she told

272

herself as she hit the opposite corner of Park and waded into the business lunch crowd of pedestrians heading north. Just an average yokel. She was just being paranoid.

Seven blocks north, on the north side of East 57th, she pulled open the door of a bank. Instead of going inside the bank itself, she did a right face and crossed the empty vestibule of its ATM lobby. On the other side of the machine, she did another right face and stopped by the sill of a window that faced south back down Park, toward the Waldorf.

For five minutes, she searched the passing pedestrian crowd for the Chicago hot dog. But there was no one. No one on the sidewalk. No surveillance car. No one. She was clean.

She lifted her phone as its text vibration went off.

It was from her husband. Two words.

Start it.

'Yes, love,' she said in the empty vestibule as she brought up the new app.

Timing was of the essence here, she thought as she took in and let out a long breath.

Perfect timing.

CHAPTER 90

Because of its heavy armor plating, capable of repelling high-powered rifle fire and rocket-propelled grenades, the rear seat of the presidential Cadillac limo, known as the Beast, is smaller than one would think.

President Buckland thought it was even smaller than usual as he sat directly across from the governor of New York's pushy wife, Janet Haber.

'I loved your wife's shoes at the inauguration ceremony, Mr. President. Were they Louboutins? Zanottis?' she asked as Buckland signed the third of the seven inaugural invites she had brought with her.

'I don't actually know, Janet,' Buckland said, smiling. 'I'll have her send you a note.'

Right away, too, Buckland thought. *It's not like I'm in the midst of some of the testiest international relations in world history or anything.*

Buckland glanced over at the woman's husband, the smug Governor Martin Haber himself, sitting beside her. His big legs crossed. His long, haughty face glued to his smartphone.

He was feeling right at home in Cadillac One, wasn't he? Buckland thought. He was an even bigger jerk than the wife, it seemed. But Haber had, after all, helped them win New York for the first time since Reagan. This UN General Assembly appearance at the president's side was the least – and hopefully last thing – they could do for him.

There were actually six people in the vehicle in total. Beside President Buckland was his adviser, Ellen Huxley-Laffer, with the Habers facing them. Beyond the Habers, in the front seat, past the open glass partition, was his driver, Secret Service vet Vince Kellett, along with Secret Service ASAC Luke Foldager.

The Secret Service head, John Levitin, had wanted to come to New York as well, but Buckland wouldn't let him. The entire group of tireless agents had enough pressure on this stress-filled important trip without having their famously meticulous big boss busting their chops.

'We're right on schedule, Mr. President. We'll be rolling in five,' Foldager called out as Buckland signed the last invite. He looked up as Vince gave him a wink in the rearview.

Though they were great at hiding it 99 percent of the time, today the agents' faces revealed their stress, their hope, their doubt, the president noted. Most of them had kids. Saw where the country was at. A crossroads. Maybe the most important one in its history. They knew how big the stakes here were.

Please, God, help me to not let them down, Buckland prayed.

He was putting away his pen when he felt the index card in his inside jacket pocket. He pulled it out. On the card, there was a marker drawing of an Evel Knievel-looking guy on a USA motorcycle jumping a bald eagle, with the following message.

Dear Dad, You're my hero. Grekov is a zero. Ha-ha. Love, your son, Terrence

Buckland laughed.
'What is it?' Huxley-Laffer said.
He showed her the card.
Huxley-Laffer chuckled. 'What am I doing here? You already have an excellent adviser, sir.'
I hope the rest of the world agrees with you, Terrence, Buckland thought, tapping the card against the bulletproof window as the car began to roll.

CHAPTER 91

At exactly 11:50 A.M., a thirty-two-year-old UPS driver named Howard Navarro was standing on the street at the back of his brown box truck, double-parked on the avenue side of the southeast corner of 72nd and Lexington Avenue.

Loading packages on his hand truck, he suddenly heard a shriek of air brakes and jumped back as a massive, grumbling blue dump truck passed by on his right so close that it knocked his passenger side mirror askew.

'You stupid frickin' meathead! Are you kidding me?' said Navarro as he hurried forward toward the dump truck, stopped now at the red light.

Navarro squinted as he noticed right away that there was something off about the driver. Up there behind the closed window, the guy just sat there, expressionless and unmoving. It was some strange-looking black dude with dreads and aviator sunglasses under a light-blue hard hat.

'Yo. What are you, stoned?' Navarro said as he banged on the guy's door. 'I'm talking to you!'

As if in response, the truck pulled immediately forward through the intersection, almost running over Navarro's feet, as the light turned green.

Lexington Avenue rolled by smoothly outside the truck's windshield. Taxis went past on both sides. Parked cars and city buses. Pedestrians on the sidewalk. A Gristedes on the left. A Sbarro on the right.

Buildings got noticeably nicer as the truck, picking up a little speed now, arrived at the midsixties. Sidewalk awnings began to appear on apartment houses, as well as flags and doormen outside hotels.

The dump truck had been getting a bunch of green lights at each of the cross streets, but on 60th, it went through a yellow. A block later, at 59th, it rolled on through a just-turned red, almost clipping a guy in surgical scrubs by the corner, talking on his phone.

'Whoopsie,' the assassin's wife said in the vestibule of the bank, where she was piloting the remote-controlled dump truck with her smartphone.

Far in the distance on her screen, she could see the flashing lights of the president's motorcade passing right to left through the Lexington Avenue intersection at 52nd Street

'Shit! Shit! Shit!' she mumbled. Was she too late?

With a swipe of her thumb, she steered the truck into the center lane and dropped the hammer. In a blur, 58th Street went by, then 57th, 56th, 55th. On her screen, she read the remote speedometer. The massive truck, in its top gear now, was hurtling at an incredible seventy-three miles an hour.

It was all about math now. Math and physics, she thought as she blasted the truck through the wooden sawhorse detour at 54th Street like a runaway freight train.

Two blocks and closing.

She swallowed, her thumb down on the accelerator.

This was going to be very close.

On her screen, at the intersection of 52nd and Lexington she could now clearly see the rapidly closing white sides of the massive city sanitation trucks that were being used to protect the intersections along the entire motorcade's route.

But instead of T-boning a sanitation truck, she flicked the control with her thumb again, and the blue dump truck suddenly lurched and moved hard left.

Straight toward the front doors of 599 Lexington Avenue, on the corner of 53rd Street.

Five ninety-nine Lexington was one of those massive midtown office buildings that are practically a whole block wide, and because of this, they have lobbies that pass through the full length of the building. Five ninety-nine Lex's lobby was unique, as it actually crossed the block in a diagonal, from the southeast corner of 53rd and Lex to a quarter block east of 52nd and Lex.

Directly out in front of the building's entrance, the hell-bent-for-leather speeding dump truck bounced up like it was about to do a wheelie as it smashed up off the high curb. Then, as it bucked down on the sidewalk, its twenty-five tons of rolling steel ripped through a sidewalk Citi Bike rack like it was tissue paper and burst through 599 Lexington's doors and glass wall with a breathtaking eardrum-crushing smash of pulverized glass.

Sparks and an ungodly grinding sound roared from its steel dump bed sides as it rode the interior lobby's left-hand marble wall. It ate the lobby's security desk in a splintering explosion of mahogany, then continued its hurtle down the marble interior concourse.

Pouring off plumes of smoke and dust behind it like a square steel meteor, the massive truck rocketed toward the presidential motorcade, which could clearly be seen now, passing obliviously by on the side street, through the glass wall just beyond the lobby's far end.

CHAPTER 92

The Governor of New York's smartphone, as well as his wife, Janet, flew forward into President Buckland's lap as the presidential limo screeched to a sudden dead stop.

Buckland, in shock, looked down at the governor's wife, whom he now suddenly held in his arms, and then looked forward, out through the limo's windshield, trying to believe what he was seeing.

A moment before, there had been a terrible sound off to the left, like metal ripping. Then a massive blue dump truck had emerged, impossibly, out of the side of a glass office building on the left and punched through the pedestrian sidewalk barriers, smashing a direct hit into the dummy limo directly ahead of them.

The hurtling truck had T-boned the dummy limo center mass and flipped it up and over, onto its side, and sent it spinning up onto the south sidewalk. The truck's momentum had carried it straight through the opposite sidewalk's barrier, and it now sat embedded in the front of a restaurant.

Through the rising dust, Buckland could see that the cab of the truck was in flames. One of the steel walls of the dump truck's bed had become detached and was quivering back and forth like a just-used diving board. As he watched, the tailgate it was attached to ripped free and fell into the street with a hollow clang.

'Move! Back!' screamed Secret Service agent Luke Foldager to the driver as he somehow leaped through the open driver's partition and into the rear of the limo and pulled the governor's wife out of Buckland's lap.

'Are you hurt, sir?' Foldager said.

A high-pitched metallic radio twirping was coming from the dashboard as the limo began reversing, its tires squealing.

'Is Bronco injured?' Agent Kellett yelled from the front seat, not waiting for an answer.

'Hotel Seven, we have contact! We have contact! Fifty-Second between Lex and Third!' Kellett hollered into his radio. 'Do you hear me?!'

'I'm fine. I'm fine,' Buckland said.

'That's a negative. Bronco is secure,' Foldager said to Kellett.

There was more radio chatter, and then horns and sirens were honking outside in the street. The blasting and bleating were head-splitting. Like the heralding of the end of the world.

Buckland turned in his seat and could see that they were reversing the entire convoy. Through the blur and motion, he could also see people on the street and sidewalk standing frozen in sheer panic. People everywhere with hands to their mouths, standing as still as model people in a train layout.

He put his hands to his own mouth, wondering suddenly if this was it. If he would die now. His mind cleared of everything except how much he missed his wife.

'Where to now? Back to the hotel?' Buckland said as he heard the governor's wife start weeping.

'Negative. The situation is too volatile, sir,' Foldager said as the limo did a hard sliding lurch to the left and pinned it up Lexington. 'We are going to go to our failback, Sanctuary One.'

'Sanctuary One?' asked Huxley-Laffer.

'Park Avenue Armory, ma'am. That's our fallback position. You'll all be safe there until we get this thing sussed out.'

CHAPTER 93

Thirty seconds before the impact, we had heard a blast of sudden screaming chatter on the radio.

From the Black Hawk hovering over 57th and Lex, we had actually witnessed the whole scene unfold. The blue dump truck crashing through the barrier on 54th and then hurtling down Lex toward the 52nd Street motorcade route like a bat out of hell.

Once the dump truck had swerved at 53rd and entered the building, I thought the driver was ditching it, that it was over. But when I saw the truck exit the other side of the block-wide building on 52nd and smash through the sidewalk barrier into the first limo, my hands went to my mouth, and all I could hear was someone on the radio crying *'No! No! No!'*

The next long minute reminded me of 9/11 – that same helpless, terrifying feeling of how something impossible can be happening right before my very eyes – as smoke and dust billowed up out of the narrow slot of the Manhattan street.

An absolute chaos of radio chatter and people screaming followed. When it subsided a little, we got the word. It had been the dummy limo!

Leroux, beside me, gave me a painful high five. Buckland was fine!

We were immediately assigned to provide air cover as Buckland was transferred to Park Avenue Armory, at 67th Street, the predesignated secure area.

We zipped up and then tilted down over the MetLife Building just in time to see the presidential limo come out in reverse from beside the Waldorf and haul ass north up Park Avenue.

It was a truly terrifying sight. The limo had only two SUVs flanking it. At every cross street, it seemed like some new threat would suddenly emerge – another truck, or who knew what the hell else.

'They're going to take Bronco in through the back southwest corner of Sixty-Seven and Lex,' Leroux told me as we came to a still hover over the massive castlelike building that was Park Avenue Armory.

I vaguely remembered that the old redbrick building was used for art shows and events now, but it had in the Civil War era been a barracks that housed horses and soldiers.

'Look sharp, Mike. I got seven to eleven. You take from one to five,' Leroux said to me as he got on his spotting scope. 'Remember, anything up to two thousand yards.'

Under the hard flutter of the rotors, I stared down at the limo, then out at the Upper East Side's daunting number of surrounding buildings. The rooftops and terraces and window after window after window.

CHAPTER 94

Five hundred eleven yards and one hundred forty feet above the corner on 67th Avenue, the British assassin lay prone on his elevated shooting platform, breathing calmly, stilling himself.

He'd removed the glass of the living room window, and he was happy for the cold air that blew in and cooled the sweat on his brow.

In front of the now glassless window was a decorative Asian bamboo folding partition, and above it was the valance of a curtain covering the top of the window. In between the two was his blind's offset shooting slit. He could shoot down through the slit without being spotted from the outside.

The British assassin thought that with its highly

varnished walnut stock and blue steel barrel, the L39A1 Enfield English sniper rifle up on the small tripod before him was a glorious Stradivarius of a gun. It was loaded with ten soft point .303 British rounds, a favored cartridge of choice for many deer hunters because of its high twist rate and excellent penetration.

The locked and loaded bolt-action rifle had been fitted with what was simply the finest high-precision riflescope in all the world, a German-made Schmidt & Bender PM II.

He didn't know if it was an intentional nod to the bloody medieval history of the fatherland or something, but to him, the intricate mill marks along the S & B's reticle gave it the distinct look of an elaborate Gothic cross.

The red intersection of that cross was dead-centered now on the sidewalk at the southwest corner of 67th and Lexington.

To the left of the reticle was the Armory's rear doorway.

And to the right was the just-arrived limousine of the president of the United States of America.

To be precise, the scope was zeroed in sixty-nine inches up above the corner, just a skosh under Buckland's six one height. The protective agent would come out and open the limo door and allow the president onto the curb first, the British assassin knew.

The moment Buckland stepped from the street onto the sidewalk would be exactly when he was going to drop him with a head shot. One shot center mass, just above Buckland's left ear, would shear the entire top of his head clean off.

The greatest assassination in the history of the world, after all, deserved nothing less than a one-shot clean kill.

The preparation was over. The windage determined. The elevation adjustments calculated.

As he lay there, certainty came to him. As if it had all been recorded already in the history books.

The sniper who wouldn't quit, they would call him. The ultimate professional. The greatest shot who ever lived.

CHAPTER 95

Low above Park Avenue Armory in the trembling helicopter, Leroux and I frantically did a systematic visual search of the surrounding windows and rooftops.

The president's limo was there below us on the southwest corner of Lex. We had word that the president was still inside it. They had cordoned off 67th between Park and Lex, and the bullet- and bombproof vehicle had been determined to be the safest place for him until the situation on the street was better put under control.

It was the strangest thing. I don't know if the attack on the motorcade had been tweeted or something, but there were now about a couple hundred people on the side street and avenue sidewalks near the limo.

Most of them seemed to be students from

Hunter College, located not far from the Armory. Were they trying to get selfies? I wondered. Just bizarre. Thank God a bunch of uniformed cops from the Nineteenth Precinct, halfway down 67th, had arrived to deal with it, but it was still quite a volatile, kinetic scene.

I swung my spotting scope down to the street toward a sudden surge in the crowd surrounding the limo. *You've got to be kidding me,* I thought. The cops were trying to arrest some dreadlocked white boy who had gotten too close to the limo.

Now was no time for a sit-in. Where the hell were the rest of the Secret Service people to take care of this circus? I wondered. It was becoming a riot down there.

Just as I wondered it, I caught something in the edge of my scope, down there on the street. On the northwest corner of Lex, opposite the president's limo, among the crush of students, there was a tall preppy guy in an overcoat standing beside the pillar of the Hunter College building.

It was Matthew Leroux's CIA boss, Mark Evrard.

'Matt, three o'clock, on the corner. Is that Evrard? That's your boss, right?'

'Yeah. It is,' Leroux said, looking down through his own scope. 'That's weird. I thought he said he was heading back down to DC.'

I had a strange feeling right then, staring down at Evrard. He just looked wrong. Out of place. Foreboding. Everything was moving around him, but he was as still as the post he stood beside.

Then something in the back of my mind shifted

286

and knocked against something else.

This was really no time to be checking my phone, but I checked it anyway. I opened the message from Doyle that had been sent sometime in the last ten crazy minutes.

Mike, we did it!!! The link to Levkov!!! Here's a video still of the SUV off a camera at the nearest gas station in Yonkers. Witness has already ID'd. These are the guys who dumped Levkov's body.

I tapped the photo and nodded my exploding head.

I looked down at the corner, then at the photo, then down at the corner again.

In the photo was Evrard.

Mark Evrard with that goon of a driver I had met the night I followed Leroux from the gallery. I didn't know why, but it was Evrard. Evrard was behind the whole thing. The man behind the curtain. Evrard had hired the assassin.

But he was here now. Why? The attempt at the motorcade had failed.

Because here and now was here and now, I realized.

The assassin's intent was to get the president to the Armory all along. We had no time. It was about to happen.

'They're about to bring the president out,' the pilot called back to us.

'No!' I screamed. 'No! Tell them not to! Tell them to leave him in the car!'

'What's the matter? What's going on?' said Leroux anxiously, still focused on the limo.

'It's Evrard. He killed Levkov! He's the one behind everything!'

'Are you sure?'

'This is the photo of the guys who killed Levkov,' I said, showing Leroux my phone.

'You mean...'

'Yes,' I said. 'He set you up. He set all of us up.'

I pointed my spotting scope at the street. Down on the corner, Evrard was looking east down 67th, then looking up. He glanced at the presidential limo as he took out his cell, checking something. Then he looked back east, back up.

'Matt, watch Evrard! He's looking up. East up Sixty-Seventh. He keeps looking up!'

Leroux lifted the Secret Service radio.

'This is air cover one. We have a problem on the outside of the vehicle. Do you copy? Keep Bronco in the vehicle. Copy.'

We listened to the radio. There was nothing. There was just static. White noise.

'Hey, can you get them?' Leroux yelled up to the pilot.

'No, it's not working,' he said. 'Nothing.'

'They're jamming the signal or something!' I cried as I looked frantically up 67th Street with the spotting scope. 'They're going to kill him now!'

'I see it! I see it!' I said a second later. 'That white building! Farthest window on the right, two floors down! See how the other windows in the building have a sun glare on them? But that one doesn't have any. He must have taken out the glass!'

I zeroed in tighter with my scope's zoom. Instead of shades or blinds in the window, there was some kind of Chinese screen and a little curtain. Between them were what looked like the aluminum legs of a ladder or a painter's scaffold.

That's when I remembered the sniper's blind in the MetLife Building. The shooter had been up high, near the ceiling of the space, far back to get a down shot angle on the street.

When I took my eye off the scope, I saw Leroux pounding on the shoulder of the pilot.

'Down! Down! Put me on the roof of the Armory!'

CHAPTER 96

Because of the raised structures on the Armory's roof, the helicopter could only get us to about ten feet above it.

We had to hang off the sides and jump, and I went first. It was farther down than I'd anticipated, and I landed off balance and went over onto the rough tar paper, the breath knocked out of me.

I was standing, looking up, waiting for Leroux to follow when his sniper rifle fell out of the chopper's side door and clattered to the rooftop beside me.

What the hell? I thought, looking down at it. Then I looked up again and saw Leroux himself drop sideways out of the helicopter, crashing hard onto the roof.

'I'm shot,' he said as he clutched himself with both bloody hands above his groin.

What?! I thought. It was unbelievable. Impossible. Just like that?!

'I saw the muzzle flash,' he gasped as blood began to pool out onto the tar paper beneath him. 'It was from the window, the one you spotted.'

'Medic! Help!' I yelled up at the chopper.

'No time,' Leroux said as I knelt to help him. He took one of his blood-covered hands off his wound and pointed toward the huge sniper rifle.

'If you don't get help, you're gonna die, Matt.'

'No, the president is. You have to save the president,' he said.

'But–'

'There's no *buts!*' he screamed, his face clotted with pain. 'Get over to that corner of the roof and drop that son of a bitch! Shoot the bastard!'

I ran across the roof with the rifle. At the corner of the crazy old building was an actual battlement like you'd see on the top of a rook chess piece. I set the huge rifle into the battlement's chest-high indentation and looked up through the scope.

Even at this lower angle, I still couldn't see the shooter in the window. Just the crazy Chinese screen, the little curtain, the ladder in the gap between them. There was no target!

I glanced down to the street as a roar came from the crowd. It was the president's limo. One of the Secret Service agents was at its rear, opening the door.

'No! Get back!' I screamed. But I knew it was fruitless. He couldn't hear me over the crowd and chopper rotor wash.

There was no more time.

Do or die.

I looked back up at the glassless window two blocks to the east and I knelt as I put the rifle to my shoulder.

CHAPTER 97

In one oiled, pistonlike motion, the British assassin cleared the brass casing of the bullet with which he'd just gutshot the cop out of the chopper and reclosed the Enfield rifle's blue steel bolt.

He'd been alternating his aim from the limo to the chopper from the moment it arrived. He didn't know how the sniper team had spotted him, but they had. When he had looked back up from the limo a moment before, the two-man team had both of their scopes on him.

Reorienting on his target, he watched in the scope as the other cop scurried and ducked behind one of the Armory roof's battlements a split second before the British assassin was going to blow his brains out.

Smart man, he thought. *Run for your life.*

When he looked back down at the limo, there was a Secret Service agent at its rear, ready to open the door. Buckland was coming out.

There still was a chance.

The British assassin adjusted the Enfield a milli-meter down as the president stood up from behind the limo door and stepped onto the sidewalk.

He sucked in his breath, held it.

Just as he slipped the center of the Gothic cross

reticle onto Buckland's head, he saw the muzzle flash from the Armory's roof.

The .408 CheyTac round traveling at thirty-five hundred feet per second came in at him just under his own rifle. As it struck home, it cut a perfectly circular groove through the bones of the ring and pinkie fingers of his left hand, holding the Enfield's stock.

Then it bored a perfect quarter-size hole through the center of his chest cavity and blew his spine and heart and much of his back out across the wall behind him.

EPILOGUE

CHAPTER 98

A week later, Old Glory snapped in the wind along with the coattails of the honor guard, standing out on the grass as the marching band played the national anthem.

When it was established that we had, in fact, somehow managed to still keep our flag waving o'er the land of the free and the home of the brave, at least for the time being, there was much hooting and cries of 'Let's go! Let's go!' from the field and the stands.

We were at Fordham Prep's famous homecoming Turkey Bowl game against Xavier, and Mary Catherine and Seamus and all my kids and I went nuts as Brian and Marvin took the field with the rest of the Rams for the kickoff.

'Well, they made it, the two knuckleheads, despite all their own efforts to the contrary,' Seamus said.

I shook my head. I didn't want to even think about what could have happened to them once I had gotten to the bottom of the saga of Marvin and Brian and the drug dealer. Sometimes, if you're wise and like to sleep at night, as a parent you say, 'All's well that ends well,' and leave it at that.

Which is exactly what I did say as I handed Seamus and Mary Catherine brimming plastic cups.

After I clicked cups with two of my twelve

favorite people in the world, I took a long, much-deserved sip out in the cold air as Fordham booted the ball high and long for the kickoff.

Marvin, of course, being the biggest and yet somehow fastest kid on the field, made the first tackle, sending a Xavier kid into a sideline tuba player.

I patted Marvin's uncle, in front of us, on the back.

'Tuba players, be warned,' I said, smiling. 'We expect nothing less than the Bronx's version of Bo Jackson.'

Mr. Peters, who was almost as big as his nephew, gave out a bellowing laugh. The sweet old man had finally made it up from North Carolina to stay with Big Marv, who had moved out of the Bennett abode amid many teary good-byes and hugs two days before. We were all going to miss the big galoot.

'And remember, Mr. Peters, he's to play basketball at Manhattan College,' Seamus said, patting the man's huge shoulder. 'Not Manhattanville. Just plain old normal, Catholic, meat-and-potatoes Manhattan. In Riverdale. Don't forget, now.'

CHAPTER 99

I was heading down the bleachers for the next round when I got the text from my good buddy Paul Ernenwein.

How's it hangin, Miss Oakley? it said.

Rootin tootin, I texted back, laughing at our little inside joke.

There had been a lot of hoopla about the shot that had dropped the assassin. Especially the fact that he had been shot through the hand holding his rifle before he'd been killed. World-famous snipers had weighed in with glowing reviews of the shot's professionalism, which suggested years and years of training. The *Post* even did a detailed mock-up of it. Where the chopper was. Where I was. Where Matthew Leroux was. A dotted line showing the trajectory of the bullet up 67th Street.

I had to struggle to stifle my laughter every time I looked at the 100 percent wrong mock-up or read one of these lauding reviews.

Because the whole thing, the famous world-class shot, was actually a complete accident.

Before I was able to adjust my aim, the big awkward CheyTac rifle had slipped from where I'd placed it between the crenellations. Grabbing at it to keep it from falling, I'd hit the damn thing's hair trigger.

Call it dumb blind luck. The hand of God. But I had nothing to do with shooting the Brit through his hand holding the rifle.

Since I knew hoopla to be far more trouble than it's worth, I had actually insisted that Leroux had done it. After the shot, Matthew Joseph Leroux died right there on the roof as we were trying to get him back into the chopper. Crediting him was the least I could do for his poor family after all the sacrifices he had made for us.

The Brit's real name, it turned out, was Andy Heathton. The FBI had sent a photo of the body to British intelligence, who had finally been able to ID the shooter. The thirty-nine-year-old professional killer had been born and raised in Leeds, England, and had been taught how to shoot by the British Royal Marines at age twenty-one. Apparently, he had spent the next several years of his life as a mercenary, killing folks all over the world.

His wife, Holly Heathton, thirty-three, who was thought to be responsible for the remote-controlled dump truck that had rammed the motorcade, was caught by customs out at JFK, trying to leave the country the night of the attempted assassination.

You hear? Paul texted me a second later.

About what? I texted back.

'About the *Times* article,' Paul said from behind me.

I turned and stared at the redheaded fed.

'No,' I said. 'But something tells me I'm about to find out about it.'

'C'mon,' Paul said, patting me on the shoulder as he pocketed his phone. 'Let's walk and talk.'

CHAPTER 100

'We arrested Secret Service SAC Margaret Foley late last night,' Paul said as we walked down a breezy drive past Fordham's beautiful old stone buildings.

'Is that right?'

'Yep. We got up on a phone we found in the

shed of her house in Silver Spring. There were hundreds of calls between her and Mark Evrard. Photos on there as well. Startling ones.'

'Of an intimate nature?' I said.

'The most highly intimate. She'd been sleeping with him for years, apparently. They met down at the pile after nine eleven.'

'Love among the wreckage,' I said. 'Romantic.'

'She finally broke last night,' Paul said. 'She had given Evrard the president's route and itinerary, which he then passed along to the assassin through back channels. They'd been planning this for over a year.'

'She happen to mention why she and Evrard wanted to off their own country's leader? Nothing new on Netflix?'

'She said it was about Buckland's call to slice the federal budget to the bone and do a thorough audit of all the books, including Homeland Security. She said she had misappropriated a few dollars here and there over the years and didn't want to wind up on the unemployment line or in jail.'

'Wow. Correct me if I'm wrong, but didn't she have a family?'

'Yep. Married, with three kids,' Paul said.

'How do you go from skimming off the top at the Secret Service to planning your boss's funeral because there might be layoffs?' I said. 'Are things really that corrupt, I wonder? Or have we gotten to the point where we don't catch it anymore?'

'That's if you even buy that story,' Paul said. 'Evrard was a spy. And I think, like all spies, Evrard sold her and played her like an asset. Used her own fears and desires to manipulate her. He needed the info she could access.'

'Too bad we can't ask him to confirm, huh?' I said.

Evrard had hung himself with a tied-together pair of sneaker laces in his cell down at the federal detention center in lower Manhattan, on the second night after his arrest. No one knew how the sneaker laces had gotten into his solitary confinement cell, but I wasn't worried because it was 'under investigation.'

'Why do you think Evrard did it? Was he a double agent? Hired by someone else?'

Paul shrugged. 'He was hired by somebody. And my gut says not the Russian government. I think he just got the Russian mob involved in order to make it look like it was coming from Grekov's direction, but it wasn't. It was just a smoke screen.'

'But who could fund an operation of this scale?' I said. 'It would have to cost a pretty penny these days to assassinate a president. Who has that kind of juice?'

Paul looked at me. 'You're right. The Brit didn't work cheap. I heard a rumor that he had a numbered account in the kind of Swiss bank they won't let you into the lobby of unless you're there to park eight figures. But don't forget, Evrard's been in the business a long time. He definitely had the connections.' Then he shrugged. 'Buckland did mention he wanted to audit the Federal Reserve.'

'Ah, the central bankers,' I said. 'That's true. Auditing them is probably something they don't want. Making money out of thin air must make it easy to fund an assassination. Let's face it: there isn't anything that's really too much of a problem for them with that kind of power.'

'True,' Paul said. 'But perhaps it'll all come out in the congressional commission that's being assembled.'

I stopped walking. A gust of cold wind blew up, hammering the trees as the branches cracked against one another like kids playing swords with broomsticks.

'We'll never know, will we?' I said after a beat. 'Just like JFK's assassination, we'll never know.'

'No, Mike,' Paul said. 'I don't think we ever will. But look on the bright side. Whoever it was, we squashed them. We checked their shit. We could be going to a presidential funeral right now.'

'We stood our watch.'

'We did. All of us. You, me, Matt, your detective friends. Sometimes it's all you can do.'

Then I shook Paul's hand and turned on my heel and went back down the drive toward the cheers and the field.

At this point, I was wise enough to no longer give a care. One day at a time and all that, and this one day was one of my favorites of the year. I wasn't about to waste one more second of it on work.

CHAPTER 101

'And it's no nay never, no nay never no more!' Seamus sang as he played the accordion in the living room after the turkey was demolished. Turkeys, to be exact.

'How do you like Irish Thanksgiving?' I said to Mr. Peters as I was stacking cleaned plates from the dining room table. 'We also do an Irish Halloween, and even, impossibly, an Irish Fourth of July. Because nothing enhances a fireworks display like green beer and a hearty jig.'

'I like it just fine,' Mr. Peters said, laughing and looking like he was ready for a long tryptophan nap. 'That gravy Mary Catherine made was divine. And those biscuits' – the Southerner winked – 'rivaled my own mama's.'

I smiled as I headed into the kitchen.

Mary Catherine had insisted we do Thanksgiving early, for Marvin and his uncle, who were just settling into their new place. I dropped off the china next to Mary Catherine, who was rinsing a platter in the sink.

I stood there looking at her for a second. She'd put her hair up, and she was smiling to herself about something – a memory, maybe a joke. She looked so incredibly beautiful and sweet as she stood there in her apron that I felt a physical pulse, an almost electric shock of happiness, pass through me.

It suddenly dawned on me then, like a name that's been on the tip of your tongue.

I knew that I loved her and only her, and that I would never want anyone else but her for the rest of my days.

'Yes, Michael?' she said, suddenly hitting me with her blue smiling eyes. 'You look like you want to say something.'

'I, eh, uh...' I said, smiling, stalling, blushing.

'You eh, uh, what?' she said, turning, now face-to-face with me, pinning me with those eyes.

'I, um, brought you my plate,' I said, pointing at the counter.

'So you did. So you did. A fine plate it is, too.'

I hugged her then. Fell into the nape of her neck. Never wanted to stop falling.

'You had my plate at hello, my Irish beauty,' I whispered in her ear. 'Cross my plate and hope to die.'

The publishers hope that this book has given you enjoyable reading. Large Print Books are especially designed to be as easy to see and hold as possible. If you wish a complete list of our books please ask at your local library or write directly to:

Magna Large Print Books
Magna House, Long Preston,
Skipton, North Yorkshire.
BD23 4ND

This Large Print Book for the partially sighted, who cannot read normal print, is published under the auspices of

THE ULVERSCROFT FOUNDATION